the Myth of You and Me

This Large Print Book carries the
Seal of Approval of N.A.V.H.

the Myth of You and Me

Leah Stewart

Thorndike Press • Waterville, Maine

Published in 2006 by arrangement with Crown Publishers, a division of Random House, Inc.

Thorndike Press® Large Print Basic.

The tree indicium is a trademark of Thorndike Press.

The text of this Large Print edition is unabridged. Other aspects of the book may vary from the original edition.

Set in 16 pt. Plantin by Carleen Stearns.

Printed in the United States on permanent paper.

Library of Congress Cataloging-in-Publication Data

Stewart, Leah, 1973–
     The myth of you and me / by Leah Stewart.
          p. cm.
     "Thorndike Press large print basic" — T.p. verso.
     ISBN 0-7862-8307-6 (lg. print : hc : alk. paper)
     1. Young women — Fiction.   2. Female friendship — Fiction.   3. Inheritance and succession — Fiction.   4. Loss (Psychology) — Fiction.   5. Historians — Fiction.
     6. Large type books.   I. Title.
     PS3569.T465258M98 2006
     813'.54—dc22   2005029579

For Matt, Eliza, and Carolyn

National Association for Visually Handicapped
--------------------- serving the partially seeing

As the Founder/CEO of NAVH, the only national health agency solely devoted to those who, although not totally blind, have an eye disease which could lead to serious visual impairment, I am pleased to recognize Thorndike Press* as one of the leading publishers in the large print field.

Founded in 1954 in San Francisco to prepare large print textbooks for partially seeing children, NAVH became the pioneer and standard setting agency in the preparation of large type.

Today, those publishers who meet our standards carry the prestigious "Seal of Approval" indicating high quality large print. We are delighted that Thorndike Press is one of the publishers whose titles meet these standards. We are also pleased to recognize the significant contribution Thorndike Press is making in this important and growing field.

Lorraine H. Marchi, L.H.D.
Founder/CEO
NAVH

* Thorndike Press encompasses the following imprints: Thorndike, Wheeler, Walker and Large Print Press.

And I'm left to wonder, What is this place? This room, this house, this life accountable to no one but myself.

— A. Manette Ansay, *Sister*

One

1

"What if you had never met me?" Sonia says. "What would your life be like?"

Sonia has been my best friend for only a few months, but already life without her is difficult to imagine. All I can muster is an image of myself alone in a room. "Boring," I say, and Sonia laughs.

We are lying on her four-poster bed, staring up at the pink canopy, our feet propped on the wall above her headboard. We are fourteen. When I turn my head to look at Sonia, her hair brushes against the side of my face.

"If you hadn't been standing in the right place in the parking lot," she says, "we might never have spoken."

"We have three classes together," I say.

"If you hadn't come into the gym that day, we might never have become friends."

"Maybe we were destined to be friends," I say. "Maybe we would've been assigned a group project."

She waves her hand in the air above us, dismissing this. "Every decision we make," she says, "affects the rest of our lives."

"Yeah, yeah," I say, because I've heard this from her a million times.

"For example," she says, "what if you had to choose between being my best friend forever and having the boy of your dreams?"

"I can't have both?"

"No."

"Why not?"

"That's the game."

"Maybe you'd marry his brother and live next door."

She shakes her head, and the movement shakes the mattress. "You have to choose," she says.

Eight years from now I will abandon Sonia. I'll drive away from a gas station in West Texas, my eyes on the rearview mirror, where I'll see her running after my car, a shocked, desperate expression on her face. Here in Sonia's bedroom it's all still there before us, every decision between that moment and this.

Sonia rolls over onto her elbows so she can look me in the face. "Choose," she demands. "Choose."

2

In February of my thirtieth year, a letter came to the house where I was living, addressed to me in my own handwriting. I didn't notice it when it arrived. Though I was the one who went to the mailbox every morning at ten-thirty-five, five minutes after the mailman came, I'd stopped flipping through the mail a long time ago, as there was never anything in it for me. That morning I just dropped the stack on the kitchen table as usual and went to the counter to make bologna-and–American cheese sandwiches on white bread, favorite lunch of my employer, the historian Oliver Doucet.

Oliver liked to declare that all times exist simultaneously, and when he did I'd say, teasing, that he thought that only because all our days were exactly the same. I'd been living with him in this house, just outside the town square in Oxford, Mississippi, for nearly three years, and I'd long since adapted to his schedule — we ate lunch between ten-forty-five and eleven, dinner between four-thirty and five. Then we watched a black-and-white movie, and Oliver went to bed before nine. Most nights I stayed up with the television or a book, even though he exhorted me to go out. What he didn't know was that every so often I crept into his bedroom to make sure he was still breathing. When I went out I worried that his heart had stopped, as though by my presence alone I kept it going. In the mornings I was always relieved to find him sitting at the kitchen table, wearing the ridiculous velvet robe his daughter, Ruth, had given him, and drinking cup after cup of coffee, each with three dollops — he always called them dollops — of heavy whipping cream. Oliver was ninety-two to my twenty-nine. He was the one who liked to say, sometimes teasing, more often with solemn portent, that this was my thirtieth year.

The kitchen had been remodeled several times since the house was built — the last time in the eighties — but each time, Oliver had insisted that certain aspects of the previous versions be allowed to remain. With its dinette set, inoperable dumbwaiter, early-model microwave, and stone fireplace with a spit, the kitchen lent credence to Oliver's notion about the simultaneity of time. I was singing "They Can't Take That Away from Me" — we had watched *Shall We Dance* the night before — as I spread mayonnaise on slices of white bread. Standing at the counter, I had a view out the window of Oliver's lush flower garden. I felt pleased about the brightness in the room, as if my own happiness were the source of the light. There was no particular reason for me to be so happy. I was just grateful for my ordinary life. Lined up on the windowsill were figurines of chickens, awkward bodies and spindly feet rendered in wood, glass, cloisonné. Even the beautiful ones were ugly. But now I stopped what I was doing to study them, and felt a surge of awe at how intricate they were — the ruffled feathers, the grooves in the feet, the devotion that must have gone into the task of their making.

"Cameron, my dear," Oliver said, and I jumped. I turned to see him standing in the doorway of the kitchen, one hand on his cane, one braced against the doorframe. He looked as though he'd been watching me for some time. Today seemed to be a dress-up day. He wore a crisp white

15

shirt tucked into black pants. Unlike most old men, he wore his pants low, cinched tight with a belt that had a rodeo buckle.

"Happy Valentine's Day." I smiled at him. Minutes before, I'd noted the date on the kitchen calendar. In Oliver's house we tended to lose track of the days.

"Is it?" he said. "I had forgotten." He pushed off the doorframe and came into the room. He started to ease into his usual chair, then checked himself and withdrew a small hand mirror from the back of his waistband before he sat. He pulled a comb from his shirt pocket and held it out for me to take. His damp hair was tufted to one side of his head. Oliver was vain about these wisps of white hair, which he insisted be slicked back in an approximation of the pompadour he had worn in his youth. He could have combed it himself, but he liked for me to do it. Every morning after he showered and dressed he came into the kitchen for his styling.

While I worked, smoothing hair with the comb and my fingers, Oliver studied his features in the hand mirror. He liked to say that he had the face of a bird of prey, and though this made him sound more menacing than he really was, it was true — he had an eagle nose and bright, watchful eyes. As a young man he had been very handsome. Though his nose was aristocratic, almost haughty, his lips were full and soft. In old pictures he seemed to be thinking of a private joke.

Oliver inspected his hair with approval as I held the mirror. He grabbed my free hand and pressed it to his cheek. "Ah, youth," he said. "Am I not handsome?"

"You're terribly handsome," I said.

"The most handsome of all your beaux?"

"Of course." I kissed him on the forehead, his skin soft as well-worn cotton.

"In that case," he said, and slipped a ring onto the third finger of my left hand, "Happy Valentine's Day." He laughed at my surprise.

The ring was beautiful — gold, obviously antique, set with five small opals. He'd given me books before, some of them rare, but never a gift like this one. "Oliver —" I started, but he cut me off.

"It belonged to my aunt," he said. "Now we're engaged. Call off your other beaux."

"I love it," I said. "Thank you."

"You've been good to me." He held my gaze, his expression serious. He was rarely this earnest, and I felt a flush of gratitude mingled with embarrassment. Before I could speak again, he waved me away.

"Don't get spoiled," he said. "Finish that lunch."

I went back to the counter, but instead of picking up the knife I stood there looking down at my hand, admiring the way the sunlight caught the opals in the ring.

Behind me Oliver was opening the mail. I heard the usual sounds of paper tearing, the skidding of envelopes across the table as he tossed them aside, and then a silence as he read. I assumed he'd gotten one of the many letters praising him or asking for a blurb or recommendation, letters he enjoyed but never answered. Sometimes I took pity on the senders and wrote them back, saying that Oliver was grateful for their kind words, that he'd be happy to comply with their request if only he weren't so busy writing his memoirs. Oliver rolled his eyes at these carefully worded replies. "Lies, lies, all lies," he said.

Now he said, "This is interesting."

"What?" I turned to see him holding an envelope up toward the light, squinting in an attempt to make out what was inside.

"This is addressed to you," he said. "In your handwriting." He raised his eyebrows. "You seem to have written yourself a letter."

"That's odd." I crossed to the table and reached for the envelope, which he handed over with some reluctance. He was right — there were my name and his address, on the front in my own script. I thought I must have misaddressed a reply to one of his acolytes, switching the *to* and the *from*. But the return address had no name, just a street and an apartment number in Cambridge, Massachusetts.

"Why would you write yourself a letter?" Oliver asked.

"I don't think I did."

"This is delightful," he said. "You have a secret identity. Hidden even from yourself. Maybe you're another person."

I rolled my eyes at this, but it did give me a strange feeling, to see my own name in my own handwriting like that, as though somewhere out there was indeed another me. Oliver pushed out a chair. "Sit down," he said. "For God's sake, open it."

I sat down. I opened it. Of course I hadn't written the letter, but I felt no less strange when I saw who had. The letter was from Sonia Gray. In high school we practiced until our handwriting was so similar even we couldn't tell it apart. This made it easy for me to do her math homework for her, and for us to sometimes leave

19

our names off our math tests, so that I could claim hers, and she mine, because my math grade could survive the occasional fifty, while hers could not. We called this "falling on the fifty," and every time I did it I felt flushed with an exhilarated beneficence. Because I couldn't imagine why Sonia was writing to me now, nearly eight years after we'd parted, it did seem to me that all times existed at once, that she'd mailed the letter from someplace years ago. That was why our handwriting was still identical, neither of us having altered at all the elaborate girlish loops in our *L*s and *Y*s.

"Well?" Oliver asked.

I ignored him, holding the letter away from his curious gaze.

Dear Cameron,

I had a dream about you tonight, and now I can't sleep. I can't even remember exactly what the dream was about — there was something about snow cones, though you and I never ate snow cones together, that I can recall. We did eat a lot of those Oreo shakes from the Taco Box. And remember how we used to stir syrup into milk and make those vanilla wafer sandwiches with peanut butter? It all sounds ridiculously disgusting now.

I've been thinking about you ever since I got engaged. My first impulse afterward was to call you with the news. Isn't that odd? It was like I was a kid again, and we were planning our imaginary weddings, back when I was certain you'd be my maid of honor and I'd be yours. It took me a moment to remember we weren't friends anymore. Ever since, I keep having this feeling I'm forgetting to do something. I look at my list — I've called the caterer and talked to the florist — and it takes me a while to realize, because it's not on the list, that the only thing I haven't done is talk to you.

I have that middle-of-the-night strangeness, when it feels like you've fallen out of your normal life, and maybe that's why I'm writing to you now, as if we were friends like we used to be. Somewhere somebody's playing Madonna, her first album, I think it is. Why do they have that on at three in the morning? Isn't this traditionally a more melancholy time? Maybe they're trying to counteract melancholy. Maybe "Borderline" is the only thing between them and suicide.

You and I used to make up dance routines to Madonna songs. Remember the

21

playroom at my house? All those boxes along the wall, full of childhood discards — an old dollhouse, the Ewok village, a box of stuffed animals loved into ruin. You and I dancing in the middle, doing what we thought were sexy moves. Don't you think that's symbolic? Loved into ruin. I just invented that phrase. I like it. On occasion I've felt like that's what's happened to me. Remember the sock monkey with no mouth? I hated that thing. The bottom half of its face was just a blank. I think my mother still has it in the house, probably to spite me. Remember when we were walking across campus to take a final exam and a bird fell dead at our feet? It wasn't some small brown finch, either, but a cardinal. A red splash. You poked it with a stick. It was truly dead. We were juniors in college but we held hands the rest of the way, we were that unnerved. Remember when we drove up to Sewanee to see that boy I was dating, I can't even remember his name now, and the three of us went skinny-dipping in the reservoir? It was so black, and the stars were everywhere, and the boy was stupid and kept splashing around, but you and I floated away on our backs, and you said that floating there and looking up at the sky was like not existing in the best possible way. I said we should make up a myth about two maidens and the water, but we never did. I guess it's a myth now anyway.

Maybe that's the point of this letter. Is it a myth? Is all of this a myth, what it was like when we were best friends? What I'm wondering now, in the middle of the night, is did those things actually happen? Sometimes without you to confirm these memories I feel like I've invented them. It's a little like being orphaned. That sounds really dramatic, I know, but since I'm a half-orphan I think it's okay for me to say it. There are things about my life that no one else has ever understood.

I wonder about your life now. Do you think about any of this, the myth of you and me? Do you wonder why we were friends, why we aren't anymore, why we made the choices we did? Do you wonder how things might be different if we hadn't? You were never as enamored of this kind of thinking as I was, but even you must admit that parting was a turning point in both our lives. For a while we were practically the same person, you and I.

I don't know what I want from you. I

23

can imagine you dismissing this letter — I think that would be your first impulse, to consider it ridiculous of me to contact you after all this time, no matter what the reason, especially if the reason is this strange feeling I have that you should still be my maid of honor, that if you're not, some part of my past is erased, something left unfinished. I think this even though I know if you were it would be terribly up-setting to Suzette. So I don't know if I'll even send this, though I did track down your address.

I don't know how to sign this, so I'll just put my name.

Sonia

Oliver was waiting for me to speak, but I couldn't formulate a thought. Somehow it seemed even stranger that the letter had come from Sonia as she was in the present, a woman about to get married, than if it really had been mailed years ago by the girl I'd known. She'd gone on getting older, but my memory had frozen her in time, running after my car at that West Texas gas station. I suppose I'd imagined that if I went back, I'd find her still waiting there.

"Huh," I said. I folded the letter, put it in the envelope, and set it back on the table. Then I returned to the counter. There were still sandwiches to make.

I tried to concentrate on the task at hand, peeling the plastic off a piece of cheese, but it was impossible not to think of the letter. I did want to dismiss it, but couldn't, because Sonia had suggested that I would, and I was annoyed by the presumption that she still knew me that well. I remembered our dance routines, of course, and the sock monkey and the skinny-dipping. I remembered the bird, too — that bad omen — but I didn't remember Sonia being there when it hit the ground. I saw only myself staring at it, a red splash, as Sonia said, next to a clod of dirt and someone's lost earring. It unnerved me now, to picture her there with me. It called other memories into question. When were we together? When was I alone? Had I erased her from the picture, or had she added herself? I couldn't shake the eerie feeling that my past was imaginary, that I really had written the letter myself. Did I want to be her maid of honor? Wasn't that stupid after all this time?

Behind me, I heard Oliver rising from his chair, but I didn't move to help because I knew he hated to be seen struggling with a simple task. I listened to the shuffle of his feet, the soft thump of his cane as he approached. He stuck his finger in the jar of mayonnaise. As I turned to scold him, he put his finger in his mouth, licked off the mayo, and grinned. "So, my dear," he said, "what is this great and terrible secret? My curiosity is piqued."

"What do you mean?" I asked, though I knew. He'd read the letter, of course.

"I mean this girl. And how you parted. Why have you never mentioned her before?"

He reached for the mayonnaise jar again, and I snatched it back and replaced the lid, tightening it with unnecessary force. "That's unsanitary," I said. "And *that*" — I pointed at the letter — "is my personal mail."

"You left it there on the table," he said. "In full knowledge of my nature. You knew I'd read it."

I recognized the expression on his face, the mixture of intensity and detachment. I'd seen it on other occasions when he caught a hint of something he didn't know about me, some avenue he hadn't yet explored. "I'm not a research subject," I said.

"At this moment you are. If I tell you you're far prettier and more interesting

26

than any of my other subjects, will you tell me the story?"

"I'm prettier than William Faulkner?" I took the mayonnaise back to the refrigerator and got out the milk. "How flattering." I didn't look at Oliver, instead keeping my gaze on my hands as they lifted down two glasses, poured the milk. I was sorry to have a witness to my reaction to the letter, even Oliver. I was sorry to be pressed for details before I'd even decided what my reaction was.

Oliver followed me to the table, where I set down the glasses. He eased into his chair while I went back for the plates. I sat and reached for my sandwich, but he ignored his. He didn't even turn toward the table, just sat watching me with both hands on his cane. "I think lunch is under control," he said. "Now we can talk about this." He nodded at the letter.

I took a big bite of my sandwich. The chewy white bread stuck to the roof of my mouth.

"Come now," he said. "What's the story? What happened?"

I swallowed. "What always happens," I said. "She did something wrong. I did something wrong. The end."

"And was that end a turning point?" he

27

asked. "Is she right?"

I had wondered, in self-pitying moments, if Sonia had dismissed me, what she'd done, what I'd done, the instant I disappeared from view. I found that I was oddly gratified to learn that the end of our friendship had been a significant event in her life, even as I resented the suggestion that it had somehow shaped the course of mine.

Oliver thumped his cane against the floor. "Are you listening to me?"

"I'm listening. But it's an impossible question."

"I don't see why," he said.

"Are you telling me there are moments in your life that you can pinpoint, you can look back on and say, 'This is the turning point; this is where everything changed'?"

"Yes," he said. "And there are some I would go back to if I could and make things turn another way." He leaned toward me, his gaze intense. "I've often wondered why you're living the way you are."

"Because of you," I said. "I wouldn't eat bologna on my own."

"No, no," he said. "I'm asking you, of all possible versions of your life, why have you chosen this one?"

"What's wrong with this one?" This line

of questioning seemed like it might lead to one of Oliver's attempts to plan my future. From time to time, he'd list potential husbands from among his distant relations. He'd begin letters to old friends at universities, trying to find my next job. These projects were always abandoned quickly. Neither of us wanted to consider what my future really meant. Oliver was no more reconciled to the idea of his death than I was.

"You know what's wrong with this one," he said. "You are too much alone."

"I know everyone in town," I said, and immediately felt ridiculous, though it was true — I knew a lot of people. I knew the curator at Rowan Oak. I had friends who taught in the English department, and there was a graduate student I slept with on occasion. I had had drinks at the City Grocery with a group that included the mayor. I resisted the urge to list my friends and acquaintances, trying to resist as well the feeling that I had to testify in my own defense.

He snorted. "Everyone in town," he said, as though I'd just claimed a friendship with the rabbits in the garden. "You're not close to any of those people. You don't have a beau. You hardly ever talk to your parents. There's a distance between you and the rest of the world."

"But I'm never alone." I got up from the table and took my unfinished sandwich to the counter. "I'm always with you. Don't you count?"

He picked up the letter and waved it at me. "Are you going to write her back?"

"No," I said, because it was the easiest answer.

"She's getting married," he said. "She misses you. You can't ignore that."

"Well, I'm going to."

He still held the letter, extended toward me, but now he let it go slack in his hand. He let his face go slack, too, so that he didn't look curious, or menacing, or handsome. He looked old and sad. He looked, for the first time that I could remember, defeated. "What will become of you?" he asked.

I knocked my plate into the sink, suddenly furious. "I don't know," I snapped. "What will become of *you?*" Before he could answer I stormed past him out of the kitchen and took the stairs two at a time, trying to outrun my anger and my shame. I knew the answer to the question I'd just asked. I'd seen on his face that he knew it, too.

3

My room was the smallest in the house, and when I moved into it Oliver scolded me for my choice. He never went upstairs; he didn't even really like to leave his part of the house — a bedroom, bath, and living-room suite added on when the house was more than a hundred years old. Oliver had been a traveler for most of his life, but as he aged, he told me, he found that he wanted less and less freedom. First he came home for good, and then he moved, gradually, into a smaller and smaller part of that home. "There's a whole world back here," he would say. "If you're the dormouse, the world is a teacup." But he said I was too young, and too tall, to live in a teacup, and it disturbed him that I limited myself to such a small portion of a completely unin-habited space.

Despite what Oliver thought, I didn't choose the room out of compunction about my status as an employee. I chose it because it reminded me of the bedrooms I had imagined for the heroines of books I'd read as a child. At first I was worried that the room had belonged to Ruth when she was a little girl, but hers was the large one down the hall, still furnished with her four-poster bed. My room was up three stairs from the rest of the second floor, tucked high in a corner like a tower. Inside were a double bed, a coarse round rug, a wardrobe, a bookcase lined with old children's books — *The Five Little Peppers and How They Grew*, *The Bobbsey Twins on the Deep Blue Sea* — and a desk that had a hidden drawer. I checked that drawer occasionally, but I never found anything except the 1936 penny that had been there the first time I looked. There was a window seat in the front window, overlooking the lawn and the street. From that vantage point I could watch the cars, the joggers, the dog walkers with a pleasurable feeling of secrecy and remove.

I sat there now, but for once there was no comfort in feeling like I was up in a tower, at a distance, as Oliver had said, from the rest of the world. I'd run upstairs jittery with anger, but it was ebbing away — I could feel it draining out of my body as my face cooled and my heart rate slowed — and I was sorry to see it go, because I was left feeling guilty and lonely and, in some way I couldn't explain, like I had failed. I was surprised by a sharp desire for Eric, the graduate student I sometimes slept with. I might have called him, if he hadn't gone to Oregon to attempt a reconciliation with his ex. Even though I didn't love him, at that moment I missed him, and was sorry that he could so easily leave me behind. Sonia was engaged. Oliver's gift of the ring was the closest I'd been to romance in quite some time. I'd dated several men in the years since college, but I hadn't loved any of them, something that, since I'd come to live with Oliver, had more or less stopped bothering me. I'd been in love only twice in my life. Both boys were best forgotten, as was Sonia, as was all love that ended in failure and grief. Of course, if Oliver was right about time, then that love still existed, and so did the grief.

What's the story? Oliver had asked me, because he wanted to know the end.

When I was fourteen we moved to Clovis, New Mexico. My father was in the air force. It was the sixth time I had moved since birth, and this time I was angry. We had left Fairfax County, Virginia, with its proximity to malls and monuments, where everybody's parents drove the beltway to play some part in the large and mysterious doings of government, for this cow town, dusty brown and flat, like an old postcard. While my friends went on to high school together, I was set adrift again with no one but my family, three passengers afloat on a dirt sea.

We arrived in Clovis at the beginning of August. It was 105 degrees, and already I took issue with everyone who had ever insisted that dry heat was somehow less difficult to bear. The skin on my hands seemed to crack like clay the moment I stepped out of my father's van onto the driveway of our new house. My father came and stood next to me. "You'll be okay, Cameron," he said. "Maybe the heat will shrink you." I was already five ten, and still growing. My father had nicknames for me: Green Giant, Tammy Tall, Camazon.

"Shut up," I said. "It's your fault I'm so tall." He was six three; my mother was a far more reasonable five seven.

He punched me lightly on the arm and laughed. My father was one of those rare people — so often portrayed in Hollywood as drill sergeants and tough-as-nails professors — who really did like you better once you faced him down. There was nothing he hated like he hated a crybaby.

My mother pointed out the yucca growing in the yard and wondered aloud if we'd see any chaparrals in our subdivision. All across America she had read to us from guidebooks. She made the best of things, my mother. She said the move would be a good chance for me to learn Spanish. Sure, our furniture wasn't arriving for a couple of days, but we could put our sleeping bags on the floor and it would be like camping. Once we had gotten settled in the house, she said, we could go out for pizza.

I lived in Clovis until I graduated from high school, but I never went back to the pizza place again. I remember it only because two significant things happened there. In the bathroom, while my parents were still eating, I looked at my underwear and realized I had started my period. Even though I had known it was coming — I was later than many of my Virginia friends — I was shocked and a little dismayed, and it made me feel even more alone to have it happen on my first day in a new town, in a shabby public bathroom. It all seemed symbolic, though of what, I wasn't sure.

I couldn't bring myself to go back to the

table. I didn't want to see my father, and I didn't know how to separate my mother from him without raising suspicion. So I went outside to the parking lot and walked through it, toward the road. I thought that I was going to be miserable there, that the entire place looked like it had been made out of dirt.

And here came the second significant thing, although I didn't at that moment realize it. A girl was walking toward me down the sidewalk. It didn't occur to me at the time to wonder why, in this town where no one walked anywhere, she was on foot. Later I'd find out she'd had a fight with her mother in the parking lot of a fast-food place, that her mother had driven off and left her to make her own way home. What struck me about her at that moment was that she was much closer to my height than most other girls my age — probably only three inches shorter. The sun brought out the red gold in her brown hair. She moved as though she were at home in her skin in a way I never could be. It was already hard to remember when I had been unembarrassed by my physical presence in the world. Not a day went by when some stranger didn't tell me I was tall.

She reached me and looked up, shielding

her eyes from the sun. She had a wide, country-air sort of face, a French farm girl face, one of her boyfriends would later say. Her eyes were blue and so big that even into adulthood she would retain a quality of innocence.

"Don't be so unhappy," she said, pausing a moment beside me. "Look up. It's a gorgeous day."

I looked up and saw, rolling above me in the endless blue sky, perfect white clouds, so puffy they could have been picked like cotton.

The girl went on by me, and I felt an urge to follow her, a tug, as though I were caught in her wake. To counteract that urge, I stepped, without looking, off the curb and into the path of a car with a long, dark body and wicked headlights. It sped toward me like a destiny. But somehow the girl was there, and her hand was on my arm. She yanked me back so hard that I seemed to leave the ground. I landed beside her on the sidewalk as the car flew by, its horn blaring. My first thought was that she was incredibly strong.

"That car almost hit you," she said. We were both shaking. She was still clutching my arm.

I said, "You saved me."

She let go of my arm and took a deep breath. She shook back her hair. "What's your name, anyway?" she said. "I should know it now."

"I'm Cameron Wilson," I said. "I just moved here."

"I'm Sonia Gray," she said. "I've lived here all my life."

"Nice to meet you," I said.

She said the same. We looked at each other a moment, and then she said, "Okay, well, I'll see you later," and she walked away.

"Thank you," I called after her, and without stopping she turned, waved, and then turned back around. I watched her go, frustrated that I hadn't been able to say more, that I hadn't been able to say what I wanted to — I'd felt a jolt when she touched me, as my life passed into her hands.

I didn't see Sonia again until the first day of school. Although I had three classes with her — French, English, and algebra — I didn't talk to her during school that day. She seemed to be very popular. In the halls she always had a crowd of girls around her, and I noticed that even upperclassmen spoke to her, especially the boys. I spent most of that day feeling like a circus freak — taller than the other girls, and with bigger breasts. I didn't have a perm or wear blue eyeshadow. I didn't go to church or listen to country music. I hadn't arrived at school in a pickup truck. To make matters worse, I was wearing a silly shirt my mother had bought, with bright appliqué patches that looked like labels: a Campbell's soup label, a Dole banana label. She had insisted that in it I'd make an impression, and I was afraid she was right. In each class, I arrived early and sat in the back. For her part, Sonia swept in at the last moment it was possible to be on time and took a desk in the front row, offering a grateful smile to the person who'd saved her the seat.

French class was half over before I learned that the teacher — a woman whose soft voice suggested a tight and frightening control — was Sonia's mother. I wouldn't have guessed from her appearance. She was not as pretty as her daughter. She was farsighted, and her big round glasses rendered her already large eyes startlingly huge and emphasized the sharpness of her nose. Her chin was more pointed than Sonia's, too, and when she was angry she seemed to jab the air with it as she talked.

I learned who she was when Sonia accidentally addressed her as "Mom." Madame Gray whirled on her like she'd shouted an epithet. Before Madame Gray resettled her face, I saw the anger beneath her control. She reeled off a few sentences in French that, judging from the puzzled expressions around me, no one understood. I caught the word *l'école,* which I recognized from skimming through the textbook. Sonia listened with her head cocked. *"Pardonnez-moi. Je suis désolée,"* she said when her mother was finished. *"Vous êtes Madame Gray."* She went back to taking notes. I admired her self-possession. If I were to be called out by a teacher like that, mother or not, I hoped I'd be able to remain that steady and calm.

It's possible that Sonia and I would never have become friends, certainly not best friends, if I hadn't stumbled on her two most closely guarded secrets at once. That afternoon, my mother, with her terrible sense of direction compounded by the move to an unfamiliar town, was already an hour and a half late to pick me up after school. I'd been wandering up and down the curb, trying not to look friendless or, increasingly, as the afternoon wore on, motherless, when I heard raised voices coming from the gym. I remembered

40

hearing that there were cheerleading try-outs, and I followed the sound into the cool interior, hoping to watch the auditions unseen. But they were already over. There, under the basketball hoop, was Sonia. Her schoolbooks were scattered around her on the floor, along with a few pens, a stick of gum, an empty duffel bag, and the skirt she had been wearing that day at school. Now she was wearing running shorts and Keds. Her eyes were fixed on the person who paced in front of her — her mother, Madame Gray.

"What's seven times eight?" her mother said.

"Sixty . . . five?" Sonia said.

Her mother slapped her across the face. I jumped like I was the one who had been hit.

"Twelve?" Sonia said. I heard panic in her voice, all the more startling after the composure she'd shown in class.

"Seven times eight!" her mother said.

"Uh, uh . . ." Sonia was breathing hard.

"Uh, uh . . . ," her mother mocked. "Fifty-six, Sonia. It's fifty-six. A second-grader knows that. You're never going to learn, are you? You're never going to try hard enough. Pretty face. Big breasts. You're never going to get anywhere but some man's bed." Madame Gray looked Sonia up and down and then said, in a cold, flat voice, "It's incredible that you're my daughter. Sometimes I wish you were never born."

This was the worst thing you could wish on a person, worse than wishing they were dead. I wondered if my mother ever felt that way about me, and felt a stab of fear at the thought. It had never occurred to me that your mother's love was something you could lose, even if she was ninety minutes late to pick you up on your first day at a new school.

"I'm sorry," Sonia said. "I'll try. Seven times eight. It's fifty-five."

"Fifty-*six*," her mother shouted, her hand flying again to Sonia's cheek. The crack of the slap echoed off the walls of the gym. Madame Gray made a strangled sound. Then she turned and fled like she was trying to outrun her own anger. She didn't see me standing there. After the metal door clanged shut behind her, there was that eerie silence particular to places that should be filled with noise.

Sonia looked up at me. She wasn't crying, as I had expected her to be. A red handprint faded from her cheek. Without a word she walked out of the gym, toward the locker rooms. I hesitated only a moment before I followed.

I found her standing a few feet from the pool, near the deep end. She watched me approach. "I heard you come in. I thought it would be better if she didn't know you were there," she said. "It's not her fault, you know. It's because I'm stupid. It's hard for her, because she's so smart, to have such a stupid child." She held out her hand. "C'mere," she said.

When I reached her, she clasped my hand. "On the count of three, we jump into the pool," she said. "We stay under until we can't stand it anymore."

I didn't think to protest, to say that I was fully dressed or that my mother might by now be waiting.

"I had a feeling about you, when I saw you the first time," Sonia said. "And now we have to be friends." Although it seemed to me that she was right, I didn't at the time know why. "Count to three," she said. "Then we run."

"One . . . two . . . three." I took a deep breath as she tugged me toward the pool, and then I was under. I felt the shock of cold, the drag of the water on my clothes. I opened my eyes. She was watching me. She kept her eyes fixed on mine. I counted in

43

my head, slowly at first, then faster, and by the time I got to sixty I was desperate for air. How calm she looked, like a mermaid, her hair floating around her, her blue eyes wide, and yet her grip kept tightening on my hand. I pointed toward the surface, and she shook her head. Her mouth shaped a *no* and a stream of bubbles rushed out. I knew it was silly, I knew we were just in a pool, but I started to panic. I had the sensation that there were sharks all around, a tail whipping just out of my view. I reached for the ladder, even as Sonia pulled on my hand, and when I managed to grab it I burst out of the water, gasping for air. I clung to the ladder with one hand, and with the other I held on to Sonia. I held on to her until she was ready to come up and breathe again. I felt that if I let go she would let herself drown.

In my head I began to compose a letter to Sonia I knew I'd never write. This is why we were friends, I told her, because when we met, you grabbed hold of my life and then, in exchange, offered me your own. We rescued each other, not only from a speeding car and a swimming pool, but from our separateness, each of us at once the savior and the saved.

4

Downstairs, it was quiet. Oliver wasn't in the kitchen, and he hadn't eaten his sandwich. He had, however, picked the broken pieces of my plate out of the sink and put them in the trash. I felt a pang of guilt, looking at the three china triangles on top of a wad of paper towels. The plate was old, thin, and delicate. I fished the pieces out, thinking I could glue them back together, a notion I abandoned when I saw that the edges were jagged, the sink still full of little shards. My guilt increased — Oliver shouldn't have been handling such sharp pieces. He was on anticoagulants, and bled easily. I tended to forget how vulnerable he was.

I went next to Oliver's suite, expecting to find him in his favorite chair in the den, but he wasn't there. He wasn't in the library, either, or in the little room adjoining it. Oliver called this room the Hall of Ancestors because of all the genealogies he kept there. He collected them from sources all over the country. They arrived regularly in the mail from used-book stores, many of them homemade, stapled affairs with scrawled notes in an old lady's crabbed handwriting. For a long time he wouldn't tell me what he was doing with them.

On the back wall of this room hung an enormous, framed family tree from Oliver's mother's side. Ruth was his only child, but she had had five children, and they had had children, and while I was with Oliver, two more great-grandchildren had been born. When this happened, he had me lift the family tree from the wall — it was surprisingly heavy — and pry it open so that he could add their names in his shaky block print. This seemed to give him enormous satisfaction. "I never guessed, when we had Ruth, that it would lead to so many descendants," he told me more than once. He'd smile in a faraway manner, as though contemplating all the ways the branches on that family tree would grow and split.

There was very little Ruth and I agreed on, including her father's refusal to move into what she called "an assisted-care facility," and I imagined how she would look at me now if she'd witnessed the morning's scene — with an expression of triumphant reproval. Just a few months ago she'd shouted at me that I couldn't keep Oliver safe. She'd slammed her coffee cup down on the counter after I dismissed her concerns by saying that I could take care of him, that we were doing fine. "He's doing fine now," she said, "but what are you going to do if he falls in the middle of the night? He's an old man."

"If you put him in that place, you'll kill him," I said.

That was when her face flushed red. She looked away from me for a moment, and when she looked back her expression was hard, her voice steely. "You've been very good to him," she said. "But I'm his family."

"Yes, but I . . ."

"You're not his family," she said. She kept her gaze fixed on me. How did she know this was the way to win the argument, the worst thing she could have said? She was right. For a little while I had forgotten.

Oliver had found me in my room an hour later. I was sitting cross-legged in the window seat, thinking about where I could go if I left here. I'd lived so many places already, it seemed to me in that hour that I

47

had exhausted all the possibilities. Because I could not retrace my steps, I'd simply have to disappear. A little out of breath, Oliver said my name, and I started. "How did you get up the stairs?"

He grinned at me. "I crawled." He leaned forward, hands on his knees, and took a deep breath. "She's gone, you'll be happy to know."

I nodded.

"I heard what she said to you," Oliver said. "I'm sorry."

"She's right," I said. "She's your family."

He nodded. "She is," he said. "Get up now. Help me down the stairs." I obeyed. As we made our way down the stairs he clutched my arm like I was the only thing keeping him upright. I started to lead him to his recliner, but he stopped me. He pointed down the hall toward the genealogy room.

"Was somebody born?" I asked. He gave me a mysterious smile.

We stood in the center of the room for a moment. He was leaning heavily on me, and I thought guiltily of my argument with Ruth. Maybe I couldn't take care of Oliver. Maybe my desire to keep him here was two parts concern, two parts selfishness. "So," he said. "What do you think?"

"What do I think about what?"

He sighed impatiently and pointed at the family tree. I walked us both closer to it. He pointed to his own name. There, he had added another branch beside the one that led to Ruth, and above it he had written my name. I stared at it, stunned, tears starting in my eyes. "Oliver," I finally managed to say.

He patted my hand. "I know you have your own family," he said. "But I wanted you to know you belong here, too."

"Thank you," I said. I turned to him. "Ruth's going to be pissed."

He gave me his wicked grin. "I know," he said. "Why do you think I did it?"

"How did you get this down by yourself?"

"I just pretend to be a weak old man," he said. "So you'll let me lean on you awhile."

I looked around the room, at shelf after shelf of carefully bound pages, list after list of names. I wiped tears from my eyes. "Are you ever going to tell me what all this stuff is for?"

He sighed, serious again. "I had this idea, a long time ago, of making a family tree that connected everyone. *The* family tree. I knew even at the time that it was impossible. It's like trying to map every star in the universe."

"But you started collecting them anyway."

He shrugged. "My dear, I couldn't stop myself. I couldn't bear to think of them languishing in used-book stores, unless the Mormons took them to save some souls. This is my way of saving souls. Making sure they're not forgotten." He pulled from the shelf a booklet with yellow construction-paper covers, opened it, and ran one finger down a list of names. "Susannah Waverly Howse," he read. Then he smiled at me. "See?"

"Susannah Waverly Howse," I repeated.

"That's right," he said. "Now someone remembers her name."

I found Oliver, at last, in the parlor, a room we rarely used, dark and heavily furnished in what he described as "the great-grandmother style." He didn't look up when I walked in, so I hesitated just inside the doorway. "I'm sorry," I said.

"Have I ever told you this house survived the Civil War?" Now he did look up, though his eyes slid off my face. He made a sweeping arm gesture, like a tour guide. "It survived, even though General Smith

50

burned much of the town."

"Oh," I said.

"It was briefly a boarding house for university students." He frowned. "I'm afraid I've forgotten the dates."

"I'm sorry," I said again.

"No matter," he said. "It's only one among the many things I know."

"No," I said. "I mean, I'm sorry about before."

He looked at me. I must have looked upset, because he held out his arms to me, as though I were not a six-foot-two woman but a child who could crawl into his lap. I perched on the arm of his chair. He took one of my hands in both of his. He sighed. "Whenever you don't know what you're feeling, you reach for anger."

"I know." He had told me this many times before.

"There are other emotions."

"I know." I tried a smile. "But they're so much harder to express."

"Perhaps I shouldn't have latched on to the letter the way I did," he said. "It was this idea of her marriage, of the turning point . . ." He stopped. "Did I ever tell you I got married in this house?"

I shook my head. He rarely spoke of his wife, and in this I sensed judgment held in

51

polite reserve, and perhaps regret as well.

"I remember that feeling, the one your friend Sonia is trying to describe," he said. "I remember standing at the bottom of the stairs, waiting for my bride, and on this momentous occasion being more aware of the people I'd lost than of the people who were there. Those lost people passed in front of me like a parade. My parents. My best friend growing up, a boy named Tommy. I don't even know what happened to him. Sometimes, even now, I see these people, all the ones I lost because of choices I made. Some of them I haven't seen in sixty years, and still they show up and ask me, 'Where did you go?'" He stopped and shook his head. "Especially Billie."

"Another friend?"

"No," he said. "Billie was my girl. The girl in the picture you showed me."

A few months before, I'd found in the attic an old tinted photograph of a girl, about sixteen, in a scoop-neck dress, a pendant at the hollow of her throat. She was smiling, and her cheeks were painted pink, her pendant gold, but her gaze was inward and her eyes were sad, as though, at the moment the photograph was snapped, she had a painful vision of the future. The day I found her I brought her down to show Oliver. He adjusted his glasses for a long time before he said, "Now there's a story, but I don't want to tell it." He gave me back the photo without appearing to see me, his eyes as sad as hers. For weeks I longed to hear the story, but I couldn't bear to see that sorrow cross his face again.

"What happened?" I asked him now.

"Oh, Cameron," he said. "I did what you have done. I left her behind." He said this as if he judged me for leaving Sonia behind, as if he knew just how I'd done it. He couldn't know, of course, but I bristled anyway.

"Sonia wasn't my lover," I said.

"No," he said. "But she was someone you loved. And you could go back for her now. That's something I can no longer do."

"I can't do it, either," I said. "She's not there anymore. She can't possibly still be the girl I knew. She's a stranger."

"But she matters to you still," he said. "Or you wouldn't be so upset."

"She shouldn't matter," I said. "She was a long time ago."

"So was Billie," he said. "A much longer time. I don't know what I've taught you, if not that time is meaningless."

"When something is over it's over."

"But she still dreams about you."

I knew what he meant by this. He'd read an article once about how there was no essential difference between the mind's experience of waking life and the mind's experience of dreams, and he'd talked about it for weeks. Sometimes he had memories, he told me, that were as vivid as his life in the here and now. This, he said, was time travel — exactly what I had no wish to do. I wanted to stay in the here and now, in this house where I'd been happy, where Oliver said I belonged.

When I didn't answer, he sighed. "All right," he said. "I won't talk about her anymore." He squeezed my hand. "I love you very much," he said. "I can't possibly be the only one."

"You're enough," I said. I put my other hand on his. He leaned over to brush his lips against my cheek. Then he rested his head on my arm. We sat like that a long, long time.

Two months later, Oliver was dead.

The whole time I lived in that house I wanted to take a particular kind of photo of Oliver in front of it. In the photograph I envisioned, he was dressed in one of his southern-gentleman suits — not unlike the ones Faulkner wore in the postcards for sale at Square Books — with both of his hands resting on his cane. But the one time I tried to pose him, he looked so unsteady that I couldn't bear to leave him standing there unsupported. I settled for a picture of him sitting at an open window. In it you can just make out the shock of his white hair, a glint of light off his glasses, his lifted hand, blurry with waving.

5

Oliver used to tell people that he had found me wandering in the woods, taken me home, and adopted me, and though this couldn't have been further from the truth it was certainly how I felt. I didn't see my parents very often — my mother, remarried, lived in California; my father, retired, lived in Montana and volunteered at Yellowstone. Between dropping out of graduate school and going to work for Oliver, I had a series of unsatisfying jobs — cataloger in a used-book store in Austin, waitress in a vegetarian restaurant in Asheville, copy editor for a university press in Chapel Hill. I had even gone back to Nashville, where Sonia and I went to college, for a summer, and had a brief tenure as a secretary in the Vanderbilt English department. When I left Austin, the man I dated there said that I thought that because my father was military, I was, too. He said I'd treated my life there, and my time with him, like a tour of duty, and that the only reason I was leaving was that my year was up. I said, "You're probably right," and then he was quiet. I accepted this view of myself as restless, and thought I would probably move around forever, and most of the time that was fine with me. There were times, though, usually late at night, in a new apartment, when I was lonely, and sorry that I'd never found a place where I wanted to stay.

Oliver's daughter, Ruth, was the one who hired me. She'd been trying for years to get her father to accept a live-in aide. He was almost ninety and, while mentally acute, he was frail. He had refused her offer to hire help until she began to call this hypothetical employee his "research assistant." That was me. Ruth heard about me from my undergraduate advisor, who had never given up hope that I would do something with my education, maybe even go back and finish the doctoral program I'd abandoned after less than two years. Every few months, he wrote me an impassioned letter about his latest scholarly interests, meant to convey to me the pleasures of the life of the mind. I appreciated his efforts, but I hadn't found graduate school to have any pleasure in it at all. Ruth's husband knew this professor, and through him she tracked me down in Chapel Hill. I'd already begun to have the feeling that signaled an upcoming move — that my life was a piece of paper I wanted to ball up and throw away — so Ruth had no trouble convincing me to relocate to Oxford. She wanted me to encourage Oliver to write his memoirs. He had written many books about other people, and was famous for doing so. In high school I'd read his biography of Faulkner; in college, his history of southern race relations. Among other things, he had once won the Pulitzer Prize.

At first I actually tried to do the job I had been hired for, getting out my little tape recorder and doggedly asking Oliver questions he was usually in no mood to answer. "Tell me about your parents," I said, and he said, "She was a cold woman. And he was a philanderer. The end." He tried to turn the conversation to me, wanting to know what I thought of Oxford or what my social life was like. He said that he could tell I was wicked, like his old-maid aunt had been. It was true that when I did go out, which was seldom, I went to the City Grocery and sat at the bar drinking bourbon. And then there was the graduate student I had met there. But I couldn't tell him about that, and so I beat back his questions with my own. My persistence made him irritable. He began to seem bored and frustrated with me, but I didn't know how else to interact with him. I was miserable because I lived and worked with him, and I admired him, and so he was like a father and an employer and a respected professor — all of them impossible to please.

After three months of this, he said, "That's enough."

"Okay." I clicked off the tape recorder. "Enough for today."

"No," he said, with a sweeping gesture. "Enough for forever. I've been humoring Ruth, but I'm not interested in my own life. Please note my all-consuming interest in the lives of others."

"So I'm fired." I felt at once ashamed of my failure, and relieved. "At least I can stop trying to figure out what you want."

He laughed. "Of course you're not fired." He leaned forward in his chair. "As for what I want . . ." He directed me to the window of his den, which looked out on the driveway, where a burgundy Crown Vic peeked out from under a blue tarp.

Oliver hadn't been behind the wheel in almost a year — Ruth had forbidden him to drive after he blew out a tire hopping a curb in a McDonald's parking lot — but that day, he got the car up to eighty-five on the interstate. He looked happier than I had ever seen him, and so I said nothing, even though I was certain he was going to kill us. When the cop pulled us over I was rather glad, but when I looked at Oliver his face was pale and his hands were trembling on the steering wheel, and I remembered that whatever else he was, he was a frail old man, and under my protection. I leaned over him to roll down the window, and when the officer appeared, I said, "I'm so sorry, officer, Grandpa isn't supposed to be driving."

"Why is he, then?"

"I ran over a dog," I said, and as I said it my eyes filled with tears. "It just ran right out in the road. We stopped, but it was dead. I was shaking so much that I had to let Grandpa drive." On cue, a tear rolled down my cheek. I've always been a good liar because I have the ability to believe that whatever I'm saying is true.

The cop let us go with a warning after I assured him that I would take the wheel. He got in his patrol car and watched us in the rearview mirror as we made the switch. Oliver was delighted with me. "Attagirl,"

he said once he had eased into the passenger seat. He banged on the dashboard
with the flat of his hand. "Getting
Grandpa out of trouble. What a performance. In the old days I would've thought
of that."

I wiped my eyes, which continued to tear
even after the need had passed. "All this
time," I said, "you just wanted to have a
little fun."

"My dear," he said. "Of course."

I busied myself with adjusting the seat,
which Oliver had pulled up so close to the
wheel that I was bent in half. It was clear
he hadn't thought me much fun before.
My entire life I had been accused of being
remote and stern, sometimes mysterious.
Many times a person had said to me, after
a long acquaintance, "At first I was convinced you didn't like me" or "I thought
you were a bitch." When I was younger I
was bewildered by these misconceptions. I
thought maybe it was my height, which set
me apart, that made other people think I
had set myself apart. By this time I had
come to accept the version of myself reflected back by others, as you cannot help
but accept the image you see when you
look in the mirror.

I put on my seat belt and looked up to

find Oliver watching me like I was his science experiment.

"Let's have fun from here on out," he said. "There's no reason to be so stern, is there? I already have Ruth for that."

I pulled out onto the road. It was on the tip of my tongue to say that he was a pain in the ass. It was what I would have said to my own father, and he would have laughed and approved. Instead — I don't know why — I said, "You make me nervous." Even this small confession made me feel wretched with vulnerability. I felt a flush rise in my cheeks and kept my eyes trained on the road, waiting for him to tease me. I added, "And you're a pain in the ass."

He laughed and patted my knee. "Tough hide, soft heart," he said. "That's my girl, all right."

I would have stayed with Oliver, if only he had not died.

In the three days between his death and funeral, I felt a righteous indignation directed at everything around me, especially Ruth. After all our bickering over the question of whether Oliver might need more care than I could provide, I imagined that I detected in her bearing an accusatory smugness, as if Oliver's death were the final point in her favor. I suspected that she intended to sell the house immediately, that she was just waiting for the dirt to cover Oliver's grave before she asked me how long until I could be gone. When I'd moved from Chapel Hill to Oxford, I'd shed every possession that would not fit in my car. Everything I owned was in my little room. I could have been packed and gone in a day. Once, I'd been proud of how portable my life had become — far better to accept a transient and unstable life than to pretend permanence when there was no such thing. Now this same idea made me angry. Every day, I looked at the suitcase on the top shelf of my closet and defiantly left it sitting there.

Late to Oliver's memorial service, I slipped into the last pew in the middle of a testimonial from an old friend, or maybe a cousin — some story about Oliver wading into a stream, trying to catch a fish with his bare hands. "He was so sure he could do it," the friend/cousin said, shaking his head in sad amusement, as the people in the pews laughed or murmured or dabbed away their tears. Who were these people? I'd seen only a few of them at the house, but it seemed to me that every one of them arose on cue, one after another, and went up to speak. There were dozens. Ruth was the last. In the middle of her speech she tilted her head back abruptly and looked up at the vaulted ceiling, trying not to cry. She waited a long moment, and then lowered her head and went back to talking. Not a tear escaped. I tried not to be hurt by the fact that no one had asked me to speak. At the graveside I stood outside the tent that sheltered Ruth and the other close relatives, who sat in folding chairs. I couldn't hear anything the minister was saying. I stared at the spot of sun on the grass near my feet and thought that soon it would be summer. I had not yet cried.

Afterward, back at the house, I stood in a corner of the living room with a glass of wine in my hand and watched people eat. Ruth and her husband had added the extra leaves to the dining- room table, which was now covered with food. Three different people had brought deviled eggs, which seemed to me food more suited to a picnic than a death. Ruth's son manned the bar in another corner of the living room. There was a silver ice bucket like something out of a bantering 1940s comedy. I'd never seen the bucket before, but it was a big house, and Oliver owned a lot of things. All day I'd had the feeling that I was outside whatever room I was in, watching the action on a movie screen.

Ruth stood in the center of the room, surrounded by an endless flow of people kissing her cheek and pressing her hand. Ruth had Oliver's big, sharp nose, without his plump mouth to offset its haughtiness. Her lips were thin. In old pictures she had a severe, spinsterish look, but age had softened her face. And she wasn't a spinster — she'd been married for forty-two years to a sweet, quiet man named Bill, who seemed an odd choice for a woman raised by Oliver. Ruth's mother, Oliver's wife, had died in her late thirties. She had been pretty, with large eyes and a baby-doll mouth, which Ruth did not inherit.

Ruth had gone to the beauty parlor to have her hair fluffed into a cloud of white curls. Over the other conversations I heard her say, "Daddy would have been so happy you were all here," and I thought that if she believed that, she didn't know her father very well. I also thought how strange it was for a sixty-year-old woman to call her father Daddy.

Ruth glanced over at me and then looked away. She hadn't bothered to introduce me to anyone, and so I'd spoken only to the handful of people I already knew. I'd caught several of the others staring at me with expressions that said, "Who are you and what are you doing here?" Now, listening to Ruth use the words *Daddy* and *my father* from her position at the center of the room, it struck me that to the world at large Oliver was not anything to me but my boss. It was unfair. Perhaps he was not my father, but he was my something. I couldn't find a word that measured both our relationship and my grief.

A large man in a black suit appeared next to me, a plate piled high with food in his hand. He was sweating, and he mopped at his brow with a cocktail napkin. "Hot in here, isn't it?"

I agreed that it was.

"He was a great man," he said. "I'm a cousin."

I wondered if he was one of the cousins Oliver had meant for me to marry.

He sighed. "I wish I'd been able to see more of him," he said. "I'll miss him."

At the sorrow in his voice, my own throat tightened. "Me, too," I managed to say.

The man looked at me like he was seeing me for the first time. "So what's your story, anyway?" he asked. "Who are you? What are you doing here?"

After that I finished my glass of wine and

drank two more in rapid succession. I had just gone back to my corner with my fourth glass when a woman I knew from Square Books squeezed my arm. I'd seen her just a few days before, when I went to pick up a book Oliver had ordered. "Give him a kiss for me," she'd said. Now she asked me what I was going to do next. The truth was, I had no idea, and when I thought too hard about it I felt blank, empty, and scared.

"Bartending school," I said.

She laughed. "Will you finish Oliver's memoirs?"

"No," I said.

"Why not? Don't you have lots of material?"

"Not really."

"Why not?"

"Because most of what he told me wasn't true."

"Like what?"

"Let's see," I said. "He used to say that he had his first harem at the age of five. Every little girl in town followed him around, and he put them in order — first wife, second wife, and so on. He said his nickname was Beau, and they used to fight over him, screaming, He's my beau, he's my beau."

The woman laughed again. "I love it," she said. "What else?"

I was drunk. I didn't want to use Oliver to entertain. "He told me he'd live to be a hundred," I said. I looked into my empty wineglass until she moved away.

I threaded my way through the crowd, avoiding Ruth. I passed through the library, swallowing the urge to tell the couple pawing Oliver's precious books that he didn't like people to touch his things, and found myself in the Hall of Ancestors. I looked at my name on Oliver's family tree. "I just pretend to be a weak old man," Oliver had said. "So you'll let me lean on you a while."

I lifted my wineglass and remembered it was empty.

"Do you have a cigarette?" somebody behind me said.

I glanced down to see a kid, no more than nineteen, looking up at me. He was not especially attractive, but I had a sudden, fierce urge to take him upstairs and remove his clothes. "No," I said.

"You look like you smoke," he said. "Do you?" He opened his palm to show me two dented cigarettes.

I shrugged. "Okay." I set down my glass and followed him outside, where he led me around to the side garden, like we were guilty children, and lit both cigarettes in his mouth. When he handed me mine, I let my fingers linger a moment against his. I had never been a smoker, and hadn't had even a casual cigarette in years, but I inhaled like a professional.

"What were you doing in there?" the kid asked.

"Trying to escape the deviled eggs," I said. "Why?"

"You looked like you were thinking about something really cool," he said. "I saw you earlier, at the funeral. There's something about you. You really stand out."

"I'm six foot two," I said. "All I have to do is stand up."

He laughed like this was the funniest thing he'd ever heard. "I've never seen a girl as tall as you."

I blew out smoke and raised my eyebrows. "No?"

He shook his head. "I wonder how much taller you are than me."

I took a step closer to him. "Turn around," I said. He obeyed, and I turned, too, so that we stood back to back. I felt the heat of his skin through his shirt, felt him move to press his back more firmly

69

against mine. I reached around and touched his head, then lifted my hand to my own. "Four inches," I said, with total authority. I stepped away, disappointed that the warmth of his body offered no comfort. I licked my fingers and pinched the lit end of my cigarette until it went out, dimly aware through my wine-induced haze that I was burning myself.

The boy looked up at me like he was about to run up a mountain, then darted in for a kiss. He had to reach up to pull my head closer, and when he did I stepped back and slapped his face so hard that tears popped into his eyes.

"Shit," I said. "I'm sorry."

He pressed a hand to his reddened cheek. A plume of smoke rose from his cigarette, which he must have dropped when I hit him. I stepped on it, bent to pick it up, and said apologetically, "Oliver doesn't like litter in his garden."

"Fuck," he said, rubbing his eyes with his fingertips. "That hurt." He sounded plaintive as a child.

"Good Lord," I said. "How old are you?"

"Fifteen."

I felt unhinged — drunk and flirting with teenagers like a character in a Tennessee Williams play. "Is this really happening?" I asked the boy. "Am I really standing here?"

He dropped his hands and treated me to a disillusioned stare. "You seemed so cool."

"Yeah," I said. "I'm good at that."

Back inside, I waited until Ruth's son wasn't looking to snatch a bottle of red wine from the box behind his bar. I stopped in the kitchen for a corkscrew on my way up to my room, where I found the box of photo albums I had been hauling, unopened, from town to town for years. I hefted all of this up the attic stairs. The attic was my favorite place in Oliver's house. Up there, on the other side of that door, I couldn't hear anything that went on below — no small talk, no platitudes, no come-ons from teenagers.

I set down my box and my bottle and stood for a moment in the dusty silence. The attic was vast, stretching so far ahead of me that it seemed to grow fuzzy at the outermost edge, like a far horizon. In the dim light everything looked brown, each mysterious shape a rumor of itself, not an object so much as a possibility. I was reluctant to turn on the light. For a moment I allowed myself to live in the mystery. Then I pulled a chain and the world brightened. Things were things again.

I'd been exploring the attic for years, and yet every time I climbed those stairs I stumbled upon a treasure I'd never seen before. There were pieces of furniture — a child's armoire containing one black shoe, a cedar washstand, an old rocking chair for a very small adult. There were hardback suitcases, copper kettles, an enormous piece of stoneware with two handles on the lid. There were boxes — packing boxes, old liquor boxes, boxes for vacuums and fans and televisions. There were wooden crates stamped with pictures of fruit or the name Coca-Cola in swirly script. There was a wicker chest, a blanket chest, a steamer trunk, a footlocker in army green. Inside one box were telegrams announcing the combat deaths of sons, love letters between husbands and wives, a diary kept by Oliver's grandmother that contained the entry, *Henry is dead. I am utterly alone.* Her grief lived in the attic, that single line on an otherwise white page as stark and sad as the day she wrote it.

In many of the other boxes were pictures — daguerreotypes and tintypes of unsmiling men with mustaches, unsmiling women with their hair in tight buns centered atop their heads. And there was my favorite — the tinted photograph of Billie, Oliver's girl. Now I wondered how he'd left her behind, and why, and how it changed his life. Now I would never know.

I sat down next to the dollhouse, nearly as tall as my waist, a perfect replica of Oliver's house. I had the stupid thought that if I opened it I would find a tiny version of him, not dead, but asleep in his blue recliner. I resisted the urge to check, muttering, "Stupid, stupid," to myself as I wrested the cork from my wine bottle. I should have thought to bring a glass; straight from the bottle, the wine went down harsh and left me spluttering. From my own box of photos, I selected the album from the final trip I took with Sonia, a long, meandering drive from Tennessee to New Mexico after college graduation.

It amazed me that I'd made this album, considering how the trip ended, and I tried to remember, but couldn't, if I was angry or sad when I arranged the photos on the pages, smoothed the wrinkles out of each plastic sheet. The last picture was of Sonia, in the motel room in Big Bend, wearing a green clay mask. I remembered how pores were her latest beauty obsession, how I had been threatening to take her women's magazines away if she didn't stop talking about cleansing and tightening, how I raised the camera to freeze her there, half laughing, half annoyed, her hand flying up to conceal her strange green face. After that there was a blank page.

One night, late in that trip, Sonia had lined up all my exposed film in a row on the motel-room dresser and made me count the rolls. There were twenty-six. After that, whenever we stopped to admire something beautiful — the red mountains of New Mexico, a river winding deep between canyons in Big Bend — I tried to resist the urge to reach for my camera. I tried to look, really look, as though this took a kind of effort far greater than the movement of my eyes. You are here, I would say to myself, no part of this moment melting into the future. You are only here and nowhere else. But I could never believe it. So I would take a photo, to stop the world, so that I could keep moving. The photo was just an approximation, the world flattened and made small. But I could paste it in an album, put that album in a box, pack the box in my car, and drive. The best I could do was record where I had been before I kept on going.

Of the two of us, Sonia had the gift for photography, but she'd just stand there, arms on the guardrail, and gaze at the landscape like it didn't matter what her memory lost.

I'd never answered her letter. I wondered how long she'd waited for a reply before she stopped hoping, whether she was married by now.

"I saw you slap my nephew," Ruth said, startling me. I hadn't heard her come up. I looked up from Sonia's face to hers. "I went outside for a breath of fresh air, came around the corner, and pow."

"He's your nephew?"

"Well, grandnephew," she said. "My husband's, really. I don't claim him." She groaned, lowering herself to sit beside me. "It's okay. I've no doubt he deserved it." I saw her eyes go to the opal ring on my left hand, and moved it out of her line of sight. No doubt she'd think I wheedled a family heirloom from an old man.

"That's a beautiful ring," she said in a neutral voice. "Opals, right?"

"Oliver gave it to me."

"Oh?" She reached for my hand, and reluctantly I showed it to her. She touched the ring. "Looks antique."

"It belonged to his aunt. Your great-

75

aunt. The one who lived here. You don't recognize it?"

"No, and I'm surprised."

"Surprised he gave it to me?"

She sighed. "Surprised she wore it. She was a superstitious woman, and her birthday was in June."

"Oh." I looked at the wine, wanting to drink it, wishing she would leave so I could. "I guess I'm braving the bad luck."

"I guess so." One corner of her mouth lifted in a rueful smile. She ran her hand down the roof of the dollhouse. "What are you doing up here?"

"I'm looking at photos." I flipped back a few pages, to a picture of Sonia leaning on an old-fashioned gas pump, somewhere on Route 66.

"Daddy's?" Ruth asked.

I shook my head. "Mine."

She leaned in. "Who is that?"

"An old friend."

"She's right pretty," Ruth said. "As somebody used to say. Can you pass me that wine?"

Surprised, I handed it to her and watched her throat work as she drank. "My God, those people," she said, wiping her mouth with the back of her hand. "They're never going to leave." She looked around the attic. "I haven't been up here in a long time," she said. "I'm not surprised you like it up here. Daddy always did. You and he are a lot alike."

This disarmed me, although I wasn't sure she meant it as a compliment.

"I was sorry we didn't hear from you at the funeral," she said.

"What do you mean? No one asked me to speak."

She looked puzzled. "Didn't you hear me at the beginning? It was an open mic."

"Oh," I said, chastened. "I came in late."

"That explains it." She smiled. "I'm glad to know that. I was rather offended."

"I guess I was rather offended, too."

Ruth sighed. "You always assume the worst of me, don't you," she said gently, and then she patted me on the leg. "Daddy always said you like to say no first."

I was stung. "He said that?"

"He didn't mean it as an insult," Ruth said. "Although I'm not sure how it's not. Oh, hell." She took another swig of the wine. "I shouldn't have said that. I'm not trying to insult you. I know you took good care of my father, and that he adored you. I'm grateful."

I was staring at the photo album, blinking and blinking. Sonia's face swam in

77

and out of focus. "I was up here when he died," I said.

She looked at me.

"I was reading your uncle's letters from the war. I didn't hear a thing," I said. "He might have called out, I don't know."

Ruth picked at the label on the wine bottle with her thumbnail. She had a French manicure.

"I found him at the bottom of the stairs." I swallowed. I could see him there, sprawled out, facedown, one hand on the bottom step, like he was trying to reach me. "I ran down the stairs so fast I stepped on his hand."

Ruth flinched.

"I feel like I killed him, Ruth."

"He was already dead," she said.

I swallowed again. That didn't matter. "I thought I could keep him from dying."

Now she gave me a sympathetic look. "Oh, my dear," she said, just like her father used to. "He was ninety-two. How could you possibly?" She handed me the bottle of wine and urged me to drink it, like it was medicine. When I had choked some down, she patted my shoulder. "Have you thought about what you're going to do now?" she asked, brisk as a career counselor. Her thin lips were stained purple.

"You must be qualified for any number of jobs. You could work in the bookstore. I assume you're planning to stay in town. Where else would you go?"

I shrugged, too weary to bristle. That was Ruth, managing to insult you even when she was trying to be kind. I looked at a picture of myself striking a conqueror's pose on the side of a mountain, both hands on my hips. "When do you need me to be out?" I asked.

Ruth clicked her tongue against her teeth. "My dear, that's not what I meant. For God's sake, you make me feel like a foreclosing bank. This is your home, and you belong here. You can stay here as long as you need to." She looked around the attic. "I don't know quite what to do with the place, anyway. Maybe you could be the caretaker for a while."

I wanted to say yes. It would have been so easy to stay up there in the attic and become a ghost. But hearing Ruth say that I belonged, I knew that I didn't. My name penciled in on the family tree didn't make me family. Once, Oliver told me I was lucky not to have the kind of past embodied in this vast, treasure-filled attic, where for more than a hundred years his family had stored their memories. He said,

"You make your own history."

Now he was dead, and the history I'd made fit in a single cardboard box. It hadn't rooted me in anything, just brought me to a place where there was nothing guiding me, nothing telling me which way to go. I shut the photo album on Sonia's face and told myself that in a way Oliver was right about my luck. To belong nowhere is a blessing and a curse, like any kind of freedom.

6

When I was a child, my father encouraged me to belong nowhere, to immerse myself in the culture of each new place and then just as easily leave it behind. I learned not to complain about moving, about the friends I'd lose, because he'd just shake his head, amazed and disappointed by my cowardice, and ask, "My God, are you going to cry about it?" He didn't believe in living on base; he said there was no point in moving if every place we lived was essentially the same. In England this meant that we rented a house in a village complete with real British people and a village green. The kitchen had a tiny British refrigerator that my mother never stopped complaining about for three years. It was the one adjustment she couldn't make.

We had been in England for two weeks when I started all-day school at Stanton Primary. I was four and a half. I had a bad first day. In the morning the lesson involved reading aloud words printed on little plastic rectangles. Each word we could read, each punctuation mark we could identify, we could put inside folders marked with our names. The teacher said that the words in our folders were the only ones we would be allowed to use when we wrote stories. I wanted them all.

When it was my turn I read everything without hesitation until I came to a square with a black dot in the center. "That's a period," I said.

"No, it's not," the teacher said.

"Yes, it is," I insisted. My mother had taught me to read six months before, and I was very proud of my knowledge. In Idaho I had been well ahead of the other children in my preschool. The teacher there had said, "Oh, very good," and "Aren't you smart?" She had been pretty and young and quick to smile. This teacher was square-jawed and gray-haired. Her accent made everything she said seem clipped and disdainful.

"That's a period," I said again.

"No, it's not," she said. "It's a full stop. Read the next one."

I went on, but I couldn't recover my confidence. A voice in my head kept insisting, "It's a period," but it grew increasingly uncertain. Maybe what I had thought was a period actually was a full stop. Maybe, more alarmingly, my mother was wrong. And now I had a folder full of words, but without full stops they'd never make sentences.

As the day went on I found again and again that I didn't know the names of things. In the line at the cafeteria, a lady asked me if I wanted pudding and then gave me something that looked more like pie. I had learned my lesson. I didn't try to explain to her that it wasn't pudding. I just went quietly to a table and sat.

For a moment, I ate happily. This was uncomplicated — I was hungry, and the food was good. Then a lunch lady appeared at my side. She said, "Oh, no, that's wrong." She took my silverware from my hands and switched them, knife in the right, fork upside down in the left.

I said, "But I don't do it this way."

She said, "Now you do."

I said, "But I'm American."

She said, "Not here, you're not."

She left me there at the table, clutching the silverware like a monkey at a dinner party. Even after she was gone I was afraid to switch the silverware back. She had been so plump and stern, so certain that I was wrong. I tried to go on eating, but my hands didn't seem to work anymore. The whole process, which had been so natural only moments before, was now unwieldy, impossible. I began to cry, but quietly. Even at that age I was embarrassed by tears. They trickled down my cheeks as I struggled to push peas onto the back of my fork. The peas just rolled right off.

Across the table a girl my age was watching me with interest. She had long brown hair, like mine, held back at her temples with two barrettes. Her cheeks were pink. "Do it like this," she said. She pushed a few of her peas onto her fork, then, without removing the knife, she mushed the peas down. They stuck. She put them in her mouth, slid the fork out, and grinned at me as though she had done a magic trick. It must have been a pleasure to astonish with such a basic and common skill. Surely no one had ever found her ability to eat remarkable before.

I sniffed and swallowed and tried to stop crying. My breath was still coming in little hiccups. I copied her movements. Some of the peas escaped but several made it into my mouth. I watched closely as she cut her meat. I imitated her. This was much easier.

"You're American, then?" she asked.

"What's that like?"

"I don't know," I said. Just two weeks before, I had had nothing to compare it to. "I say Mommy, not Mummy." I had noticed this difference at the corner shop, where my mother had given me fifty pence, my strange new allowance, and let me pick out an Enid Blyton book.

"Well, that's odd, isn't it," she said. "You'd better change that."

"Okay." I was willing to make any number of accommodations for her. She had taught me to eat, and with that small triumph, a few little peas, it had become possible once more to negotiate the world.

After that, every time we moved I was on the lookout for what changes in me would be required. Like the friends I'd had elsewhere, Sonia enjoyed teaching me about life in her town, everything she took for granted. She said showing me the ropes made her feel like she knew all there was to know about this life, like she'd already lived it a thousand times over and because of that would always know just what to do and say. She taught me that on weekend nights teenagers cruised Main, driving up and down in their pickups and El Caminos and red or silver Camaros, bouncing to the music that drifted out their open windows. She taught me that the high-school girls who dated airmen were called barracks bunnies, that the Future Farmers of America wore Wranglers and hung out behind the Ag building, that at the Trinity Church, a strange little box of a place downtown with no visible windows, people were rumored to speak in tongues.

But unlike other friends, Sonia showed me what was different about this new place without ever seeming to require me to change. The slight Texas accent I acquired, the knowledge of how to two-step — I picked up those things on my own. With Sonia, I belonged for the first time with a person, instead of pretending to belong to a place. When one of us walked into a room alone, "Where's Sonia?" or "Where's Cameron?" was the first thing said.

Sonia didn't explain to me, at first, why I'd seen her mother hit her, why she couldn't multiply seven times eight. That time in the gym, we climbed out of the pool and walked in silence outside, where we stood dripping in the courtyard, wringing out our hair. I asked her how she was going to get home.

"I don't know," she said, like it didn't much matter.

"We can give you a ride."

"That would be nice," she said. "Thank you."

After that she was silent. I took her silence to mean that I was a reminder of the scene I'd witnessed, that she now wished I'd disappear, and that she'd avoid me in the future. I knew this was how I'd behave if I were her, but the thought that Sonia might ignore me made me sad. I wanted to be her friend. Already I wanted to protect her, less because of pity than because of my admiration for her resolve, which seemed to me to make her deserve protection all the more. There she was, soaking wet, her clothes clinging to her body, and for all I knew she could still feel the sting of her mother's slap against her cheek. But she stood without hunching her shoulders or twisting her legs, with no appearance of self-consciousness. When a boy from our English class walked by, I crossed my arms over my chest — my nipples were showing — but Sonia just said, "Hi." She met his gaze like there was no need for explanation, and he didn't ask for one. She embodied the lesson I'd learned from my dealings with my father: Show no weakness. The world will use it against you.

At last my mother arrived. She didn't

offer her usual explanations for her lateness; she was too busy staring at me and Sonia. "Mom, this is Sonia," I said, opening the front door. "She needs a ride."

"Nice to meet you," Sonia said. "Do you mind taking me home?"

"Of course not," my mother said, and only then did Sonia climb into the car. "What on earth happened to you two?" my mother asked.

I didn't look at Sonia. "It was freshman hazing," I said. "Some of the upperclassmen pushed a bunch of us into the pool."

"That's terrible," my mother said.

"No, no," I said. "If they haze you it means they think you're cool. It would be worse if they ignored us."

"It's hot out, anyway," Sonia said. I chanced a look back at her. She met my eyes and smiled, this smile she had that made her look like a child given an unexpected gift, a smile that said she was delighted with you, and amazed at her own good fortune. I'd passed a test. She knew I'd keep her secrets.

Sonia's house was in a subdivision not far from the one where we lived. It didn't have any of the southwestern flavor of our house. It was gray brick, tall and narrow, and I imagined that her mother peered at us, witchlike, out of a second-story window, malevolence in her eyes. Before she got out of the car, Sonia asked if I wanted to come over after school the next day. "If that's all right," she said to my mother, and my mother, surprised by her politeness, said of course it was.

"Okay," I said, resisting the urge to ask if she wouldn't rather come home with me. As Sonia walked to her porch and climbed the steps to her front door, I felt like we were delivering her back to captivity, like she was a princess returning to the castle of her long imprisonment.

"I'm glad you made a friend," my mother said.

During French the next day, Sonia passed me a note that said, *Wait for me at the end of class.* So I did, lingering awkwardly among the desks while Sonia told two other girls she'd catch up to them later. Madame Gray was flipping through a stack of papers — she'd given us a pop quiz on the night's reading, and even though it was only the second day of school, the class already knew better than to complain. The other girls dispatched, Sonia waved for me to join her at her mother's desk.

"Madame Gray," she said, and then waited for her mother's attention. When she got it, she said something in French. I caught only my name and the words *après l'école.* Madame Gray looked at me, surprised, and I was sure she was going to say no. She narrowed her eyes, appraising me. Then she pulled out my quiz and scanned it.

"You did the reading," she said. Now she looked up at me with a smile. "You got every question right." She addressed her daughter without looking at her. "She's a smart girl, Sonia."

Despite myself, I was gratified. *"Merci, Madame,"* I said, and then — I don't know what possessed me — I made an odd, abbreviated curtsy.

"You're welcome," Madame Gray said, with the gracious nod of a queen. "Okay, girls," she said. "Meet me in the faculty parking lot after school."

As we went out into the hall, Sonia appraised me in a way not unlike her mother, and I wondered if she thought perhaps I'd gone too far with the curtsy, that I might not be an ally after all but a potential teacher's pet. To distract her, I asked, "Why are you in this class, anyway? Shouldn't you be in French Four or something?"

"What do you mean?" she said. "I've never taken French before."

"But you speak it so well."

She looked at me like I was crazy. "No, I don't," she said. She turned as if to go, and again I worried that she'd changed her mind about being my friend. But she stopped. "Well done, by the way," she said, and then she disappeared into the crowd.

I anticipated the end of the school day with a mixture of excitement and dread. In my mind, that narrow gray house assumed gothic proportions, with Madame Gray a woman of the sort who tormented poor orphan girls in Victorian novels. I imagined her shouting questions at me in French, then sending Sonia to fetch the rod. When I got to the faculty parking lot, Sonia was already leaning against a car, and I was glad to see that her mother wasn't there yet. Sonia was excited — she'd made the JV cheerleading squad. She started describing for me the girls she'd been up against, the whole process of the tryouts, but she stopped abruptly when she saw her mother approaching. "Don't say anything to her," she said.

Madame Gray insisted I sit in the front seat, to accommodate my long legs, and all the way to their house she asked me questions about myself — where I'd lived before, what my parents did, what I liked to study in school. I tried to give minimal answers. It was clear I needed to be polite to Madame Gray to be allowed to spend time with Sonia, and yet every politeness I offered her felt like a betrayal.

When we got inside the house Madame Gray went up the stairs, Sonia followed, and I brought up the rear. To my relief, at the top of the stairs Madame Gray went one way, Sonia the other. I followed Sonia, jumping when Madame Gray shut her door with a bang. I turned in the direction of the sound and saw that every door in the hall was closed. I couldn't tell which room Madame Gray was in. "Don't worry," Sonia said. "She won't come out again for hours. Sometimes she spends the whole day in there, with the lights out and the curtains drawn."

She pushed open one of the doors. "This is my room," she said. She walked in first, and then turned as if to see my reaction.

It was a room for a little girl. The furniture was white, painted with sprays of pink roses. The carpet was pink. There was a four-poster bed hung with lacy curtains. On the walls were paintings of ballerinas, none of the posters of actors or rock stars I favored. "It's crazy girly, isn't it?" Sonia said. "My father had it decorated for me when I was seven. I'm afraid it would hurt his feelings if I changed it."

"It's really . . . clean," I said.

She gave me a rueful smile, and then bent to lift the bottom of the pink-and-white bedspread. I crouched to look underneath the bed and saw a crazed jumble of clothing, books, candy wrappers, crumpled paper, and, pushed way back against the wall, a few old Barbie dolls.

"Wow," I said. We straightened up. "Your mother doesn't check under here?"

Sonia shook her head. "It's the same under her bed," she said. "The whole house is like this. You don't want to look in the kitchen cabinets." She sat on the edge of her bed and fixed me with a hard stare. "Can you keep a secret?" she asked.

"Sure," I said.

"No, I mean, really. Can you really keep a secret? Can you swear to never, ever tell?"

"Yes," I said, growing annoyed.

"Even under pressure? Even if someone asks you questions?"

"I can lie," I said. "I'm a good liar."

"That's true," she said. "I noticed that yesterday." She looked away, moving her fingers in the air like she was playing invisible piano keys. I'd learn to recognize this gesture as a sign of anxious thought. At that moment it just seemed as strange as everything else about her — her crazy mother, her childish room, the unnerving intensity in her manner. Even with all that, I didn't feel any urge to retreat from the friendship we were beginning. She fascinated me, and whatever she was thinking of telling me, I wanted to know what it was.

"So, yes, I can keep a secret," I said.

"Good," she said, her tone suddenly brisk and decisive. "I've decided to tell you everything." She pointed at the digital clock on her bedside table. "What does that look like to you?"

"A clock."

"No, but what does it say?"

"It says three-fifty-three."

She shook her head. "Not to me, it doesn't. To me it says, 'Hello, I am a bunch of little sticks.'"

"I don't get it," I said.

"Numbers," she said. "Sometimes I can't read them. They reverse or turn themselves upside down. They come loose and float around in space. Sixes look like nines. Fives look like threes. And sometimes they all just fall apart into a bunch of little sticks."

I squinted at the green display on the clock until the numbers blurred, but I couldn't make them do any tricks. "Why?" I asked.

"I'm dyscalculate," she said. "It's a rare condition that usually occurs only in the brain-damaged. No one knows why I have it."

"What does it mean?"

"It means I'm stupid," she said. "I can't do math. Sometimes I think I'm doing math, and then I realize I've just written a bunch of little lines. Who would do that besides a stupid person?"

"You don't seem stupid," I said.

"I'm good at hiding it." Her voice was almost angry now, and she was watching me with a narrow-eyed intensity, as if she expected that at any moment I'd denounce her, slap her across the face like her mother had. "I have good days, when I can read numbers. On bad days, if I'm in class and I can't find the right page number in the book, I let it fall off my desk. The person who picks it up automatically turns to the right page before they give it back. If the teacher asks me to read numbers on the board, I squint and say I forgot my glasses. If I'm supposed to call someone and I can't dial their phone number, I'll tell them I got a busy signal or that my parents were on the phone all night. Some numbers I can dial because I've memorized the pattern on the phone." She punched a number on an imaginary phone in the air. "If I have to pay for something, I just hand someone the bills and hope they'll give me the right change, and if they say, 'This is only a five,' I laugh and say, 'What's wrong with me today?' and hand them another bill. I know it's George Washington on the one, but sometimes I still get confused."

"No one knows about this?"

She shook her head. "My parents. The people who tested me in Albuquerque when I was little. You."

"Why don't you just tell people?"

She looked at me like I'd suggested she run naked down the hall. "Would you tell people if you were brain-damaged?"

"But you're not."

"No," she said, but she didn't sound convinced. "I'm lazy. I should work harder."

"That's what your mother says," I said. "Isn't it?"

She sighed. "I bet you don't realize," she

96

said. "Numbers are everywhere."

I sat beside her on the bed. She didn't look at me, but stared at her hands, which she twisted in her lap. Her hair fell forward across her face. The bed was so tall her feet dangled off the edge. She looked like the child she'd been when her father decorated this room. I touched her hair, tucking a strand behind her ear. It was sleek as seal fur and soft — almost unbearably soft. "I think you have to be really smart to hide it so well," I said. "It's impressive."

She glanced at me shyly. "Really?"

"Show no weakness," I said. "That's my motto."

"I like that." She looked away and then back again. "Show no weakness," she said.

Later, Sonia would say that I was her negative and she mine, and by that she meant that our qualities were reversed, that she seemed less guarded than she was, and I seemed more. She used to say I did a fine job of seeming to care about nothing in order to hide the fact that I cared about everything. I used to say her best defense was a good offense; she used to say mine was a wall. She said I was hiding a big, bleeding heart, an assertion I always disputed, though she meant it as a compliment — she admired my ability to hide it.

I think I knew, even when we were fourteen, what a relief it was to Sonia that I had witnessed that scene in the gym, that she never had a chance to put up her guard with me. Because my own strangeness was physical, there was little I could do to conceal it, though I tried — avoiding heels, slouching, wearing baggy shirts to hide my substantial breasts. The best I could do was to pretend invulnerability, roll my eyes at my father's jokes about my height, at the guy at my old school who referred to me as Melons. I understood the impulse to disguise, and I understood, too, the longing for one person to know the truth, the weakness of spies and superheroes everywhere.

"Can I ask you something?" I said.

"Okay."

"Why did your mother look so surprised when you said you wanted to bring me home?"

"Because you're the first friend I've had over since fifth grade."

"But you're so popular," I said. "You're a cheerleader, for God's sake."

She shrugged. "I want those people to think my life is normal, that I'm normal," she said. "I want you to know what I'm really like." The darkness in her mood suddenly lifted. She smiled, looking pleased with herself. I couldn't tell if she was pleased by the thought that finally she'd have someone who knew her or by the thought of how successful she'd been at making sure no one else did. She said, in a stage whisper, "My eyes aren't really blue."

"Really?"

She nodded. "I wear tinted contacts."

"What color are your eyes?"

"They're brown," she said. She raised a hand, her fingers hovering near my face. "Same as yours."

7

One morning, about a month before Oliver died, I woke at seven, as usual, and went to the kitchen only to find it empty. There was no sign of Oliver, no coffee in the pot. In the three years I'd been living with Oliver, I hadn't once reached the kitchen first. I put my hand against the coffeepot and when I felt its cold glass surface I was certain Oliver was dead. I ran to his suite, the word *no* beating time in my head with my steps.

I saw his figure in the bed and came to an abrupt stop. I don't know what I would have done if he hadn't at that moment raised his head. I pressed my hand to my heart. "Jesus," I said. I took a deep breath, struggling to disguise my relief. "What are you doing still in bed?"

"Jesus, yourself," he said. "If I sleep in, is that a national emergency?"

"Are you sick?"

"No." He spoke to the ceiling. "I've decided that I'm going to spend the day in bed."

"You should get up." I put my hands on my hips.

He regarded me. "Why?"

"Because." I couldn't think of a single reason. He snorted and put his head down. "Fine," I said. I went back to the kitchen, where I made coffee and put two full mugs, each with three dollops of heavy cream, on a tray. When I returned, Oliver had propped himself up on pillows and turned on the television. A morning news show anchor was interviewing an attractive young actor about his new movie. Oliver kept his eyes on the screen as I went around to the other side of the bed and set the tray carefully in the middle. I climbed in on the other side.

"What are you doing?" Oliver asked.

"Joining you," I said. "This is what we're doing today."

Oliver lifted his mug and then, with a movement so startling I sloshed hot coffee onto my thigh, he threw it at the television. It was a weak throw. The mug made it just past the end of the bed and dropped to the floor with a thunk. On television, the anchor and the actor laughed like they were immensely pleased with themselves.

"What's wrong with your own life?" Oliver said. In his fury he looked like the bird of prey he always claimed to resemble. "What do you want with mine?"

In the week after Oliver's funeral, I woke up at seven every day. For lunch I made two bologna sandwiches and ate both of them. At night I watched *The Philadelphia Story* — one of Oliver's favorites — so many times I could have acted out all the parts. During the day, when Oliver would have been reading or, more likely, nodding off over a book, I went to the attic and searched for old photos I'd never seen before, trying to guess who the subjects were — all those serious and smiling mouths, uplifted chins, hair bows and bow ties, striped bathing suits and carriages, hats and furs, cigarettes, lost lives. I didn't cry. I avoided Oliver's suite, and so a feeling persisted that Oliver was not dead, just perpetually in the next room. No one else came to the house that week, and I never left it.

On the seventh day, I was standing in the kitchen, eating a bologna sandwich, when I heard the front door swing open. I froze. After a moment I finished chewing, and swallowed, but I stayed where I was, like an animal convinced that if it keeps very still no one will see it.

"Cameron?" It was Ruth's voice. "Cameron? Where are you?"

"Here," I said, but my voice, unused in days, came out small.

Ruth appeared in the doorway. She wore paint-splattered jeans and a T-shirt, a huge cardboard box under her arm. She had a red bandanna over her white hair. "There you are." She made a face. "What are you eating?"

"Bologna. Are we going to paint?"

She set the box on the table. It was empty. "No." She rolled her shoulders and one of them cracked. "We're going to clean. We're going to sort. We're going to give stuff away."

"Right now? Why?"

She gave me a disgusted look. Then she pointed at the sandwich in my hand. "Isn't it obvious?" she said. "Don't tell me you like bologna. Now, come on." She picked up her box and marched from the kitchen, heading in the direction of Oliver's suite.

This was a dilemma — not only did I not want to sort and clean Oliver's suite, I didn't even want to go in there, but I couldn't bear the thought of Ruth making all the decisions alone. What did Ruth know of the value of the ballpoint pen on Oliver's bedside table, his favorite pen, without which he wouldn't write a check or even sign his name? To her, that pen would look ordinary, would look like trash. The longer I stood in paralyzed indecision, the more likely Ruth was to be ripping through Oliver's bedroom like a natural disaster, turning all his treasures into debris.

I expected to find Ruth flinging the closets and dresser drawers open, grabbing clothes and books by the armload. But she was standing stock-still in the center of Oliver's bedroom, the cardboard box on her hip. When she turned to me there were tears in her eyes. "The sheets are still rumpled," she said.

I made a quick survey of the room, letting my eyes skip over the bed. There were three dressers topped with bookcases. There were two closets, an armoire, two wooden chests, and two bedside tables, each with a drawer. That was just the bedroom. There was also the bathroom, with its shelves, cabinet, and medicine chest, and then there was all the built-in storage in the den. "Okay," I said briskly. I clapped my hands at Ruth like a coach. "Let's do the big job first." I pointed at the wall of dressers.

Ruth stared at me. "I changed my mind. I can't do it."

"Yes, you can. Come on, let's go."

She set down her box, and we turned toward the dressers. We each opened a drawer, and sighed in unison at the chaos revealed.

It's astonishing what a single life accumulates. The belts, lightbulbs, AAA batteries, bud vases, safety pins, expired medications, eyeglasses, rubber bands, picture frames, birth announcements, buttons from old coats, boxes that once held jewelry — all the things we think we just might need someday. These things we endow with a certain life — the possibility that we might use them, the memory we attach to them — and then, when we die, they become just things again. Again and again Ruth and I turned to each other, holding up a broken travel alarm or a never-used date planner from 1979, and said, "What on earth was he saving this for?" More than once one of us held up an unidentifiable object — a black plastic rectangle, a twisted piece of metal — and said, "What the hell is this?"

After three hours we had emptied the dresser drawers. Ruth shut the last one with an air of weary victory, and then reconsidered. She reopened each one and ran her hand all the way to the back.

"I think we got it all," I said, but she kept looking. As each drawer came up empty, she seemed to grow more certain that there was something still to find. In the last drawer she checked, she found a small gray jewelry box, printed with the name of the jeweler in gold.

"Another one?" I said. "He really loved those empty jewelry boxes."

Ruth shook it. "There's something inside." She made an excited face — a pirate about to open the treasure chest — and then she took off the lid. In a tone of wonder, she said, "I thought these were lost." She showed me two slender gold bands — her parents' wedding rings.

After that, Ruth didn't want to clean anymore. She sat on the floor and turned the rings over and over in her hands, reading the inscriptions inside. I was glad she had found something that meant so much to her, but I couldn't conquer the envy I felt at the emotion in her voice. I wanted to find something, too. On my own I lost the focus that had gotten us through the first task. I wandered from closet to dresser and back again, opening and closing drawers.

At Oliver's bedside table, I picked up his favorite pen. "Can I keep this?"

"What?" Ruth looked puzzled. "Of course."

I slipped the pen into my pocket. Then I bent to open the drawer, and found my reward. There it was — the exact thing I had been hoping to find, without quite knowing it — an envelope with my name on it atop a package wrapped in thick brown paper. I lifted it out with reverence, and felt immediately possessive, like Gollum with his ring. I didn't want Ruth to see. I sat on the floor beside the table, hoping the bed would hide me from her view.

The package was rectangular in shape, big enough to hold a hardback book, but too light for that to be its contents. Oliver had cut up a brown-paper bag to wrap it, and had not done a terribly good job of either the cutting or the wrapping. The paper puffed out in some places, stuck out in jagged triangles in others, and I could see where he'd struggled with the tape, jammed it on in sticky little bunches and started again with new pieces. He'd tied a piece of red yarn around the package, a loose knot where perhaps he'd wanted a bow. I turned the package around in my hands, imagining what, out of all his things, he might have chosen especially for me — a necklace that matched his aunt's opal ring, one of the chickens from the collection on the kitchen windowsill? Maybe he'd secretly tape-recorded his memoirs and was leaving them for me to edit — a plan for my future he'd finished making after all. I knew exactly which picture of Oliver I'd choose for the cover — a studio shot of him as a young man, his thick hair combed back, his eyes bright, his sly smile suggesting a wealth of clever thoughts. He looked in that picture like a man on the verge of an adventurous life.

My excitement made me hesitant, hoping that whatever was inside the package would equal my joy at discovering it. I opened the letter first, tearing the envelope as carefully as I could.

My dear Cameron,

I suppose you think yourself now relieved of duty — alas, I have one final task to charge you with before I release you from my employ. Deliver this wedding present to your onetime friend, the charming Miss Sonia Gray. Do not mail it — it must be delivered in person, by you. You will, of course, be compensated, at twice your normal rate, for however long it takes you to complete this task. Please show this letter to Ruth (unless of course I have outlived her) as a sort of invoice.

Your Miss Gray thinks perhaps you never replied to her letter because you are genuinely indifferent to her. She imagines you have at last become as detached as you always wanted people to think you were. I differ from her in this opinion. Still, I can well imagine your indignation at being sent to her. Right now you are thinking that the package is empty and its delivery just another scheme I have devised to torment you. I assure you this is not so. Remember that you have a long life yet to live, as I do not. I know you will not refuse me the time it will take to do this one last thing.

Yours, as ever,
Oliver Doucet
P.S. Don't open the package. I invoke your overdeveloped sense of honor. And if there's life after death, I'm watching you.

There were many things in the letter to upset me, but at first all I felt, like a punch in the throat, was disappointment that the package was not for me. Three years together, and Oliver's parting words were instructions to deliver something to another, instructions not even signed with love. He'd never even met Sonia, but he'd chosen her over me.

I read the letter again. What did he mean when he said Sonia thought I was indifferent? How did he know what Sonia thought about anything? It took longer than it should have for me to realize that he was telling me he'd corresponded with her. He must have taken it upon himself to answer her letter when I wouldn't, the way I answered the letters that he ignored. And what had they said to each other, these two people who had nothing but me in common? What other opinions on my psychology had they shared as they formed their secret bond? What had they told each other that I wouldn't have wanted them to know?

I stood and paced away from the bed, then back. "Son of a bitch," I said. My voice came out funny, like I was about to cry.

"What?" Ruth said.

I looked up to find her watching me from the foot of the bed.

"What do you have?" she asked.

I didn't want to tell her. The thought of her reading the letter pained and embarrassed me. I didn't want to explain about Sonia. I didn't want her to know I merited not a final, sentimental gift but a task. "Nothing," I said. She looked at me sharply, and I braced myself for more questions. But then she blinked, and her face relaxed. She gave me a sad smile. "Okay," she said.

I picked up the package and headed for the door. Ruth said nothing as I passed her, but when I looked back, she met my gaze. She looked so small there on the floor, dwarfed by the large room and the enormous quantity of Oliver's things. When Oliver was alive, she and I had fought about the best way to care for him, but now there was no one else in the world who could understand how much I missed him, how hard it was to accept that he was gone. I went back, sat beside her, and put the package between us on the floor. I handed her the letter.

As she read, I tried to imagine the other letters, the ones that began *Dear Sonia* or *Dear Oliver,* and went on to dissect me. I felt like I'd joined a laughing crowd only to have a hush fall over them at my arrival, everyone looking away. After the day we argued about Sonia, Oliver had never mentioned her to me again. I'd never seen him writing her a letter, never come upon any replies from her in the mail. I prided myself on being a good liar. Why, then, was I amazed over and over at other people's capacity for deceit?

Ruth looked up from the letter. To my relief, she didn't ask for explanations. She said, "You don't have to do it, you know."

"He pulled out all the stops to make sure I would."

"You could just mail it."

I shook my head. As betrayed as I felt, I couldn't bring myself to dismiss the last lines of the letter. *I know you will not refuse me,* he'd said. "I need the money," I said.

"I could pay you whatever you would have made. For someone who lived the life of the mind, he actually left behind quite a bit of money."

I took the letter back from her. "He said I had to go."

"I know how much you hate to disappoint him," she said quietly. "I know what that's like. But now he's dead. You can't disappoint a dead person."

My throat tightened. I certainly felt like I

could. Rereading the letter, I heard Oliver's voice as clearly as if he were in the room, giving me a set of instructions to follow — how to make a sandwich, how to interpret an event, how to deliver a package. When he wrote those words, he was still alive. We both looked at the package. "What do you think is in it?" I asked.

"Well," Ruth said. "It's smaller than a bread box."

"It's also smaller than an elephant."

"Yes, but that's imprecise. Better to say it's smaller than a bread box."

"I'm pretty sure there's no bread in it," I said.

Ruth picked up the package and turned it gingerly in her hands. "He said it's a wedding present, right? It's so light. Maybe there's jewelry in it. Something like the ring he gave you."

At this, I felt a surge of anger. "Or maybe it really is empty," I said. I snatched the package back and gave it a good shake.

Ruth gasped, her hands flying up. "What if it's fragile?"

"Then it's broken." I shook it again. A rustling and thumping. So Oliver hadn't been lying — there was something inside, something for Sonia. "This is going to be awful." I set the package down, gently now.

My anger drained away as I began to worry that I had indeed broken something precious. "Why would he do this to me?"

Ruth didn't answer. She was staring at the package, a half-smile playing on her lips. After a moment she said, "Because he was a bit of a bastard. Didn't you know?"

I got Sonia's number from information. A recording picked up — not even her voice, which I'd been braced to hear for the first time in eight years, wondering if I'd recognize it, but a hollow, computerized one. When I spoke, I sounded as strange and stilted as the recording. "Sonia, it's Cameron. I'm bringing you a package from Oliver. I'll be there in a few days." I paused, and let the pause go on too long. I felt like I'd dialed the wrong number and somewhere a stranger was bent over an answering machine, listening to me breathe. I hung up without saying another word.

From the backseat of my car I retrieved my battered old atlas, which I hadn't used since a back-roads trip to see a newly divorced friend in Sewanee, Tennessee, two years before. Ruth and I pored over it at the kitchen table, plotting my route. It looked to be about fifteen hundred miles, passing through seven states in three days. In spite of myself, I felt the stirrings of a certain familiar excitement — the anticipation of departure. I was not looking forward to the arrival in Boston, and I didn't know where I would go after that. But I knew how good it would feel to be driving into darkness, singing along with *Nebraska*, alone in a traveling world. With moving, I have always been partial to the in-between, the blurred highway outside the window, that suspended time when everything you were lies behind you like a molted skin, and everything you might become shimmers at the horizon. You might choose anything and make it happen, constrained by nothing but your own imagination, sure that not even gravity can hold you.

Ruth tried to persuade me to wait a week or two. She said there was no need to pack all my things, that I could come right back and take my time moving out. But I knew, even if she didn't, that once I was out of the house it would be anticlimactic if I returned. The single day I took to pack was far more time than was necessary, and so I paid many visits to the attic, looking over all the fragments of Oliver's history I would never see again. On my last trip up,

115

after some deliberation, I added the sad-eyed picture of Billie to my box of photos. When Ruth came over the next morning to say good-bye, I asked her if I could have the picture, and she said of course, she had no idea who the girl was. I didn't tell her. My request inspired her to offer me many more things. I let her press on me a carved box from Russia, a small framed copy of a portrait of young Oliver, a first edition of his first book, the value of which she dismissed with a wave of her hand. She kept insisting that I wait one more moment; she was sure there was something else Oliver would have wanted me to take.

"I doubt it." I did my best to smile. "It's not like he wrapped anything up."

She sighed. We stood at the open front door. It was already early afternoon. My car waited in the driveway, the trunk full, Sonia's package in a place of honor on the passenger seat. I was anxious to go, rattling my keys in my hand just like my father always did. I could hear him saying, "We're burning daylight!" If I didn't get moving, I'd soon be jingling the coins in my pocket in imitation of him, whistling under my breath.

"I think," Ruth said, "that it's me I want you to take."

I looked at her in surprise.

"My whole life I've lived here," she said. She touched the doorframe as she spoke. "Sixty years in one town. Maybe that's enough. Hell, I know it's enough."

"I just can't imagine that, living in one place your whole life," I said. "You might as well tell me you're from another planet."

She smiled. "I would consider you the space traveler. You and Daddy." Her eyes went past me to the car, and for a moment she looked just like her father.

"Come on, then," I said, at that instant meaning it. "Let's go."

She gave her head a regretful shake. "My dear," she said, "I am surprised to find that I will miss you."

I laughed. "Me, too." I bent to hug her. Another surprise — she gave me a firm, lasting hug, not the uncomfortable one-armed embrace I expected.

"Good luck," she whispered in my ear. She said it like there was much more at stake than the safe arrival of a package.

"Thank you," I said, pulling away from the embrace. First she, and then I, said good-bye. It was a few short steps to my car, and then my home of the last three years was in the rearview mirror. As things always do, it grew smaller until it disappeared.

Two

8

About a month after her father's death, Sonia and I are sitting in the common room of our suite. We're seniors in college. I'm flipping channels, looking at her as each new show or movie appears, to see if there's any change in the vacant expression on her face. Finally I find *Dirty Dancing*. This seems promising to me. Early in high school it was our favorite movie, and we watched it until we could quote lines — "Most of all I'm afraid of never feeling again the way I feel when I'm with you." We practiced Baby's dance steps, counting one-two-three, one-two-three.

"We used to love this movie," Sonia says.

"Remember dancing up and down your stairs?"

"I remember your crush on Patrick Swayze."

"That was you."

She shoots me an amused look. "I'm not

the one who had a shirtless poster on my wall."

"I put that up for you," I say.

"The sacrifices you've made." She pats my leg. "What a friend."

I feel encouraged, even more so when she sings along to "Love Is Strange." Since her father died, it's been so hard to know what to do, her grief like a fog we've both been lost in. Her father doted on her. He called her Princess, and when he looked at her his love was like a spotlight — it made her the brightest thing in the room. Now she seems caught up in the movie, and so I let myself pay attention to it and not to her. During the scene when Baby confronts her father, my eyes well — I'm a sucker for father-daughter scenes, especially the sentimental ones, alien to my own experience, which make me feel a weird kind of longing mixed with scorn. Normally I laugh this off, saying in a breathy, little-girl voice to the character on screen, "Oh, will you be my daddy?" Now as Baby begins to cry, I do, too. Embarrassed, I try to sniff quietly, glancing at Sonia to see if she's noticed.

She's not paying attention to me, her eyes riveted to the screen without seeming to see what's on it. Her face is frozen in a mask of grief. I put my arm around her shoulders, but there's nothing I can say. "I'm sorry" seemed used up even before the first time I voiced it. She doesn't cry — she never cries — and so I feel like I'm crying for her. I rock her a little from side to side, patting her shoulder, like she's the one in tears.

Later that night, drifting on the edge of sleep, I snap awake when Sonia speaks from her bed across the darkened room. "I wasn't a baby," she says. "I was a princess."

I was neither. It's hard to say whether that's anything worth regretting. "I know," I say.

She's silent, and soon I'm almost asleep, so that in the morning I won't be sure whether I really heard her speak again. She says, "Now I'm nothing at all."

9

When you drive across country instead of flying you really know how far you've gone. You feel the miles roll away beneath you, and as each one disappears, propelling you that much farther from where you started, it's easy to believe you've left behind not just a place but everything you felt there, even grief. On the road during the day I was nothing but forward motion. I was a rocket cutting through time and space, a sealed and impenetrable metal thing.

At night in the motel rooms it was different. The first night, I drove as late as I could, until I began to nod over the wheel. On an empty stretch of highway in Virginia, the only motel I could find had a horror-movie look. There were two beds in the shabby room, and in the center of one of them lay a knife. In the bathtub there was a strange red stain. I lay down on the other bed, fully clothed on top of the bedspread, but I had trouble sleeping, haunted by the thought that murders might have taken place there. I wanted only to be moving again, and when I finally did drop off I dreamed of trying to overtake another car around a mountain curve. Over and over again my car flew off the road, I hung in the air for a long moment, and then, as in a video game, the picture froze and the race began again.

The next night, somewhere in Delaware, I stopped earlier and found a better motel, generic and clean, but still I couldn't sleep, this time because thoughts of Sonia and our impending meeting circled and circled in my mind. I couldn't decide what would be worse — if she'd changed so much I'd barely recognize her, or if she hadn't changed at all. I imagined that what I'd always considered the falser side of her had prevailed, the side that had been a cheerleader and a sorority girl. The man she was marrying was a grown-up frat boy, a lawyer or an investment banker who wore baseball caps on the weekend, made dumb-blonde jokes, and talked about his golf game. She'd be dressed like she was going to a country-club luncheon, in a sweater set and a string of pearls, and she'd kiss both my cheeks, flash me a cocktail-party smile, one that didn't quite reach her eyes, and tell me that if I was at loose ends it was a perfect time for me to travel through France. Or perhaps the strain of maintaining her persona had become too much — rather than poised she'd be brittle and too thin, heavily made-up, a drinker of martinis with an uncertain laugh. She'd insist on how happy she was, how perfect her life was — she'd insist she was thrilled to see me, while again and again her eyes would dart past me to the door.

Then I imagined another Sonia, one who'd emerged from the part of her that worked at the college newspaper with me. This Sonia wore vintage clothes she spent hours scouring thrift shops to find. She'd abandoned her tinted contacts in favor of angular red glasses. She worked for a non-profit organization or made documentary films. Her fiancé was thin and earnest, an artist of some kind, or a political activist. When I arrived she'd insist we go to a funky neighborhood bar that had local beer on tap, and after a couple of pints she'd want to talk, really talk, about what had happened to us. I populated my mind with a crowd of different Sonias — she was an advocate for kids with learning disabilities; she was a girlish dilettante with a father complex, marrying a much older man

126

— but I knew that none of them was real. I was dividing her into her parts — forthright and secretive, insecure and confident — as though she wouldn't still be all of those things.

Near dawn, I finally fell asleep, and dreamed that I was up in Oliver's attic. I was sitting on the floor and crying, though in the dream it wasn't clear to me why. The door opened, and Oliver and Sonia appeared. They approached me with serious expressions, making urgent gestures with their hands. I knew they were telling me something important, but I couldn't hear them, and when I tried to tell them that, they just looked bewildered. They started talking to each other, and I knew they were talking about me. They seemed less and less aware of my presence, and as they receded from me I grew increasingly frantic to know what they were saying. But I couldn't understand them. I couldn't make them understand.

I didn't find Sonia's apartment until after dark. I'd gotten off to a late start, and then miscalculated the length of that day's drive and spent too long in a Cracker Barrel, picking out candy-stick flavors in the country store after my meal. I chose root beer for Sonia, because it used to be her favorite. Back in the car I remembered that Sonia thought me detached and indifferent, not the sort of person who'd show up bearing candy, but the sort who'd hand her Oliver's package, shrug off goodbyes, and climb back into the car. Why bother trying to be nice? I might as well be what she expected. Stuck in traffic in New York, I ate the candy, every sugarsaturated, crunchy, sticky bite. "That'll show her, huh?" I said to the package, still resting on the seat beside me. It had come to seem like a passenger over the long three days of the drive.

By the time I found the apartment, my shoulders were tight with the stress of negotiating directions and traffic. The Cambridge street signs were hard to spot or sometimes missing altogether, as though navigation of this town were a privilege only for locals. I had been honked at more than once, and shouted curses at people who couldn't hear me. This was not Oxford. But at least I'd found a parking space, just the size of my car, across the street from Sonia's building. Sonia was in apartment one. For a couple of minutes I watched the dark windows on the first floor like a private detective, waiting for lights to come on, waiting for proof that Sonia was home. I'd tried to call again from the road, but only the computerized voice answered, and the long beep on the answering machine signaled that the tape was full.

The front door to the building — an old house that had been subdivided — was locked. There was a row of five buzzers beside it. Beneath the first, the nameplate read gray, in Sonia's handwriting, which of course I recognized as easily as my own. I rang the buzzer. I stood on the porch with the package in my hand. I waited a long time before I rang the buzzer again.

It used to be that when I found the front door of Sonia's house locked — her mother often kept it locked, even during the day — I'd go around the right corner to find a green ceramic frog nestled against the wall with the house keys in his mouth. His name was Frank — Sonia had named him that as a little girl. I used to take the keys from him rather than risk disturbing Madame Gray with the doorbell, and then I'd slip quietly up to Sonia's room, to find her pacing, singing something from *The Sound of Music*, or sitting at her window doing a careful, intricate drawing of a bird.

I remembered all this, and it seemed to

me that if I went around the corner of this building, I'd find that things were exactly the same. I was right — there was Frank, waiting with the keys in his mouth, as if he'd known all along I'd be back. I unlocked the exterior door quietly, like I was still trying not to disturb Madame Gray. I had the feeling that inside the apartment Sonia would turn to me with no surprise on her face, her mouth shaping the words to "Climb Every Mountain," and that she'd be not a woman but a fourteen-year-old girl.

I stepped into the entryway. Judging from the mail jammed inside Sonia's box, she hadn't been home in two or three days. This was odd, no doubt, but certainly no cause for the shot of fear and adrenaline that went through me at the sight. Sometimes Sonia was scattered and impatient. Most likely she just hadn't bothered to bring her mail inside. Not everybody was going to turn up dead. Still, as I gathered all the envelopes and magazines and newspaper flyers and fumbled with the door to her apartment, I felt like I was watching myself in a horror movie, yelling, *No, no, don't go inside!*

The apartment was small but beautiful, with high ceilings, crown molding, shiny blond hardwood floors. There was a small table in the foyer, and on it was a note.

C,

Oliver told me he wanted to send me something — did he mean this package or you? Either way, I can't be here. No doubt you want to get back on the road, so I suppose you can just leave the package. I know you've had a long drive — feel free to spend the night. Clean sheets on the bed.

— S.

For a moment I stared at that last line, *Clean sheets on the bed,* as though that were the most significant part. How odd that she'd taken the time to make her bed for me, but hadn't left me a note about the keys. Somehow she'd known I'd find them and come inside. We used to send each other pictures with our minds, trying to develop ESP. We never saw any of each other's pictures, but still there were times when each knew exactly what the other one was thinking. Now I had the sudden conviction that there was a connection between us I'd never managed to sever after all. Sonia knew what I would do as clearly as if she were watching me.

She was wrong, though, to imagine I wouldn't wait for her return. I couldn't abandon the package without seeing what was inside. I didn't want to sleep in her apartment, but I felt so weary at the thought of braving Boston roads and traffic again that it seemed I might as well. The truth was, I hadn't really considered what I'd do once I delivered the package, though Sonia was right to think I'd had a vague notion of getting back on the road. When I thought of this now a pit opened in my stomach. Get back on the road to where?

I picked up the note and stacked the mail on the table as neatly as I could. I looked at the note again. "I can't be here," I read aloud. What did she mean by *can't?* I'd thought she was eager to see me. The note even suggested that I was Oliver's wedding gift, as though my presence continued to be something she wanted. Had she changed her mind and decided to avoid me, or was something else keeping her away? I wanted to believe that she had a pressing need to be elsewhere — for all I knew she might already be on her honeymoon — but something told me she just didn't want to see me anymore. How ridiculous, when I'd been the one to ignore her attempt at contact, that this should make me feel abandoned. I'd never spoken to Sonia, never told her exactly when I was arriving, but it seemed I'd nevertheless expected to find her waiting here.

"Sonia?" I called, just in case, and waited. There was nothing, although I had the haunted feeling that the place itself was listening to me.

Above the table on the wall was an old mirror with a wide frame on which someone — Sonia? — had glued, at artistic intervals, tiny black-and-white photos of women wearing 1920s clothes. I looked closer and saw that they were all the same woman, here posing in a fur, here in an evening gown, here in a swimsuit with a boardwalk behind her. The mirror, hung at Sonia's eye level, cut off the top of my head, and the glass was slightly warped and blackened at the edges. It seemed a strange, imperfect mirror for Sonia to use, as I knew she did, for checking her face and hair every time she left the house.

I went to the living room and put the package on a fan of magazines on the coffee table, which matched the end tables, just as the couch pillows matched the rug. The room could have been a catalog picture. It was pin neat, with a blanket thrown over one arm of the couch as if to prove someone inhabited the place. I touched the magazines — they were all, every one of them, about architecture. This did not seem to be the home of anyone I knew.

The kitchen was small, the cabinets full of items for someone who didn't cook but did entertain — white and red wineglasses, tumblers, champagne flutes, martini glasses, but only three pots, stuffed haphazardly under the sink, their lids in a drawer full of takeout menus. In the refrigerator I found Diet Coke, eggs, and, strangely enough, a box of sugar cereal and one of yellow cake mix. The front of the refrigerator was a riot of snapshots, fanned out in a way that both looked chaotic and suggested much time and thought had been given to their arrangement. I skimmed them for someone I recognized. I saw Sonia on a sailboat with another girl — Suzette, her sorority sister. They were smiling, squinting into the sun, the wind whipping their hair. There were, of course, no pictures of me, but there was a picture I had taken, of Sonia and her high-school boyfriend, Will Barrett, on the night of a homecoming dance. She was laughing, looking at the camera — at me — as Will looked at her, a smile of adoration on his face. I had an urge, which I repressed, to turn that picture's face to the wall.

The bedroom door was closed, and when I opened it, after knocking first, I found that the room was empty. It wasn't empty of things — there was a bed, nightstand, dresser, television — just empty of Sonia. She was really gone.

The bedroom was as neat as the living room. I circled the room, running my fingers across the top of her dresser, over the seams of her white bedspread. After what must have been at least a dozen laps, I sat down on the bed, dizzy. I was no judge of furniture, but it seemed to me the things Sonia owned were expensive. Perhaps I'd been right in my first vision of her life. After all, she'd moved here after college with Suzette, a honey blonde with plucked eyebrows who, Sonia reported not long after meeting her, had a wedding fund of eighty thousand, established by her wealthy father when she was only a baby. Suzette was not a natural blonde, but she spent enough money to achieve a convincing simulacrum, and Sonia hadn't been in the sorority a month before Suzette persuaded her to do the same. I remembered how Sonia came into the room, exuding a sharp chemical smell, so excited she leapt onto the end of my bed and bounced there, shouting, "It's true, it's true! Blondes have more fun!"

I told her I liked it, but what I really felt was bewildered — my friend had been replaced by a changeling. I was relieved when she tired of the look a month later. That time, I went with her to the salon, where the hairdresser said, dubiously, "I've never made a southern girl's hair darker before."

I said, "We're not southern."

"How dark do you want it?" the hairdresser asked, but she seemed to be addressing the question to me, and Sonia caught my eye in the mirror like she wanted me to answer.

"All the way back," I said. "Match her roots."

In the pictures on the refrigerator, Sonia's hair was still dark, but what did that tell me about the life she was leading now? If it weren't for those photos and the note she'd left me, I'd have had no evidence that it was Sonia and not Suzette living there.

"Who are you?" I said out loud.

Then I thought to look under the bed. There it was, the chaos of books and clothing and paper I should have known I'd find. Sonia was still in some way the girl I knew.

In the living room I sat on the couch and stared at Oliver's package. I could hear cars passing outside, the creaking of a floor as someone moved around upstairs — sounds that only increased my awareness of the silence inside the apartment. Here in her home, surrounded by her things, I still couldn't shake the feeling that Sonia didn't exist, that this place was my own imaginary rendering of her life. Only a few days ago I'd been in Oliver's house, sorting through his things, trying to imagine what they meant, and yet he himself was gone. And if they didn't exist, these people who'd at least left some evidence of their presence behind, then did I? I had no job, no home. No one on earth, not even Ruth, knew exactly where I was.

When I got my father on the phone, he said he had been reading — I could picture the glass of single malt beside him on the table, the paperback mystery in his hand — but he seemed happy to hear from me. I told him about my mission. I described the package and said, "What do you think could be inside?"

There was a long pause. I waited for his

theory. He said, "Remind me who Oliver is?"

I wanted not to feel it, the familiar drag of disappointment. "My boss," I said, as calmly as I could. "The one who wrote the Civil War book." I had given him the book one Christmas, with an inscription from Oliver that read: *To Cameron's father, with much gratitude for her creation. I wish she were mine.* "Think that will make your father jealous?" Oliver had said.

"Oh, right," my father said. "That old guy you lived with."

"Right." I swallowed. Strange, when I was working so hard to diminish my own sorrow, how much it hurt to have him diminish it.

"I always thought that was kind of weird." My father chuckled. "It wasn't some kind of Anna Nicole Smith situation, was it?"

"You bet," I said. "You raised yourself a gold digger."

My father laughed. "Well," he said. "I tried."

After I hung up, the apartment seemed even quieter than before. I treated the place like a crime scene, trying to disturb nothing. I drank from a glass and then washed it and put it away. It seemed too strange to sleep in Sonia's bed, so I lay down on the couch, even though I had to curl up tight to fit, with only the blanket and a fat, square pillow for bedding. From outside came the distant sound of sirens. I couldn't shake a betrayed, abandoned feeling. Every night, before Oliver went to bed, he used to kiss me good night, chastely, like a parent, but also like a child. A day seemed incomplete without that kiss to signal its end.

Many times I had been the new girl in the cafeteria, holding her tray, searching the room for that face that will smile, that will say, *Sit here, you're welcome* — and will do it before the moment goes on too long, before she and the whole room see that nobody wants her, that she doesn't, and never will, belong. Still, lying there on Sonia's couch, that might have been the loneliest moment of my life.

In the middle of the night I woke up cold, with a terrible crick in my neck. I stumbled through the door to Sonia's room, and, moving as if in a dream, I got into Sonia's bed.

10

Sonia and I used to call ourselves Cameronia, and Sonia drew a logo for us, a wreath of flowers, in the center a C and an S intertwined. It was beautiful, the fantastical shapes of the flowers, the extravagant loops of the C and the S, so long they almost didn't look like letters anymore. They ran together in unbroken curves, our two identities made one.

That was how it was when we were fifteen, when every experience was something we shared. We even wrote each other into our memories, so that Sonia would make reference to something that had happened two years before and be surprised when I reminded her I hadn't been there, I hadn't even lived in Clovis then. "That's so crazy," she'd say, because it no longer seemed possible that there had been a time when we weren't friends.

We both reached the age of fifteen without ever having kissed a boy. Even this was a problem we confronted together. When we imagined ridding ourselves of this embarrassment, we thought of finding two acceptable boys who would kiss us at the same time — it never occurred to either of us that one of us could go it alone.

One Saturday, when her mother went to bed at three o'clock, Sonia was finally able to put into motion the plan we'd been making for weeks, by asking her father for permission to go out when her mother wasn't around to say no. That evening we sat at Sonia's kitchen table while her father made dinner — spaghetti and meatballs, which was his specialty and Sonia's favorite. She was sketching my portrait, intermittently frowning at it and erasing furiously, refusing to let me see. The smell of tomato sauce filled the house.

We had our driver's licenses by then, and my father had bought me an old car, a stick shift he'd spent all summer teaching me how to drive, shouting obscenities when I ground the gears and then screaming at me to relax. He said if I knew how to drive a stick, boys would respect me more, but this was the least of my concerns when it came to boys. In seventh grade I'd had a huge crush on a boy named Mitch, but he had a friend named Ronnie who used to tease me, calling me Green Giant, asking me in a loud voice in the hall what my cup size was. One day in the cafeteria Ronnie came up to me and said Mitch liked me and wanted to go with me. I assumed this was just another plan to humiliate me, so I said no, and Ronnie turned, cupped his hands over his mouth, and shouted, "Mitch, Cameron doesn't want to go with you." Only then, when I saw the way Mitch flushed, the way he blinked, as though trying to hold back tears, did I realize my mistake. I wanted to leap from my chair and run to him, but fear and embarrassment kept me in my seat. He pushed back his own chair and took his tray to the conveyor belt. He never spoke to me again. The next year we went to different schools.

This was the story I told Sonia when she asked why I was so nervous around boys. I assumed they wouldn't like me, that they'd be intimidated by my height. I assumed that if by some chance they did like me, I'd screw it up somehow. That night, despite my nerves, we planned to cruise Main with the rest of the high-school population, and to meet up with two boys, seniors and football players, who'd told Sonia they'd look for us there.

Mr. Gray had the radio up loud, on an

oldies station. He was still wearing his tie, but he'd loosened it and flung the ends over his shoulder. His light blue shirt was dotted with red from the spitting tomato sauce, but he didn't notice, or if he noticed he didn't mind. Every once in a while he sang along to "Second Hand News" or "Stand By Me." Whenever he did, Sonia would look at him and smile, and once, in the middle of a Simon and Garfunkel song, he turned down the radio and said, "Harmonize with me, Princess," and Sonia did. Mr. Gray's voice was low, pleasant, and unremarkable, but Sonia's was beautiful, clear, and open, with none of the pinched, nasal sound of the school chorus star who always sang at pep rallies. Normally Sonia was self-conscious about singing, critical of her voice the way she was of her drawing, her piano playing, her French and Spanish, which all seemed perfect to me. She had brought these talents to her mother like offerings, but none of them was good enough, and so Sonia dismissed them as well — her French was adequate, her playing and singing so-so, her drawing embarrassingly bad. Not until we got to college and she started to take photographs did she ever admit that she had a skill beyond cheerleading and charm.

143

But when her father asked her to, Sonia would sing. Mr. Gray was broad-shouldered and sweet, with a large, comforting mustache and a patient smile. Once, torn between exasperation and gratitude, Sonia said that if she blew up the school her father would find a reason she'd been right to do it. When he was home, and his wife was sequestered in their room, their house could seem like a happy place. It was easy to pretend Madame Gray wasn't even there. Yet at the same time I went on feeling her presence, just up the stairs in the one room in the house I never entered. She was like the little voice in your head that describes for you, while you're having the time of your life, all the possibilities for trouble and regret, everything that might go wrong. I often wondered what it was like for Sonia to live with that voice all the time.

Mr. Gray crossed from the stove to the table to admire Sonia's handiwork. "That's excellent, Sonia," he said.

She held up the sketch pad, leaning back, and for the first time she looked as if she approved of what she saw.

"You two should write a book," I said. "You can write it, Mr. Gray, and Sonia can illustrate it." Sonia had told me about the bedtime stories her father used to tell her, tales that took weeks to complete. He described castles and moved his hands through the air like he could touch them. In these stories Sonia was always a princess, so beautiful the stars were jealous.

"You two should write a book," Mr. Gray said. "Your own fairy tale. The Princess in the Tower."

"How about the Princess and the Tower?" I said. My father would have laughed, might even have thought of the joke himself, but Mr. Gray shook his head like my self-deprecation troubled him.

"The Princess and the Taller Princess," he said. "And maybe no tower at all."

"In your stories there was always a tower," Sonia said. "Sometimes a dragon."

"Well, in your story let's have no tower or dragon." Over Sonia's head he winked at me. "No princes, either."

Sonia laughed. "Don't worry," she said. "No sign of a prince yet."

Mr. Gray looked at me. "Not for you, either?"

I shook my head. His expression was so sympathetic I had to bite back the urge to tell him about my unrequited crushes, to unspool again the sad story of Mitch.

"He'll turn up," Mr. Gray said. "I'm

145

sure of it." He went back to the stove and started singing again, and I thought with a quick pang of envy how lucky Sonia was, forgetting for a moment that she was her mother's sorrow as well as her father's joy.

Sonia looked up suddenly from her sketching, her gaze going over my shoulder toward the door. "Shit," she whispered.

I glanced behind me. "What?" I said, and then Madame Gray appeared in the doorway, and I knew. She had brushed her hair and put on lipstick, but there was still a line from her pillow across her face. There was a break in the music. Mr. Gray looked up. I felt that for a moment all three of us held our breath.

"*Bonjour,* Simone," Madame Gray said to me. Simone was my French name, from her class.

"*Comment allez-vous, Madame?*" I asked her.

"Well," she said with a smile. "I haven't killed myself yet."

I had no idea what to say to this. Sonia dropped her eyes to the drawing.

"Dinner's almost ready, honey," Mr. Gray said, like he wasn't surprised she'd emerged from her room, like she hadn't said anything strange. He always behaved like whatever she did was normal.

Madame Gray rounded the table and looked over Sonia's shoulder at the picture, putting her hand on top of Sonia's head. "Pretty," she said. She smiled at me. "You're a pretty girl, Cameron," she said. "Pretty *and* smart." When she said *smart,* she squeezed the top of Sonia's head, and I could see the tension in her fingers as she pressed down, like she was trying to do something to Sonia's brain. Sonia didn't move away; her face was calm, but she pressed down her pencil with extra force.

"Merci, Madame," I said.

"So," Mr. Gray said, "what are you girls planning to do tonight?" He was trying to help, but this was the worst thing he could have asked.

"Oh, I don't know," I said. I shot a look at Madame Gray, but she didn't appear to have heard. In fact, her mood seemed to have changed. She was smiling in an inward way, her hand still in Sonia's hair.

"When you were a baby your hair was like wisps of silk," she said. She began to stroke Sonia's head, letting strands of hair slide through her fingers. "Remember that, Gordon? What a beautiful child. Remember how you used to tell people we'd found her sleeping in the petals of a giant flower?"

"Hmm," Mr. Gray said. His stirring spoon had slipped into the sauce, and he was trying to fish it back out without burning himself.

"You were a beautiful baby," Madame Gray said. Sonia closed her eyes. She leaned into her mother's hand like a kitten. I wondered what she would have given for things to be like this all the time. When her mother drew her hand away, Sonia opened her eyes with a startled jerk, as though she'd lost her balance. Madame Gray went over to the refrigerator and poured herself a glass of wine. Sonia looked down at her sketch pad and for a moment didn't seem to understand what she saw there. Then she ripped the paper off the pad and handed it to me.

I studied the picture of myself. In it, I gazed off to the side, a little half-smile on my face. I looked cool and detached, which was just how I wanted to look — like a keeper of secrets. "Looks like me," I said.

Sonia frowned. "It's not perfect," she said.

"So, girls," Madame Gray said, coming back to the table, "what are you planning to do tonight?"

"Probably just go to the movies," Sonia said, but her eyes darted back and forth in a way I called "being shifty." With time to prepare, Sonia was a great liar, as good as I was. But I could lie at the drop of a hat, and she couldn't.

"I can see your eyes, Sonia," her mother said.

Sonia sighed. "We're going to cruise Main."

"I've never understood that particular pastime," Madame Gray said. "I suppose it's just a mating ritual." She took a sip of her wine. Her voice was entirely reasonable when she said, "You'll stay in tonight."

I saw our plans slipping away — I saw the taillights of the boys' truck receding into the distance, two other girls inside, and in the grip of that vision I spoke up when I otherwise wouldn't have. "But Madame Gray," I said, "all we're going to do is drive up and down."

"Oh, I trust you, Cameron," she said. "It's Sonia I don't trust."

Right at the moment Sonia had been feeling most loved, Madame Gray turned on her, like love was just the setup for a practical joke she fell for over and over. Sonia stood up, facing her mother. "Daddy already said we could go out," she said, but I could tell she had no confidence in this line of argument.

Mr. Gray kept his attention on his pot of sauce. "I'm sorry, Princess," he said. "I didn't know your mother would object."

"I wouldn't object," Madame Gray said, "if I had any faith in you at all."

"Why don't you trust me?" Sonia said.

"You just lied to me, Sonia," Madame Gray said. "Not five minutes ago. I'm supposed to believe you're not going to meet boys?"

"I wouldn't lie to you," Sonia said, "if you weren't so unreasonable." Her voice began to tremble. "You spend the whole day in bed," she said, "and then you come down here like nothing's wrong and start making rules."

"I'm your mother," Madame Gray said. "I'm doing what's best for you."

"That's not true," Sonia said.

Mr. Gray said, "Sonia," but she ignored him.

"You're unhappy," she said, "so you want me to be unhappy!" She was shouting now, her face red. I stared, paralyzed. I'd never seen Sonia lose her temper like this. "You want me to be as miserable as you are!" she shouted. "You don't care about me! You wouldn't care if I was dead!"

Her mother threw her wineglass at Sonia. It missed her and shattered against the wall, spraying wine and shards of glass. Then Madame Gray grabbed Sonia by the ears and began to shake her. "Don't you ever talk to me like that," she said. "You little slut." Sonia went limp as her mother rattled the life out of her.

I'd known from the first day I saw her that something was wrong with Madame Gray. But the behavior of a parent still seemed as inevitable as the weather, as the fact that we had to go to school. You could complain about it, but it didn't call forth the sort of anger that led to action. For the first time, as I watched Madame Gray shake Sonia like she was trying to pull loose her ears, I felt enraged. I wanted to knock that woman down, to take Sonia by the hand and lead her to a place where these sorts of things would never happen to her. Without planning to, I stood up. I felt my fists clench. I might have tried to intervene if Mr. Gray hadn't been there.

"Stop it," he said, stepping forward to grab his wife's arm. "Stop it right now."

For a moment she didn't seem to hear him, and then abruptly she let go of Sonia. Sonia's ears were bright red. Her mother took a step back, breathing hard. Then she grabbed Sonia's arm and marched her out of the room and up the stairs. Mr. Gray and I just stood there, not looking at each other.

"Please, Mommy," we could hear Sonia saying. "Please. We had plans."

"Then you shouldn't have done it," her mother said.

"Done what?" Sonia asked. "Done what?" She asked like she was begging her mother to tell her what she had done wrong, not just tonight, but in the whole of her life.

There was no answer from Madame Gray, just the sound of Sonia's door slamming, and then her own.

I looked at Mr. Gray, and he shook his head. I couldn't tell if that shake was denial or apology, or just a request that I not speak. He reached into his breast pocket for a pack of cigarettes and went out the kitchen door to the backyard. I'd noticed before that he often snuck out there to smoke, usually when his wife was in bed. I'd never understood how Sonia and her mother failed to smell it on him. My anger at his wife extended at that moment to him. He couldn't or wouldn't protect Sonia, so there was only me.

I crept up the stairs and into Sonia's room. She was lying on her back on the bed, and as I got closer I could see the

152

tears running down her temples. She didn't look at me. "I'm sorry," she said.

"For what?"

"That you had to see that."

"It's not your fault," I said. "Your mother went crazy."

"But she was right, wasn't she? We were going to meet boys. Who knows what I would've let them do? Maybe I am a slut."

"Sonia," I said. "You've never even kissed a boy."

She closed her eyes. "You know when I was younger she used to scrub my mouth out with soap? She scrubbed out the dirty words. I wish everything dirty could be scrubbed out like that. I wish there was nothing I wanted in the world."

"Sonia," I said. "There's nothing wrong with you."

"You'd better go," she said. "I don't want to get in any more trouble."

I'd never felt so useless as I did then, leaving her there, as if I'd come to rescue her and then failed to break the enchantment. I went back to the kitchen for my purse, and Mr. Gray came in. "Oh, Cameron," he said, his voice sad. We looked at each other, and my anger at him drained away. I understood that he felt useless, too, and ashamed that I had witnessed his uselessness. But I couldn't say any of that, so I just said good-bye.

Outside the house, I stared up at Sonia's window, wishing for it to open, for her to throw out a rope and climb down. I thought of her saying that every decision affected the rest of our lives, and I wondered what it would mean for me to walk away and leave her now. That self-loathing in her voice, when she said she was a slut, when she said she wished to want nothing, that was a curse her mother had put on her, a curse that could last the rest of her life. If I could get her out, if she could kiss a boy like a normal teenage girl, that would break the spell. It occurred to me that Mr. Gray hadn't locked the back door when he came inside.

I parked up the street, just near enough to see the lights of Sonia's house, and then I waited. When the lights went out, I walked up the street and slipped around to the back of the house. The gate was unlocked, as was the kitchen door. I was so nervous as I crept inside, I felt with every step that I might turn back.

Sonia was asleep in her clothes on top of the covers. She was still wearing her shoes. I touched her arm and whispered her name. I heard a sharp intake of breath, and then she was sitting up, blinking at me. "Am I dreaming?" she whispered.

"No," I said. "I came to get you."

"You came to get me?"

"Come on," I said. "It's a jailbreak."

In the hallway, Sonia paused, staring at her parents' closed bedroom door. "What if she catches us?" she whispered.

"She won't," I said.

"I'm scared," she said.

"Pretend you're not," I said, and I reached for her hand. Because she was afraid, I suddenly wasn't. My sense of purpose overrode my nerves, so that I could observe with detachment the hammering of my heart.

We crept down the stairs like criminals. I led the way. I held Sonia's hand and waited for her to step down each stair like she'd just learned to walk. We went out the kitchen door into the backyard, still holding hands, each of us deep-breathing like we hadn't been outside in months. Sonia turned to me. "Freedom," she said. She reached for my other hand and began to spin. We leaned back and spun until I could have sworn our feet left the ground.

Later that night we'd find those boys and we'd kiss them, sitting in the waiting room of the law office belonging to one of their fathers. I'd feel a boy's tongue inside my mouth, a boy's body pressing against mine, and find it hard to believe it was really happening. Then I'd glance over at Sonia, and see her kissing the other boy, and she'd glance back at me and widen her eyes, and in that silent exchange I'd know that the moment was real, because she was there, too, because she witnessed it. But all that was later, and though kissing those boys was part of the story, boys themselves didn't matter yet. What mattered was the two of us as we were at that moment, spinning so that if one of us let go the other would fall, back when we loved each other more than anything.

11

Sitting on Sonia's bed that first morning in her apartment, I looked at a postcard with a picture of Main Street on the front, the word *Clovis* in red beneath it. On the back I read, *Ma chére Sonia, N'oublie pas ta maison. Je t'aime. Je t'embrasse, Maman.* The card was dated two days after we arrived in Nashville, freshman year. There was a little puncture in the top — Sonia had kept it pinned to the bulletin board above her desk. For the first few weeks, when our hallmates asked us where we were from, we'd point to that card. The wide, flat street. The lines of low, tan buildings leading to the redbrick box of the Hotel Clovis. The blue, blue sky, full of clouds so low and full they seemed to be alive, racing the pickup trucks below them on the street.

The card had been in a box labeled VANDERBILT, which I'd pulled down from the top of Sonia's closet. Inside the box I'd also found Sonia's bid-day photograph —

she and Suzette smiling in the center of a crowd of smiling girls, all of them wearing identical sorority sweatshirts — and a notebook from a class she took sophomore year on assessment of learning disabilities. The first two years, she was an education major, something she took on even though it required math. Only three days into the semester, her interest in assessment seemed to peter out, and she began to narrate what was happening in the classroom, the attempted invasion of a squirrel through an open window: *A flurry of blond-haired shriekers fleeing to the other side of the room, clutching a variety of Cosmos and notes.* In the margin of this page she had drawn tiny Chinese ideograms, sketched a flower, and written the word *synecdoche* and circled it. On another page I found a note that said, *I wonder what Camazon is doing right now.*

It was almost noon, and I hadn't even showered. I hadn't meant to search Sonia's apartment and yet I'd spent the morning doing just that. When I started opening drawers, I'd wanted only to find some clue to her whereabouts — something that might tell me the date of her wedding, her fiancé's name, where she worked. But even after I found a paycheck stub — she worked for a photography and literary magazine whose name I recognized because they had once done an interview with Oliver — I kept looking. In part, I wanted to see the letters Oliver must have written her, letters about me, letters she had surely kept, though not in any place I could find.

Most of Sonia's clothes were black, with only the occasional splash of red. In high school, red had been her favorite color. In college, she went through a pastels phase — the influence of her sorority. She owned an impressive number of shoes — six pairs of red alone, so she did still have a preference for it — and she kept them organized neatly, color-coded, on three shoe racks. In her bathroom was an array of half-used beauty products. She had five different kinds of eye creams, claiming to reduce wrinkles, shadows, puffiness — did she not sleep well? On the table beside her couch she had a framed photo of her father and a pair of opera glasses, decorated with what looked like mother-of-pearl. Did she regularly go to the opera, the ballet, the theater, or did she just find the glasses pretty? I didn't find any opera in her CD collection, except *The Marriage of Figaro*, which she'd bought for a class on Mozart we took in college. Her taste in music was eclectic, almost random — she had the first Garth Brooks album, the Modern Lovers, Al Green's *Call Me*, more Mozart, Papas Fritas, U2, Phoenix, and lots and lots of show tunes. She owned a Mensa puzzle book, full of difficult questions about math. Had she bought that to torment herself when her mother wasn't around to do it for her? She was a reader of contemporary short stories. And she had one of Oliver's books, which I snatched from the shelf and flipped through, but there was nothing — no inscription, no letters from him tucked inside.

Under her bed were dirty clothes, credit-card offers, magazines — she subscribed to both *The New Yorker* and *Entertainment Weekly*. There were also old receipts — she'd bought her throw pillows at Pottery Barn — and crumpled sketches, mostly of half-finished faces. And, beneath a hairbrush on her dresser, there was a small blue envelope containing a birth announcement from my college boyfriend, Owen, who, I knew now, was married, lived in Brooklyn, had a four-week-old little boy, and still kept in touch with Sonia, something that surprised and upset me. I hadn't been in touch with Owen in eight years, and yet I felt like he and Sonia, like Oliver and Sonia, were communicating behind my back. Beneath the baby's weight and time of birth, Sonia had scrawled a large blue question mark. What question was she asking? What question was I asking? What did I hope to discover about Sonia now, rummaging through her things?

When I was in graduate school, and the disastrous end to my relationship with Sonia was still recent, I told a new friend what had happened. She wanted to know why, and I did my best to tell her. I told her about Sonia's father dying the summer before our senior year. I told her about Sonia's mother. Then she wanted to know why Sonia's mother was like that. We were English Ph.D. students and we spent all of our time "unpacking" images and sentences and words, and when we weren't working we turned that attention to other people. Though my attempts to explain Sonia, and myself, satisfied my friend and made me feel better, there persisted a nagging feeling that ultimately it couldn't be done. A person is not a suitcase, with a finite number of items to unpack. A person is a world. Look at any photograph — of a stranger, your father, your very best friend. Sometimes the mystery is all you can see.

★ ★ ★

If Suzette still lived in Boston, she'd know where Sonia was, but I couldn't find a listing for her. So I got dressed, copied down the Cambridge address of the magazine where Sonia worked — that day was a Friday — and left to find someone to give me directions. On my way out I stopped at my car to repack what little I'd brought inside. I took Oliver's package with me. Walking up the street, I turned for a last look at my car, which contained everything I owned. I almost wished someone would steal it.

There was a Dunkin' Donuts in Porter Square, and as I walked in, a small child with chocolate frosting around his mouth stared at me. I smiled at him, and his eyes widened. He turned to his mother and said in an audible whisper, "Mommy, that's the biggest girl in the world."

"Uh-huh," the mother said, turning the page of her newspaper.

Waiting in line for coffee and directions, I thought of Oliver's months-long obsession with chocolate doughnuts, how I'd fetched them from every doughnut shop in town, searching for the perfect one — until I began to complain that he was never going to agree I'd found it. On the rare occasions when I grumbled about doing what Oliver asked, he'd endure only a few complaints before saying, with mock sternness, "I'm the boss." This always made me laugh, and because, in the end, what he wanted was so small, I'd stop complaining and do it. There's something to be said for living a life subject to someone else's needs — you never have those empty periods of vague discontent brought on by too much freedom, too little purpose. I never had to decide when to eat my lunch or what I was going to have. And then, too, I used to know that I was what Oliver needed, that I was necessary. I swallowed over a sudden lump in my throat.

Behind the counter was a boy who spoke awkward English. I ordered a chocolate doughnut and a cup of coffee with cream. I confirmed that I wanted no sugar and then watched as he spooned some in anyway. He caught himself and looked up at me with a guilty expression. "That's all right," I said. "I'll take it." While he made change, I tasted the coffee and tried not to make a face. I put the address on the counter and asked him if he knew where it was.

He let out a whistling breath, studying the address. I could feel the man behind me in line growing impatient. The boy said, "I think Harvard Square. Perhaps, yes."

"How do I get there?" I asked.

"You take the T," he said. "Across the street."

"That way?" I said, pointing. And then the man behind me stepped around and in front of me, jostling me out of the way so that hot coffee sloshed onto my hand and dripped onto my white shirt. I hadn't even gotten my doughnut yet.

"Can't you see you have other customers?" he said to the boy behind the counter. He placed his order, not even glancing at me, even though I continued to stand there, mopping at my shirt with a napkin. He was tall, with floppy blond hair and a gray shirt tucked into black pants with an iron crease down the leg. If this had been Oxford, he would have patiently waited his turn. He would have overheard my request for directions and walked me out onto the sidewalk to show me where to go. He would have asked about my errand and expressed interest and concern. Here, he didn't even thank the boy for his coffee. I followed him out the door, and on the sidewalk I said, "Excuse me." He whirled around, startled, and I said, "That was really rude."

He turned scarlet. He stammered, "Well . . . you . . ."

"I what?" I didn't care that my voice was rising, that people were turning to look. "This is about you and why you would be so fucking rude. I'm looking for a missing person. What's your excuse?"

"You were taking too long," he mumbled.

"Well, I'm really sorry. I've no doubt two minutes of your time are more important than my missing friend." I brushed past him. "Asshole," I said, without looking back. Because I was at the corner, and the light had just turned, I crossed the street. I went into the T station. The escalator down was so long I felt I was descending into a pit of hell.

On the train I stood even though there were plenty of seats, gripping the pole with one hand and holding my coffee with the other, the package wedged under my arm. I was still so angry I was shaking. I could still see that man's scarlet face. He hadn't put up much of a fight. My shirt was stained. My coffee was too sweet. It was only as we pulled into Harvard Square that I realized I had left the address on the counter, between the napkin dispenser and an advertisement for a frozen drink. I

165

threw the coffee away as soon as I got off the train.

I walked around Harvard Square for an hour, hoping to stumble across the office of the magazine. I tried to look through Sonia's eyes at the gourmet food shop and the chess players outside the Au Bon Pain, at the tall man who called me darlin' and persuaded me to buy, for a dollar, a newspaper about the homeless. If I could see this place the way she did, I would find her.

Finally, past the main part of the square, I found a fancy-looking camera store next to a bookstore, and knew that if Sonia and I had been together, we would've parted company here — she to look at cameras, me to look at books, saying we would find each other again later. I went into the camera store.

The clerk — he looked vaguely professorial, and I thought maybe everyone in Cambridge looked like that — knew where the magazine office was. The boy at the Dunkin' Donuts had been wrong. It was on Massachusetts Avenue — the clerk said Mass. Ave. — outside of Porter Square, not far from Sonia's apartment. He found a piece of paper and drew a little map for me. Looking over his shoulder at the carefully labeled streets, I asked if he knew Sonia. Indeed, he did. He said she was delightful, and that she came in all the time, for new lenses, for advice, for careful processing of her black-and-white film. The one-hour places, he said with contempt, never got the contrast right. Even in this big city the guy in the camera shop knew Sonia's name.

I was halfway out the door when he called after me, "Tell Sonia her black-and-whites will be ready in a couple of days."

"Okay," I said. "If I see her, I will."

As I passed a low brick wall on my way back to the T station, I saw among a group of teenagers two girls, about fifteen or sixteen, smiling and frowning and rolling their eyes in unison. In my peripatetic childhood I had had other best friends besides Sonia — Terry in Virginia, Helen in England, and in Kansas, Dana, whose flat American vowels I religiously imitated, frantic to lose my British accent. So Sonia was not my only, or even my first, best friend. She was the last. It wasn't that I hadn't made friends since, just that I thought myself past the age of that particular kind of friendship. Adult friendship doesn't grant you an exclusive, isn't meant to be ranked above romance and family. I couldn't imagine ever living that moment again, when you say, with a shy and hopeful pride, "You're my best friend." The other person says it back and, there, you have chosen each other, out of everyone in the world. You have fallen in love and said so.

The teenagers looked nothing like Sonia and I had looked at their age. We had big hair — one of these girls had dyed hers blue. We wore Coke shirts and Swatches and acid-washed jeans. We said "fixin' to" and "dang," hung out with Southern Baptists, dated boys who drove pickup trucks. These girls probably snuck into rock clubs. They did drugs and went to poetry readings. They knew all about Zen Buddhism and read articles in *The New Yorker*. What I recognized was the way they kept looking at each other even though they were each talking to a boy. Every so often they exchanged these quick, knowing glances, each making sure the other one was still there, still with her. I wondered how long their friendship would last, and I felt sorry for them, because they didn't know it wouldn't.

12

On the long escalator back up out of the Porter Square station, people huffed past me on the left while I held on to the railing and felt myself lifted. I knew where I was going now, and I could see myself handing Sonia the package, see her tearing off the paper. I indulged a brief fantasy in which the package contained not only something for Sonia, but further instructions for me, Oliver sending me on a scavenger hunt. As I rose into sunlight, I thought of how difficult it would have been for Sonia to do what I had done that day — buying a T token and telling someone the magazine's address. For her these simple daily transactions would have been fraught with the possibility of error and confusion. It was no miracle for me to count out the correct change.

I glanced over at the down escalator, and there, just passing me, looking straight ahead and frowning, was Will Barrett,

Sonia's ex-boyfriend.

When I saw him, I thought his name. But I didn't connect it to the boy I had known. That boy belonged to another time and place and was not supposed to be here.

At the top of the escalator, I stepped off and got on the one going down. I took the steps two at a time, running down the left side, halting in impatience when there was someone in my way.

I reached the bottom in time to see Will push through the turnstile. I had to wait in line to buy a token, and while I stood there, almost frantic, I remembered senior prom, dancing with him, his warm hand flat against the small of my back. The woman in the booth slid a token into the metal dish, and I nearly fumbled it away trying to pick it up, but then I was through the turnstile and running, dodging people who reared away in exaggerated alarm. I saw him again just as the train pulled into the station. I shouted his name, but he didn't turn, didn't hear me over the hissing of the brakes, and then I was close enough to touch him. I reached out my hand toward his shoulder, and then the doors opened, and he moved.

He got on the train. As the doors closed,

I saw him clearly through the window, choosing to stand, as I had, even though there were available seats. It was definitely him. Same height, same proud nose, same deep brown eyes, so dark they were almost black.

Same air of remove, as though, even on a crowded train, he was completely alone.

I stood there and watched the train pull away.

When I finally turned to leave, I found an old man behind me, leaning on a cane and watching me with curiosity. "Why didn't you get on?" he asked.

"What?" I was still rattled.

"The train? You were running and running. I was thinking, 'I wish I could run like her.' But then you didn't get on." He cocked his head, waiting for an explanation.

"Wrong train," I said.

"My dear, this is the Red Line," he said. "Only one train comes through here."

The phrase *my dear,* the cane, the white hair, the light glinting off his glasses — I was seeing ghosts. Grief, memory — they were hallucinogens.

"Are you all right?" the man asked.

"Claustrophobia," I said. At that moment it was true. I ran back up the escalator, through the glass doors, to the welcome light outside. Will Barrett, I thought, with some amazement. I was standing on a street corner, people darting around me, my heart still beating out the rhythm of his name.

I met Will Barrett for the first time late in Christmas break my sophomore year, the night my parents dragged me to a party at his parents' house. His father, like mine, was in the air force, and they'd been transferred to Clovis from Virginia, just as we had been more than a year before. Will's father was a big man, as tall as my father and wider through the shoulders, and when Colonel Barrett greeted us, his expression suggested a smile without being one.

"I see you brought your daughter," Colonel Barrett said, speaking to my father but looking at me. He pointed into the living room. "My son's over there, standing in the corner as usual." He looked me up and down, pursing his lips in a silent whistle. "You're almost his height. Do you play basketball, too? Will was the star of the varsity team last year, even though he was only a freshman." He didn't wait for me to say anything; he just took me by the

172

arm. "Come on," he said. "I'll introduce you."

I'd never been a fan of meeting new people, especially not boys, and I didn't appreciate the man's grip on my arm, or the way he marched me toward the crowd of people in the living room. Colonel Barrett pointed again at Will, who I could see now, leaning against the wall with his hands in the pockets of his jeans. He was watching the partygoers as though he were at a much greater remove from them, like someone at a play. He didn't seem to notice our approach. His black T-shirt — it said THE REPLACEMENTS on it — looked like it had been bought before a growth spurt. Worn thin, it clung to the muscles of his stomach and chest. Over that he was wearing an unbuttoned white oxford, no doubt a concession to his parents' urging him to dress up for the party.

As we got closer, dread blossomed in my stomach. This boy was so beautiful he could have posed for one of the posters I hung on the walls of my bedroom. When we were two feet away, he looked up, and I saw him wince, before he assumed an expression of resolute politeness.

"Well, Will," his father said. "Here's someone for you to talk to. Cameron, tell him all about Clovis. Do you play basketball?"

I shook my head.

"Why not?"

I had no interest in basketball or any other sport, or any activity that would cause large numbers of people to look at me. I didn't think Colonel Barrett would sympathize with that. "I can't dribble," I said.

"It's easy," he said. "You just . . ." He demonstrated with an imaginary ball, then looked at me expectantly. Will was watching me, too.

"I can't," I said.

Colonel Barrett shook his head like this was tragic. He jerked his thumb at his son. "He dominates the court. You'll see." With that, he strode away.

I did my best to smile at Will, and he nodded in response. I turned and surveyed the adults. I saw my father on the other side of the room struggling to focus on what someone was telling him, and knew he didn't want to be at the party any more than I did. At a safe distance from Will, I leaned against the wall.

After a moment, he said, "I guess somebody should talk."

I glanced at him, but he was still looking out at the room. Even up close he seemed like a photograph. It was strange to hear him speak. "How about you?" I said.

"I just did."

"Me, too."

"Okay," he said. He paused as though searching for a subject. "I bet you get tired of being asked if you play basketball."

"You're right," I said.

"If you play basketball," he said, "then you never have to explain why not. That's an advantage."

"I'll keep that in mind." I looked at his T-shirt. "So, who are The Replacements?"

"A band." His expression suggested that he was trying to suppress disappointment. "You never heard of them?"

"No," I said. "Sorry."

We lapsed into silence again. Out in the room, the laughter swelled. A woman in a low-cut red dress, fancier than anything anyone else was wearing, put her hand on the arm of the man she was talking to, and leaned in like he was so funny she couldn't stand up straight. Her breast brushed against his arm. Wine sloshed dangerously near the rim of her glass. The man, who wore a wedding ring, watched her with detached amusement. "Stop it," I wanted to say to her. "You're making a fool of yourself."

When Will spoke again, I jumped. "So what's this town like?" he said.

I thought of what I could tell him about Clovis — that the fundamentalists signed yearbooks "In His Name" and considered Mormonism a cult, that the kids who wore Megadeth T-shirts and smoked on the edge of school property were called thrashers, that people of Mexican descent were called Spanish, that Spanish kids hung out with white kids or black kids, but usually not with both, that when the fire alarm went off at school early one morning all the girls you otherwise never saw came out of the nursery, cradling their babies close. That after you suffered through the unbearable heat of summer days, you got as a reward a warm and crisp night, that the flatness of the land, the way nothing blocked your view of the sky, made you feel open and expansive, like a deep breath. "It's okay," I said.

"Somebody told me they tip cows here."

"Well, not everybody," I said. "Not me."

"That's good," he said. "You shouldn't. When you tip a cow over, it can't get up. It just lies on its back with its legs wriggling, like a beetle."

"Really?"

"Really," he said.

I stared at him, trying to decide whether to believe him. Finally he grinned. "I knew you were kidding," I said.

"Cows have a lot in common with beetles," he said. "The Beatles almost called themselves The Cows."

I laughed. Then we were silent again. Every comment I could think of had something to do with cows.

"So cow-tipping is out," Will said. "What else can I do to fit in here?"

"Let's see," I said. "Cruise Main. Join the Southern Baptist church. Change your name to Cody."

"Cody Barrett."

"That's a pretty good cowboy name."

"I like it," he said. "Let's do it. You can call me that at school, and everybody will follow your lead."

I started to say, "Really?" then stopped myself. "That's not going to work again."

He sighed in mock regret. "So," he said, "you don't tip cows and you don't play basketball. What do you do?"

"Nothing exciting," I said. "I don't play anything."

"Not even Monopoly? Or a musical instrument?"

I shook my head. "Do you play a musical instrument?"

He looked at me a long moment, like he was gauging my trustworthiness. "I play guitar," he said. "But I'm no good."

He was so intimidating, with his good looks, his self-assurance, that it was a relief to hear the uncertainty in his voice. "My father plays," I said. "I bet he could teach you." I imagined Will coming over every Saturday afternoon.

"I don't want anybody to teach me," he said.

"Why not?"

"I don't want anybody to monitor my progress," he said.

"How are you going to learn?"

"I'm teaching myself."

"But if you had lessons, you'd learn faster."

He frowned. "I don't care," he said. "I don't want anybody to hear me."

"But how will you get any better?"

"You don't get it," he said, in a tone that suggested my ignorance extended far beyond the topic at hand. "Just forget it."

"Fine," I said, as angry with myself as I was with him. "It's forgotten."

He stood there another moment, and then he said, "I'll see you, okay?" He left without waiting for my reply. I focused on the woman in the red dress, resisting the urge to watch him walk away, and then, when I couldn't stand it any longer, I looked. He was already gone.

Several awkward conversations later, I slipped away from the party, looking for the bathroom, mostly so I could have a few minutes alone. I heard music coming from the end of the hall and followed the sound to stand outside Will's room. He hadn't closed the door all the way, and through the gap I could see him sitting on the edge of his bed, guitar in his lap. He didn't see me. "Won't you let me . . . ," he sang, and then he stopped, tuned his guitar, and started again. "Won't you let me walk you home from school."

I didn't recognize the song, which I later learned, after much searching, was "Thirteen" by Big Star. The lyrics were about wanting to meet a girl at the pool, take her to a dance — they were about how he'd leave her alone if she told him to. I wouldn't have guessed this boy, with his long silences and jokes, would choose a song in which love was laid out with such bare simplicity. He played the song in a key that was too high for him, but the way his voice strained after certain notes gave the performance that much more emotion — he sang it like he meant every word. I wondered if he was thinking of a girl he'd left in Virginia. No matter what he'd said, he was really, really good. Watching him sing was like catching a glimpse of him naked.

I stood there in the hall, my heart racing, afraid that at any moment he would look up to see me spying on him, unable to walk away. I'd found him attractive before, but as his voice cracked over the word *you,* I felt a longing so big it threatened to swallow me. I was fifteen, I was familiar with longing, but at that moment I seemed to understand for the first time exactly what I wanted out of everything in the world. I wanted Will Barrett to be singing that song to me.

And then he looked up, and at the sight of me he stopped singing in the middle of a word. He jerked to his feet like I'd caught him doing something shameful, and a flush spread up his neck and brightened his ears. "I told you I'm no good," he said.

I couldn't think of anything to say that was remotely adequate to what I felt, and even if I could have I wouldn't have been able to say it. I shook my head. "I'm sorry," I said, and I pulled the door shut and walked away.

Monday morning I walked into my first-period government class, and there was Will Barrett, sitting in a desk next to Glenn, the class president, a boy with spiky hair and an easy smile who had practically climbed over his own desk in his eagerness to talk to Will. He was always trying to persuade somebody of something. When I walked in, Will was leaning back in his chair, his long legs stretched out in front of him, but when he glanced up and saw me, the muscles in his jaw tightened and he sat up straight. Glenn looked up at me and nodded, not pausing in what he was saying, which I now heard was something about school spirit and the basketball team.

I took a seat two rows back from Glenn, behind Michelle Martinez. Will's hair was a little long on top, but in the back it was razored into straight lines. I wondered if this was some kind of compromise with his father, who, if he was anything like my father, believed every man in America should have a military haircut. I wondered if Will was always going to hate me. He had a smattering of freckles on the back of his neck. He reached up to rub his neck, as though he could feel my gaze, and I looked away. As the bell rang I decided I didn't care if he hated me. I would hate him, too.

I heard Will say, "So, what kind of music do you listen to?"

"Top forty," Glenn said. "A little country, a little Christian rock."

"Oh," Will said.

"What else is there, right?" Glenn said.

"Seriously?" Will said.

Glenn laughed like he thought Will was kidding, and as the teacher began to speak I saw Will's shoulders rise and drop in a sigh. I could have told him that if he expected anyone to know who The Replacements were, this would not be the last of his disappointments. How many times had he moved? Shouldn't he be used to this kind of thing by now?

I was doodling in my notebook, a minute from the end of class, when Michelle turned and handed me a folded piece of paper with my name scrawled on the front. Inside, in small, neat letters, it said, *I hope you didn't tell anyone.* He didn't even sign his name. I hadn't told anyone, mostly because Sonia had been grounded since she came in twenty minutes past curfew on New Year's Eve, and when she was grounded her mother forbade her use of the phone. But I was annoyed by the peremptory tone of the note, by the way he assumed seeing him play guitar was so important to me I'd know exactly what he was talking about. I considered lying and saying I'd told everyone in school. I looked up at him. He was perfectly still, but something about the angle of his head let me know he was anxious about my reply. The back of his neck was slightly pink. *No,* I wrote. I folded the note and passed it back.

When Glenn handed it to Will, Will nodded once, curtly, and then crumpled the note in his hand. Glenn began to talk the moment the bell rang, and the two of them walked out together. Will didn't once glance back at me.

By the time Will asked Sonia out, three weeks later, I was thoroughly convinced I disliked him. When our eyes met, he'd give me this blank nod, like I was no one he knew, and because I often found myself compelled to look at him, I came again to feel that he was a picture in a magazine, and not a person at all. I admired, like everyone else, his skill on the basketball court. His father had been right about that. Sonia admired that, too — she spent the game on the sidelines and so was close enough to see the way he transformed when he came off the bench. "When he's not playing," she said, "he watches like it has nothing to do with him, like he doesn't even care who wins. Then the second he goes in there he looks *fierce.*"

She reported, once they were dating, that all of his apparent disinterest was a mask. He was incredibly romantic, she said. He courted her, leaving roses on her doorstep. I didn't see this side of him. When the three of us were together he was remote and serious. In my presence he didn't even hold Sonia's hand. I didn't recognize in him the boy she described, the one I'd seen playing guitar. He seemed to me impervious, made of stone, and that was what I believed until late in the spring of that year, the day the town flooded.

Clovis was not built to handle rain. The streets were flat, with no runoffs, and on this occasion, a Monday in early April, it rained so hard that the streets flooded until they were two feet deep in water. I made it to first period, thanks to a neighbor's pickup, and so did Will. We were the only ones there. We sat at opposite ends of the room, not looking at each other, waiting, for ten minutes. Finally Will turned to me and said, "Should we get out of here?"

"Okay," I said. I didn't really want to leave. I didn't know where I would go, what I would do, and I was worried that the teacher would show up to find an empty classroom. I followed Will out into the hall and then stopped. The hall was quiet and dark. I had never cut class before. Will kept walking, then looked back. He seemed surprised to see me still standing there. "Aren't you coming?" he said. It hadn't occurred to me that, wherever he was going, he wanted me to come along.

I followed him out to the parking lot. He led me to a baby blue Buick with seats like couches. He unlocked the passenger door for me. I looked at him. I felt as though I had signed a contract without reading it. Now it was too late to ask the terms, and I was to be trapped in a car, going who knows where, with a boy who was impossible to talk to. He took my hesitation for a question about the car. "It was my grandfather's," he said. "He just gave it to me." I got in.

Nothing is stranger than the familiar become unfamiliar. A house on your street that you never stopped to see before, so that it seems to have been dropped into place with its rosebushes, its bicycles in the yard, like a fairy cottage appearing from the mist. A birthmark on your back that you never noticed in twenty-five years of looking at your own skin. Why, you don't know anything, do you? The world can crack open like an egg, spill fires into forests, rivers into streets. A boy who was yesterday as unreachable as a movie star drives you today through a town underwater. He is close enough to touch.

The football field was a swamp. Water rose halfway up the equipment shed. The sight seemed to call for silence, and neither of us said a thing as we headed into town, the only sound the sloshing of the tires through water. For several minutes we saw neither a person nor a moving car. "We're the last people on earth," Will said. I had wanted to say that, but hadn't.

We drove through a downtown neighborhood of small houses, rusty old cars, parched lawns — except now the lawns weren't parched; they weren't even lawns. They were lakes, and all the houses boats. I turned to watch a child's plastic toy, bright orange, bobbing in the water, and so I wasn't ready when Will suddenly jerked the car toward the curb and slammed on the brakes. "What . . . ," I started, my hand going to my neck, but he was out the door and wading toward a house. He was straining against the water, trying to run, and it splashed out around him like it was fighting to hold him back. He'd left his door open, and the floorboard was getting wet, so I leaned across the seat and struggled to shut it. I got it shut, but in the process I brought more water inside. There was an inch of water underneath the pedals, but I didn't know what to do about that. Will had reached the sidewalk now and was crossing what would normally be the front lawn of a house, headed toward the side. I could see a cage back there, beyond the wire fence, but I had no idea what Will was doing. I couldn't decide whether to get out of the car. The water was moving around me so that I felt like the car and I were drifting, and it seemed that to step outside would be to take a raft into high seas. But I didn't like the feeling, either, that as I sat there, a river was carrying me away.

I pushed open the door, took a deep breath, and stepped out. My shoes filled with water. My jeans grew heavy around my calves. I waded after Will. He was climbing the fence into the backyard. He swung a leg over and then paused. I couldn't see his face, but his shoulders were tense and I knew he'd scraped or cut himself on the jagged edges of the fence. Then he swung his other leg over and let go, landing with a splash that soaked his shirt. When I reached the front lawn, I shot a nervous look at the door, which remained shut. There was no movement behind the windows, no sign that anyone was home. I didn't want to call after Will, for fear of alerting someone who might emerge with a shotgun, and I felt irritated with him for putting me in this position. What on earth was he doing — scavenging after a floating toy?

It wasn't until I finally reached the fence that I saw what he had seen. Inside the cage in the backyard, paddling desperately, with only its nose and terrified eyes visible above the water, was a small brown-and-white dog. Will was crouched in front of the cage, up to his chest in water, even his hair wet now as he struggled with the door. "Good boy, good boy," he was saying. "I'll get you out." His voice was calm, but then he glanced back at me, and his eyes were as desperate as the dog's. "I can't work the latch," he said.

"I'll see if they're home," I said.

"There's no time," he said. "He's drowning!" He grabbed the front of the cage with both hands and began to strain against it, trying to wrench the whole thing apart. The dog whimpered, its eyes trained on Will, who said, "Good boy, good boy," and then heaved backward with such force he landed with a splash in the water. The cage was still intact. Will threw himself back at it, grabbing the front again.

"That's not working," I said, frantic. "Try the latch again."

The dog slipped beneath the water and bobbed back up. Will let out a cry of frustration, and I began to climb the fence. But before I could swing my leg over the top, Will made another try at the latch, and this time he got it. The door opened, the dog seemed to rush out at him, and then Will was standing with the wet and shivering animal in his arms. I clung to the fence and looked at him. His wet hair had curled at the ends and rivulets of water ran from it down his back. He cradled the dog like a baby, trying to warm and comfort it, though he was shivering himself. "Will," I said, but he didn't hear me. I didn't know what I wanted to say, anyway. What I wanted was to hold him until he stopped shaking.

"It's okay now," he said to the dog. "It's okay." His voice went high on the last word, and he swallowed hard. He seemed to gather himself before he looked at me. "We have to do something," he said. "We have to take this dog to a vet."

"But shouldn't we . . ." I hesitated.

"Shouldn't we check and see if the people are home?"

He looked at me like I was crazy. "They can't be home. Who would leave their dog like this?"

"I'll just check," I said. "Stay here." I waded around to the front. I rang the doorbell and then, impatient, pounded on the door, which opened abruptly just as I was raising my fist to knock again. A woman in a pink terry-cloth bathrobe, her hair sleep-tousled, stared at me. "What . . . ," she started to say, but the word disappeared into a yawn.

"Your dog," I said, pointing toward the backyard. It was all I could manage.

She looked at me for a moment with a puzzled frown, and then she said, like she'd just dropped her keys, "Oh, hell."

"He was drowning," I said. "We let him out."

She checked behind me. "So where is it?"

"Backyard," I said. "With my . . . friend."

She sighed and waved me inside. "I was asleep," she said. "I didn't think about it back there." I followed her through the dark, dingy house. The smell of old trash wafted out of the kitchen.

Will was standing where I'd left him, up to his knees in water, holding the dog, who was licking his face. As the woman opened the back door he stared at her like she was an alien, and then when I walked out past her he stared at me like that, too. She waved him in, but he just stood there. "Is he going to bring it inside or what?" she asked. She checked the pocket of her robe, found nothing, and sighed.

I waded across the lawn to Will. "We better take him in," I said.

He shook his head, tightening his grip. "I'm not giving him to her," he said. "She doesn't deserve him."

"I don't know what else to do," I said. "It's her dog."

He looked at me like I was responsible for all the world's injustice, and then, without another word, he carried the dog across the lawn. I followed, feeling like I was somehow as guilty as this woman. Inside the house the dog began to struggle to be put down, so Will let him go, and we watched as he sniffed the floor and the woman's bare feet and then began to wag his tail.

"You should take him to the vet," Will said.

"Why? It looks fine." The woman

checked her pockets again and seemed just as disappointed to find nothing.

"He nearly drowned," Will said, his voice tight. "Something could be wrong with him."

"It's not even my dog," she said. "It belongs to my daughter. She just stuck me with it."

"So you were just going to let him drown?"

The woman looked at him. "I didn't know it was going to rain." She walked toward us, waving us down the hall toward the front door.

Will strode angrily down the hall, but at the door he turned, his face pleading. "I'll take him," he said. "If you don't want him. Give him to me."

"I didn't say I didn't want him," the woman said. "You're just a kid. Who the hell do you think you are?" She reached around us and opened the door. I walked outside. Will failed to move, and she said, "I'll call the cops."

"Will," I said, but without a glance at me he moved outside and began to cross the lawn.

The woman looked at me. "That it?" she said. Behind her the dog barked once, and she shut the door in my face.

There was one tree in the yard, and that was where Will stopped, and as I reached him, he began to kick it over and over, water flying everywhere so that I had to back up to avoid being hit. He kicked it until I was sure he was hurting himself, I was sure that woman had called the cops, and I was in a panic, I had so little idea of what to do. Then suddenly he stopped, wading as fast as he could toward the car. I was afraid he'd drive off and leave me, but he sat there with the engine running and waited for me to get in.

When I got inside he didn't look at me. He just began to drive. His face was red. I saw now that he'd torn his pants on the fence, that blood was beading along a nasty scratch on his inner thigh. I didn't know what to say. I thought he was furious with me for going to get the woman. As we left that neighborhood I realized I was holding my breath.

He yanked the wheel, and we turned into the parking lot of a strip mall. Here, we were on dry land. He stopped the car, but he went on clutching the steering wheel like we were still moving. I looked at his face and saw that he was struggling not to cry. "I'm sorry," I said. "We should have just taken him."

He shook his head. "Why does life have to be like that?" he said.

"I don't know," I said.

"My grandfather didn't give me this car," he said. "He died. He's dead."

"I'm sorry," I said again.

"I don't want sympathy," he said.

"Why not?"

He didn't say, but I knew the answer — sympathy made it that much harder not to cry. He swiped at his eyes, dashing away a tear I hadn't seen. "Guess you think I'm a real crybaby," he said.

"I don't," I said. "I think you're brave."

He shot a glance at me, as though to see if I was lying, then looked away. "Well, you don't like me."

"That's not true," I said.

"You act like you hate me," he said. "Ever since you saw me playing guitar. I guess you thought I was really bad."

"No, I thought you were good." I heard my voice tremble and took a deep breath. "I thought you were great. I just closed the door because I was embarrassed."

He shook his head. "You sort of annihilated me."

"I didn't mean to. I was afraid you thought I was spying on you."

He considered this. Then, at last, he

smiled. "Well, you were, right?"

I smiled back. "I guess I was."

He sighed, leaning back against his seat. "So you don't hate me."

I shook my head.

"Good," he said. "Sonia really wants us to be friends."

Until he mentioned her name, I'd forgotten Sonia, and at the realization of this I felt as guilty as if I'd put my hand on his leg, at that rip where the skin showed through. "She's great, isn't she?" I said.

He smiled again, but this time it was a private smile, akin to the one Sonia wore when she talked about him. "She really is," he said. "At first I wasn't sure, because she reminded me of the girl I dated in Virginia. But really just because she was pretty and a cheerleader. Sonia's nothing like her."

"What was wrong with her?"

"She just wanted to date me because I was on the basketball team. She wanted me to take her to dances and bring her corsages, you know? She didn't care about me. I thought she did, but . . ." He shook his head. "I learned that song for her, the one you heard? And then I found out she made fun of me later to her friends." His voice tightened. A flush crept up his neck. "So I guess I'm a little sensitive about that."

And I'd made it worse by shutting the door on him. I started to apologize again, then stopped myself. "Sonia would never do that," I said.

"I know," he said. "I can trust her." He nodded to himself. "I feel really lucky," he said, "because I thought I'd always be unlucky in love." He was only fifteen, but I was, too, and so I didn't laugh. In fact, my throat closed. I was the unlucky one.

Something caught Will's eye outside the window. "Hey," he said. "Look at that."

I saw nothing but the Taco Box, a local fast-food restaurant where high-school kids hung out. Their specialty was Spanish fries — actually tater tots covered with melted cheese. A squat building with a pink tile roof, it was at that moment like an island in a vast lake. "What?" I said.

"Come on."

I followed him across the parking lot. The water got deeper the closer we got, until it was halfway up my shins. Then I saw what he saw. Ducks. There were ducks, a pair of them, gliding in a graceful circle around the Taco Box.

I glanced at Will, and I could tell by the way he watched in silence that he saw it, too: the beauty in the light bouncing off the water, the graceful motion of the ducks. The ducks were not surprised to find a lake where there had never been one before. They took what was offered.

As they disappeared behind the Taco Box, Will said, "I'm glad you don't hate me. I like you."

"I like you, too," I said, and that was all, but I was as embarrassed as if I'd just confessed to love. I stared out at the water and from the corner of my eye I saw that he was doing the same. His cheeks were pink. He was not impervious, and neither was I. It was startling how wrong I could be, how quickly the old world could change. The ducks appeared again, completing a circle. I don't know how long we watched them, how long before I remembered that my feet were wet and cold. We had to go back to school.

Of course I told Sonia about leaving school, about Will's rescue of the dog, a story that made her treat him like a hero for the next couple of weeks. But I held back the part about the ducks, and because she never mentioned them, I assumed that Will hadn't told her about them, either. Almost everything I had and did I shared with Sonia. The ducks afloat in the parking lot, they were mine.

13

At times in high school I repressed my feelings for Will so effectively I could spend hours in his company without a pang. Then he'd kiss Sonia's temple or tuck a strand of hair behind her ear, and just like that I was back in the whirlpool of guilt and envy and longing. Walking up Mass. Ave. a dozen years later, I wondered if Will had just come from a visit to Sonia's office, and was stunned to find myself sick with jealousy at the thought that they might still be friends or, far worse, that he might be her fiancé. It struck me now that if they weren't still together it would be odd for her to keep his picture, a picture of an old boyfriend, on the fridge. When I saw her I'd have to repress my feelings once again. I didn't want her to know that I still cared about him, about her, about any of this. I resolved not to mention his name.

The day of the flood there were still six years of my friendship with Sonia remaining. But maybe when I kept back the part about the ducks, that was the first choice I made that led us to the end, because what I really wanted to keep was a part of Will. I didn't think about it that way at the time. Even after that day, I didn't consider myself to have a crush on him, until my father forced me to see it.

One afternoon, I was lying on my bed reading *David Copperfield* — I was going through a Dickens phase, in which I systematically read all of his books in order of publication — when someone knocked, and my father came in carrying his briefcase. I was surprised to see him home before dinner. He was wearing camouflage, which brought out the green in his changeable eyes. He had beautiful eyes, with the sort of long, curling lashes women envy in men, in contrast to the military precision of the rest of his straight-edged features, his Roman nose, his serious mouth, his abutment of a jaw. I had always been sorry I hadn't inherited those eyes.

"Hi, honey," he said. "What are you reading?"

I sat up and showed him the cover.

"Good book," he said. "My favorite Dickens." He liked reading as much as, if not more than, I did, and unlike my mother, he could remember the plots and characters from books he'd read twenty years ago.

"It's my favorite, too, so far," I said. "Why do you like it?" I thought maybe we would have one of our talks. Every now and then he had this wonderful way of engaging me like I was an adult, of sitting up with me after my mother had gone to bed to expound on topics like the difficulty he had believing in heaven and hell. For that reason, he was my favorite parent, something about which, as a teenager, I felt a mingling of guilt and righteousness.

"It's been a long time since I read it," he said. "I probably wasn't much older than you. But I think it's because I like the characters. I even like dumb little Dora."

"I just got to her."

"I shouldn't say anything else, then. I don't want to give away the ending."

"It's not like it matters," I said. "I know it will be happy. They're always happy." It had dawned on me sometime in the last year that happy endings were not an inevitability but a contrivance, and so I had begun to affect a scorn for them. I thought I sounded very adult as I said, "I mean, he writes so much about death and poverty, but then at the end he always makes it all

work out. It's so unrealistic."

"What about the poor guy in *A Tale of Two Cities*?" My father made a slicing motion across his neck. "He loses his head."

"I haven't read that one yet." I checked the list of publications in the front of the book. "I've got three more before that one."

My father laughed. "You're reading them in order?" He set down his briefcase and reached for the book. He sat on the end of my bed and studied the list. "So you haven't gotten to *Great Expectations*?" I shook my head. He stared at the ceiling, biting his lip. "If I remember right," he said slowly, "he meant to give that one an unhappy ending, but then he rewrote it to make it happy." He looked at me and smiled. "To give love a victory."

I crossed my legs and sat up straight. "But that's not what life is like. So why rewrite it?"

He paged through the book without appearing to see it. "You know," he said, "a happy ending isn't really the end. It's just the place where you choose to stop telling the story. Why not make everything work out when you have the chance?" He sat with his elbows resting on his knees and stared at his hands. He seemed to have forgotten I was there. I suppose he might have been thinking about all the things that hadn't worked out for him, the unhappy endings, the time he spent in Vietnam, the way that war had directed him into a profession he hadn't really meant to enter. I wasn't old enough then to have any real concept of regret, of the endless things that ripple out from every choice. I knew only that he seemed, suddenly, rather sad.

I said, "I guess everything doesn't always work out, does it?" I don't know what I wanted him to say to that. Part of me wanted to understand him. Part of me didn't. In the end it didn't matter, because he didn't hear me. After a moment, he turned to look at me, and his eyes slowly focused on my face.

"You're a smart girl," he said. "I'm proud of you." Then he handed me the book, picked up his briefcase, and pushed to his feet.

I held on to that book with both hands, as tight as I could, although it was the moment I really wanted to hold on to. I could have lived in it for a long time.

He paused on his way to the door and turned back. "I almost forgot," he said. "Your mother had me pick up your pictures." He squinted at me, grinning with boyish mischief. I recognized the expression and braced myself. I was about to be teased. I tried to guess what he was going to tease me about — the pictures were mostly from homecoming, which I'd gone to with Sonia, Will, and a friend of Will's who'd been drafted as my date. My father pulled the packets of photos from his briefcase. They'd been opened. I reached for them, but he held them back. "I just have one question," my father said. He extracted a photo, studied it, then turned it to show me. "Who's this?"

It was a picture of Will. It was a beautiful picture. His dark eyes, which often looked black, in this picture had a hint of gold. He wasn't looking at the camera, but at someone — no doubt Sonia — off to the side, and on his face was an expression of love. Ardent, undisguised love, such as I would never see when he looked at me.

I said, as matter-of-factly as I could, "Sonia's boyfriend. Will Barrett. We went to a party at his house, remember? You know his dad."

"He's Sonia's boyfriend?" my father said. He started leafing through the packets. "Because, hmm, there are a lot of pictures of Sonia's boyfriend." He showed me another one, then another. "More than anyone else, even Sonia."

"So?" My cheeks began to burn.

"So maybe Sonia has something to worry about."

"Don't be ridiculous." I reached for the pictures, but he held them away.

"Cameron's a snake," my father chanted. "Cameron's a snake." He waved the pictures at me, hissing between his teeth.

I tried. I really did. But I hadn't been prepared. Not after the discussion we'd been having, the way he'd taken me so seriously. All at once I stood and said, "Shut up, shut up." I snatched the packets from his hands and burst into angry tears.

"Jesus H. Christ," my father said. "Don't be such a crybaby." He picked up his briefcase. Frowning at me, he headed for the door. "Pull yourself together," he said. "I was just teasing you. You're not the first person to have a crush."

When he was gone I pulled out all the pictures of Will. I took deep breaths, furious at myself for crying, determined not to cry another tear even if I choked on the lump in my throat. I decided to keep the ones of Will with someone else. But the others, the ones where he was the center of the frame, I ripped up into tiny, jagged pieces. I let them rain into the wastebasket.

My father had looked at these pictures and seen what I was trying so hard to hide from myself. I couldn't risk anyone else coming to the same conclusion.

I tried to return to my book, but the pictures were still in the room. I fished the pieces out of the wastebasket, stuffed them inside a used lunch sack, and took the sack into the kitchen, where I buried it in the trash can under some balled-up paper towels.

Maybe I did live an old story, but I couldn't help but live it as though for the first time. The first time you fall in love, it's like you've created the first love in the universe, and the first time someone you love dies, you grieve the universe's first death. What does it help to be told that what you feel is nothing new? You want your father's respect, not as a pale copy of all the children who have ever wanted their fathers' respect, but fiercely, because he's the only father you'll ever have.

What my father didn't know was that I wasn't only envious of Sonia. I was a snake and a crybaby in other ways as well — I was envious of Will. Because of him, Sonia's time was no longer automatically mine. I didn't drop by her house unannounced anymore, because sometimes Will would be there, and, worse, their faces would be flushed, their lips red and swollen. We were often a threesome, but it was hard to endure the ends of those evenings, when they drove off together while I walked to my front door alone. I made some halfhearted efforts to spend time with other girls I knew from school. They were willing to include me, inviting me along when they cruised Main. But they knew why I was with them — that I had, essentially, been dumped — and I felt like a stowaway, squeezed into the backseat of some stranger's tiny car.

At the beginning of junior year, I started dating a boy named Dustin, because he asked me out and because I hoped if I said yes I'd fall in love with him. He was a Southern Baptist, and our relationship consisted mostly of our fumblings in the dark of my living room or his car, his guilt about these fumblings, and his attempts to bring me to Christ. Still, being with him was preferable to playing chaperone to Sonia and Will. He gave me a Bible with my name printed on it in gold, wanting me to read the Gospels, but the first time I touched it, it fell open to Song of Songs: "For love is as strong as death, its jealousy unyielding as the grave. It burns like blazing fire, like a mighty flame. Many waters cannot quench love; rivers cannot wash it away."

"You know what my mother says?" Sonia asked me. It was toward the end of Christmas break, and I was spending the night at her house. "She says we're too young for love, that in a year Will and I won't remember each other's names. She says this isn't love." She sighed. "If this isn't love, what does love feel like?"

I had no idea. I'd had no luck falling in love with Dustin, and I couldn't give that name to what I felt for Will. I shrugged. "It feels like what it feels like," I said.

She stared at me for a moment like I'd posed her a riddle, and then she laughed. "I can always count on you for the answer," she said.

I didn't particularly want to talk about love. So far this night hadn't gone the way I'd anticipated. Sonia had been calling it a girls' night, a night when we wouldn't even talk to our boyfriends on the phone. We hadn't spent enough time together lately, she'd said, and I'd agreed, repressing the impulse to be sarcastic in response. I'd imagined we'd draw pictures, watch movies, make up dance routines in celebra-

207

tion of how we used to be, but so far all we'd done was talk about Will. Sonia's father was out of town, her mother up in her room, and we were sitting on the couch in the living room, *Dirty Dancing* waiting in the VCR, talking about Will.

"I have to tell you what happened last night," Sonia whispered. "I've been dying to tell you." Her voice trembled with repressed excitement, and I knew what she was going to tell me. I wanted to hear it and didn't want to in equal measure.

"Where's your mother?" I whispered back.

"She can't hear me," she said. "She's upstairs."

"Okay, tell me," I said, but then I couldn't let her say it, so I said it first. "You had sex."

"We had sex!" she said, her voice rising enough on the last word that I shushed her, casting a worried glance toward the stairs. "I have to tell you about it, okay?" Her eyes searched my face. She wore a confused, slightly worried expression, and I realized that I wasn't behaving like a girl whose best friend had just lost her virginity. I should have been curious, giggly, exclamatory — not reluctant and subdued.

"Yes, yes," I said. "Tell me." As I listened, I did my best to think only about Sonia, to convince myself this story had nothing to do with me.

They drove out a country road to a dark and quiet field. It was only a few miles from her house, but to Sonia it felt like they had left the earth, or perhaps more like the earth had disappeared, like they were suspended in space, holding on only to each other. There was discomfort, the strange feel of the condom, but still it was perfect, so perfect that in the morning Sonia couldn't quite trust her own memory, so she got out of bed and found her shirt in the hamper. There were three little pieces of grass still stuck to it. She picked them off and lay them side by side on her bedside table. Evidence.

"Can you believe I did that without you?" Sonia said.

Taken aback, I laughed. "You had to, didn't you? It would've been sort of kinky otherwise."

"You know what I mean," she said. "All these big events in my life, you've been there. But for this one, you couldn't be. It wouldn't have been real if I hadn't told you."

"Oh, Sonia," I said. I felt myself to be on the verge of something, though I wasn't sure what — maybe I was about to confess my shameful crush or, finally, bravely, rid myself of it and reaffirm my love for my best friend. But then the phone rang, and her mother called from upstairs to say that it was Will.

Sonia hesitated. She glanced at me as if for my permission to go, but I looked away, wanting her to choose me without my telling her to. "Coming," she called. Then to me she said, "I'll be right back." She patted me on the leg as she went. I heard her running up the stairs.

Only a few minutes later — minutes I'd spent staring at the digital clock on the VCR, determined that if Sonia wasn't back soon I'd leave without a word — I heard footsteps on the stairs. I turned, awash in gratitude and relief, but it wasn't Sonia who came into the room. It was Madame Gray.

"All alone?" she asked, as if she knew exactly what I was feeling. "I'll keep you company." She sat beside me on the couch and patted me on the leg, exactly as Sonia had. "I remember when my best friend first got a boyfriend," she said. "It was hard for me. I felt left behind." She turned toward me, the most sympathetic look I'd ever seen on her face. "That's just how it is, you know," she said. "Women always choose men over other women."

I wanted to protest, but what could I say? Clearly she was right. To my great embarrassment, I felt my eyes well with tears.

"Oh, *chérie,*" she said. She handed me a tissue from a box on the coffee table and watched as I dabbed at my eyes and swallowed hard. She tucked a strand of hair behind my ear. "I know," she said. "I know." She rubbed a circle between my shoulder blades, and I forgot everything I knew about her and felt only grateful for the comfort. "Tell me something, *chérie,*" she said.

"Okay," I said.

In the same soothing voice, she asked, "Is she having sex with him?"

I almost said yes. In a flash before I spoke I saw myself repeating the story Sonia had just told me, ridding myself of it by putting it in her mother's hands. Then I caught myself. "No," I said. "Of course not."

"But you hesitated," she said.

I tried to smile at her. "I was surprised by the question, Madame," I said.

She took her hand from my back. She said, "If she's doing it, I'll catch her, you know."

"She's not." I offered her my most sincere expression, but she continued to look at me with suspicion. "I'd better go see if she's off the phone."

That night, lying next to Sonia in her bed, I couldn't sleep, even after her part of our conversation had turned to disjointed murmurs and she'd dropped off. I was shaken by that moment of hesitation, when I almost told her mother what she wanted to know. I could have lied without missing a beat if some part of me hadn't wanted to betray Sonia, hadn't wanted her mother to punish her for having what I could not. How could I want that, no matter what else I felt?

I got up and went to the bathroom, where I stood for a long time, staring at my face in the mirror. I was just about to go back to bed when I heard a whisper outside the door. "I know what you're up to, you slut," it said. "Don't think you're getting away with it." I froze, convinced the voice belonged to Sonia, that somehow she knew. I opened the door to face my accuser, and instead of Sonia there was Madame Gray. At the look of surprise on her face, I realized she'd also been expecting Sonia, but she didn't apologize, didn't speak at all. She just watched me as I inched around her out of the bathroom. She stared at me as I fled back into Sonia's room.

I climbed back into bed and lay there, breathing hard, unnerved by the reminder of what I'd almost brought down on Sonia's head, convinced Madame Gray's accusation had been meant for me, no matter what she herself had intended. Sonia rolled toward me, the warm weight of her back against my shoulder. "Did you have a nightmare?" she asked, the last word dissolving into a yawn.

"Yes," I said.

"Poor baby." She reached down and squeezed my fingers. "It's all right." She fell asleep holding my hand.

Much to Dustin's delight and surprise, the very next day I agreed to go with him and his youth group to a revival he'd been pestering me about for weeks. There were sermons, and giant video screens showing people witnessing and weeping, and a Christian rock star who wailed over some electric guitars about his love for Jesus while everyone swayed and clapped. There were hymns, and frequent altar calls, in which people made their way down the aisles to the stage and let the minister lay his hands on their heads and whisper something mysterious in their ears. They'd nod, their eyes closed, their faces suffused with joy. Through all this, I could feel Dustin watching me from his seat beside my own. "What did you think of that?" he'd ask, during every break after a sermon or a witnessing or a song. He'd search my face, hoping for a sign the songs and the videos were working.

"It was okay." I'd shrug, even though my traitorous heart swelled and yearned when three hundred voices sang "Nearer, My God, to Thee," and Dustin's face would collapse with disappointment. During the last altar call, I could feel his hope and excitement overwhelming him. He took my hand and squeezed it hard, and though I could feel his eyes trained on my face I wouldn't look at him. He wanted so badly for me to kneel in front of the stage. He wanted me to cry. I took my hand from his and gripped the armrests like I was on a roller coaster. I didn't think about Jesus. I thought about Sonia and Will, how I felt and what I'd almost done, everything I had to make up for. It came to me with the force of religious conviction that I had to rescue Sonia from her mother. I had to persuade her to apply to the same East

Coast colleges I was considering, as far from Clovis as possible. I had to take her away. That was my responsibility.

I had a strange experience then, as around me people wept and sang and hurried down the aisles, almost tripping in their eagerness to prostrate themselves before the giant video screens. I'd feel nothing like this again until I started doing drugs in college. While I sat still, hanging on to my seat, everyone and everything around me began to speed away, faster and faster, spreading and dissolving into blurred streaks of color. Even Dustin was indistinguishable. There was only me, the lines of my fingers clear and sharp, the armrests cold and hard beneath my hands. I could hear myself breathing. I watched my chest rise and fall. I didn't think about anything. For a moment I felt, with a dazzling clarity, the incredible joy of being left alone.

14

I looked up to find that I was ten blocks past where the camera-store clerk had said the magazine office would be. I turned around, telling myself that seeing Will Barrett changed nothing. I had to concentrate on the task at hand — giving Sonia the package, learning what was inside it, getting back on the road. Purpose and pride, as my father always said.

The office of the magazine was on the top floor of an old house. In the lobby I found an imposing gray desk with nothing behind it except the name of the magazine mounted on the wall. No one seemed to be there. It was four-thirty — perhaps everyone was gone for the day, but then why had the door been unlocked? I stood there a moment in indecision before I heard a woman's laughter — not Sonia's. I followed the sound past the desk into a large room with slanting wooden floors, low ceilings, and stained-glass windows divided by gray cubicle partitions. It was an odd mix of quaint and sterile.

No one was in the first set of cubicles. I ventured farther into the room, and there, gathered around a conference table, was a group of people. One of them was a girl, tall and dark-haired. I tightened my grip on the package, but then she turned her head, and no, she was someone else, an Indian girl, about a year or two out of college, with a round face and red highlights in her hair. They all looked at me now. There were five of them: a short, curvy woman in her late thirties — I was sure she had been the one laughing — the Indian girl, a broad-shouldered boy about the same age, and two men who looked remarkably alike, lanky and white, in their late twenties or early thirties, with long, narrow faces and receding brown hair. One of them had a manuscript in his hand. There was that expectant silence that follows interrupted talk.

I found myself speechless under their gaze. I crossed my arms and assumed what Sonia used to call my Egyptian statue look — legs braced, looking down my nose from a great height.

"My, my," the curvy woman said, and I waited for a comment on my size that didn't come. She waved me over. She didn't seem intimidated by me at all. When I reached her side she touched my arm, like she knew me, and then turned her attention back to the man holding the manuscript.

"Where was I?" he asked.

"She was looking for nipples in his fur," the boy said matter-of-factly.

The woman glanced up at me with amusement. No doubt I looked confused. "Just go with it," she whispered.

The man began to read what I slowly gathered was a story about a woman having an affair with the Pink Panther. He reached a graphic description of what the panther could do with his tail. "Ugh," the girl beside me said, turning away in disgust, but not leaving, and the woman let loose with her belly laugh again. When the story was over — the panther leaving the narrator forlorn, dreaming of their one night of passion — they all applauded. "Bravo, Andrew, bravo!" the woman cried, and the man who had been reading bowed and said, "Thank you, thank you."

"Look for that in our next issue," he said. "The short-fiction debut of . . ." He checked the name. "Oh, my God." He lowered the manuscript and widened his eyes.

"Her name's Kitty."

"You are so full of it," the girl said.

"Would I make that up?" He handed her the story.

"Holy shit," she said.

"What's next?" asked Andrew's look-alike.

Andrew lifted another story from the pile on the table. "A fine work of narrative, titled, evocatively, 'The Undersmell.'"

The boy said, "What about 'Big Tony Does His Business'? I thought you were going to read that one."

"All in good time," Andrew said.

The woman turned to me. "Come on. This could go on a while." As Andrew repeated, "The Undersmell" like an announcer, I followed the woman through the office. "So, that's not normal, you know," she said. "We just finished an issue yesterday, so we're blowing off steam with some atrocious fiction submissions. Not an average day at the office. I don't want you to think we always have so much fun, especially at the expense of others." She looked back to grin at me, then led me into a small corner office. It was full of books, some on the shelves, many stacked on the floor, and there were magazine layouts on the floor, too, marked with blue pencil.

There was an odd collection of twisted metal on top of one of the bookshelves and, hung on the wall, a photograph of military cadets reading *Howl*.

The woman sat behind her desk and motioned for me to take a chair. "I'm Daisy Reid, as you've probably guessed." Confused, I sat down. Daisy had an expansive, motherly sexiness, large breasts barely contained by a black shirt that snapped up the front. She wore a short denim skirt and black leather boots that seemed painted onto her generous calves. She gave a general impression of straining against her bindings, as if in medieval times she would have been a bawdy serving wench with her breasts spilling out of her gown. In fact, as she leaned way back in her chair to look up at me, the top snap on her shirt popped open. With no embarrassment, she closed it. "I have trouble staying in my clothes." She smiled. *"Buh-dump-bump."* She made a motion like she was hitting a cymbal. "I'm betting you know something about clothes not fitting," Daisy said. "How big are your feet?"

"Eleven," I said. She certainly came out swinging.

"Wow," she said. She scooted her chair closer and leaned across her desk to look at my feet. "I've got one question. Will you mail anything I ask you to?"

This was so unexpected, I laughed. She stared at me. "Seriously," she said. "That's all I care about."

"What's in it for me?" I asked.

She laughed, one loud "ha." "A paycheck, of course. The last girl quit because she didn't want to mail things. She didn't want to mail things, FedEx things, UPS things . . . I guess the job description escaped her notice."

"Was that Sonia?"

"Sonia Gray?" Daisy made that "ha" sound again. I was wondering what she meant by that — surely she didn't know about Sonia's troubles with numbers — when she said, "You know Sonia? Did she know you were coming? She's not in today."

So Sonia wasn't here. I considered lying, pretending to be whomever Daisy thought I was, taking the job, letting the package wait until Sonia returned of her own accord. Whatever this job was, it was sure to be something I could do. And I knew I'd fit in here. Those people out there had a look of pasty, indoor intensity that reminded me of our friends from the college paper. Seeing them read those submissions made me think of the way, punchy from staying up all night at the newspaper, we used to compose the sort of poetry published by the student magazine across the hall — *The moon is a blue shoe, dancing in the twilight of my soul's memory,* and so forth. I was especially fond of this activity.

It was with considerable reluctance that I told Daisy Reid I wasn't who she thought I was.

"You're not Samantha Wood?"

"No," I said. "I'm Cameron Wilson."

"Huh." She sat back in her chair. "So you don't want the job?"

"Well, I don't know. What is it?"

She seemed to think I was kidding — she laughed again, then said, "So what are you doing here?"

I explained that I was an old friend of Sonia's, that I was looking for her.

"Why?" Daisy asked. "Is she in some kind of trouble?"

"No," I said, puzzled. "I'm bringing her this package. It's a gift, from my former employer."

"What is it?" she asked.

"A first-edition Faulkner," I lied.

She pursed her lips in a silent whistle. "I used to collect first editions," she said. "I hunted used-book stores and garage sales, and bored the crap out of people, going, 'Oh, I got this for ten dollars and it's actually worth seventy-five.' Then my husband gave me the British first of *Lucky Jim* — any idea what that goes for? — and for some reason that just killed the urge."

I wanted to say something incisive or funny — I wanted this woman to like me — but all I could manage was a nod.

"I don't know where Sonia is," she said. "She called the other day when I wasn't here and left a message that she was going out of town, not sure when she was coming back. Frankly, I'm worried."

Out the window behind Daisy, a cat crouched on a rooftop. Daisy swiveled to follow my gaze. "Not out there," she said. "Unless she transmogrified."

"Is that normal? For her to just take off?"

"No." She swung from side to side in her chair. "She's very conscientious about this job. And she's been planning her wedding. Maybe she just got overwhelmed." She turned away from me to look out the window again, rubbing at the back of her head until her short hair tufted out like a duck's tail. "I don't want to be worried," she said. "I love that girl."

"Someone must know where she is," I

said. I made my voice as casual as I could. "Does she ever mention a guy named Will Barrett?"

Daisy cocked her head, thinking.

In high school, when I drove, Sonia used to sit in Will's lap in the passenger seat. Once, I turned to look for oncoming traffic and saw Will take her earlobe into his mouth. Another time, at a high-school dance, I saw him lean over to plant a kiss at the place where her breast rose above the black satin of her dress.

"I don't think so," Daisy said at last. "Her fiancé's name is Martin."

"Martin?" Suddenly I was buoyant with relief. Martin was a wonderful name.

"But what's his last name?" Daisy frowned. "Shit. I never know anybody's last name anymore. It's just, 'Daisy, meet Martin.' " She jumped to her feet. "Let's look in her office. Maybe there's something in there with his name on it."

Daisy led the way back through the main room, where Andrew seemed to have moved on to "Big Tony." I could picture Sonia among that group at the table, her head thrown back in laughter, and in my current benevolent mood the image made me smile. I should've known I'd find her working in a place like this. Sonia and I

224

joined the school newspaper together — she was a photographer, and I was a reporter — and there, where everyone prided themselves on their quirks, their thrift-store distinction from their J. Crew-wearing classmates, Sonia had been the quirkiest of all. She talked in funny voices, staged elaborate displays of mock despair over missing photos, stood on the sports desk to lead everyone in a chorus of "My Favorite Things." At three in the morning, on a sleep-deprived production night, she'd emerge from the darkroom demanding cake, and one of the boys on staff would go to a convenience store to get it for her. There at the paper, she was closest to the person I knew her to be when we were alone, though of course, no one was to know anything about her mother, and we worked to keep her dyscalculia a secret. When she screwed up a measurement on a photo, people assumed she was joking, or making an artistic choice. When she said to the sports editor, after giving him the wrong-sized print, "I thought it looked better this way," he just shrugged and adjusted his page.

We met Owen, my college boyfriend, at the newspaper. The first time I saw him he was wearing a yellow T-shirt with a wobbly drawing of a crown and the words CROWN VIC scrawled across it in what looked like marker — the name of the band he'd led in high school. He had shaggy brown hair and an angular face that made his big green eyes look even bigger and more vulnerable. Despite his slender frame, he had strong hands. He wrote for the Arts section, mostly music reviews, and when he finished a review he was particularly proud of, he'd shout, *"Ta-da!"* and dash over to twirl me around.

For a moment I wished I were back there, Sonia laughing while Owen and I twirled through the newspaper office, before everything went wrong.

As she unlocked the door to Sonia's office, Daisy said, "So who was your boss, anyway?"

I told her about Oliver. She raised her eyebrows, impressed, and I felt a flash of pride. She pushed open the door. "I know who he is," she said. "But he just died, didn't he? I read the obit in the *Globe*."

I stepped around her and into Sonia's office, hoping she'd say nothing more. I didn't want her condolences. There was nothing she could say that wouldn't remind me how irrevocably my life had changed. At this time of day I should have

226

been bringing his dinner to the kitchen table, laughing as he pretended surprise at the sight of the meat loaf we ate twice a week. My eyes had filled with tears — I hated that, how close my grief was to the surface, how easily my throat closed — and I tilted my head back so the tears wouldn't fall. The office swam. I blinked, and blinked again. Photographs everywhere. A large desk, the surface bare except for a computer and a tray of in-boxes. File cabinets with long, thin drawers along one wall. "What does Sonia do here?"

"Oh," Daisy said. "She's the photo editor, of course. I guess you don't know her that well."

I said, "I guess not." I walked over to the cabinets and opened a random drawer. A stack of photographs, the first one of a church, looming oddly, as though shot from below, with a sign in front reading SEVEN DAYS WITHOUT PRAYER MAKES ONE WEAK. Except for the green lushness of the cemetery to one side, the church could have been in Clovis.

"Other people took those," Daisy said. She opened another drawer, pulled out some more photos, and began to spread them across the desk. "These are Sonia's. I really want to run them, but she keeps saying it's a conflict of interest."

The pictures, every one of them, were of Sonia's mother. They were black-and-white. One showed her mother in bed, in a room with the blinds drawn but some sunlight pushing through. One white arm was thrown over her head. Another had her laughing, but Sonia had taken this one with two of her own fingers in front of the lens, segmenting her mother's face. In another Madame Gray looked right at the camera, her eyes tight, her mouth twisted in contemptuous anger. I knew what this expression meant, and at the sight of it my stomach tightened. I wondered if Sonia had held on to the camera when her mother slapped her face. I had to look at the prints twice before I realized that there were numbers hidden everywhere in them, turned upside down and sideways, tucked into corners, a tiny four etched into the pupil of her mother's angry eye.

"How did she do this with the numbers?"

Daisy shrugged. "I don't know, I'm not a photographer. I'm not an artist of any kind." She was watching me closely. "You didn't know she did this?"

I shook my head. "She was photo editor of our college paper, but that was mug

228

shots and frat boys playing Frisbee on the lawn. Nothing like this. These are beautiful."

"Beautiful? Disturbing, I think. But, yeah, she's fucking fantastic." She began to stack them, not looking at me. "You're friends from college?"

"High school," I said. "Actually, both."

She looked up. "So you've met her mother?"

I said yes, I had, but I was wary. Perhaps Daisy saw my presence as a chance to learn some of Sonia's secrets. When we were in high school, my mother had slipped up and revealed to Sonia that she knew about her dyscalculia — I'd had to tell her after she caught me doing Sonia's math homework once. Even though my mother had sworn to keep her knowledge secret, on that day, during a Scrabble game, she offered to count up Sonia's score. Sonia gave me a look of cold assessment, and then without a word she stood up from the table and left the house. She didn't speak to me for a week. She'd never been angry with me before, but now she hung up on me when I called, and when I approached her in the hall at school, her left eye twitched and she walked away. Sonia and I were so often together that her absence branded me. For a week I felt like the whole world looked at me with pity and scorn.

Even now, the old rules seemed to apply. I couldn't reveal anything to Daisy about Madame Gray. To change the subject, I said, "This seems like a fun place to work."

"Oh, it is," Daisy said. "It's great. Except for the boss."

"Who's that?"

"Avery Sidwell, founder of this magazine. He comes in once a month and fucks everything up. Every so often he fires somebody, or pisses somebody off so bad they quit. He thinks he's lord of the jungle. He looks at people like he's waiting for them to drop behind the rest of the pack." She sighed. "He loves Sonia, though. He thinks she's enchanting."

"Who doesn't?"

Daisy laughed. "Exactly."

I wandered to the window, where Sonia kept a large jar full of broken glass on the sill. The sun hit the jar and scattered pieces of colored light across the gray wall. When I lifted the jar for closer examination, a postcard slipped out from behind it and fell to the floor. "What's this?" I said.

Daisy picked it up. "Maybe it's a clue," she said, and handed it to me.

It was a picture of an old bathhouse in Hot Springs, Arkansas, one of the places where Sonia and I stopped on our last long road trip. On the back, Sonia had written only an address. There was no name, just the number, with one normal three and one backward three, the street, and Gloucester, Massachusetts. I had no idea where that was.

I asked Daisy if she recognized the address, and she said no, but she took the card back and studied it again. "Maybe this is where Sonia went," she said. "Who knows?" I waited for a comment about the backward three, but instead she said, "I guess you have to go there." She handed me the card.

I was taken aback. I thought, but couldn't say, that even if the address was a clue, Sonia had most likely written it down wrong. I envisioned myself stopping at every house on a street, asking a series of suspicious homeowners if they'd ever heard of Sonia Gray. "I don't think so," I said.

"What else do you have to go on?" She sighed. "I'm starting to worry. I wish you could find her."

I started to say I wished I could, too, but then someone shouted from the other room that Daisy's phone was ringing, and she darted out the door. "I wish I could, too," I said to Sonia's empty office.

I picked up one of the prints from the pile on Sonia's desk. In it, an image of Sonia's mother was superimposed over a drawing of a woman on a throne, a sword in her hand. I recognized both pieces of the composition. The photo was of Sonia's mother at about fourteen, posed like a pinup on a lawn chair. She sat on the edge of the chair in a white bikini, her toes pointed, her hands on her thighs, her hair blowing in the breeze. In high school Sonia kept this picture in a frame on her bedside table. The first time I saw it, it took me a minute to realize that it was Sonia's mother, and not Sonia, smiling coyly out of the frame. I had never seen the resemblance before, and it made me wonder what had happened to Madame Gray to make her so much less pretty than her daughter.

The other image was the Queen of Swords from a tarot deck. Our freshman year of college Sonia and I had been obsessed with tarot cards. She was the one who dragged me to my first reading, in an old house in East Nashville, a blue hand with an eye in the center of its palm painted on the door. But I was the one who believed. While Sonia waited in another room, the tarot reader told me I was in love with a new boy — Owen — after having spent years harboring a secret crush on another. She said I should tell this new boy how I felt, that this time I could trust that my love would be returned. Then she told me I had the insight to read the cards myself. She sold me a deck for forty dollars, and Sonia laughed at me all the way home.

Sonia might have teased me, might have called me "witchy woman," but whenever she got drunk she begged me to tell her future. We'd shut the door, sit on the floor, and lay out the cards. Every reading I ever did for her, the Queen of Swords came up. This queen represented the presence of a powerful and controlling woman, one who resents others' independence and whose advice will bring about ill. She sat on her throne, face hard, hand lifted in judgment, a crown of butterflies imprisoned in stone around her head. At the beginning of every reading, we held our breath, waiting to see if she would appear, knowing somehow that she would. "Oh, shit," Sonia would say, giggling helplessly, when I laid that card down. "Hi, Mommy."

By then, Sonia had formed out of the events of her mother's life a story that explained everything. There was the strict, religious upbringing in a tiny town in West Texas, chafing a brilliant girl who picked up Spanish, taught herself French, solved the quadratic equation independent of any textbook at nine, and graduated from high school at fifteen. The harsh father who would not let her date, who insisted she go to a college within an hour of home, crushing her dreams of Harvard or Oxford. And then West Texas State, in Amarillo, and the appearance of the young man, gallant and devoted, charming a sixteen-year-old who was smart and beautiful, but naïve and socially awkward. He married her the summer after graduation and took her back to his hometown of Clovis, where his father owned a bank. But after the fairy-tale courtship, there were disappointments. The miscarriages, the ectopic pregnancy, the doctorate from a local university, which subsequently turned her down for a teaching post because her brilliance cast the provincial members of the French department into shadow. Stuck teaching in the stultifying environment of a public high school, she finally gave birth to Sonia — and like any good child, Sonia was to fulfill her mother's failed dreams. "But I turned out stupid," Sonia said. "The end."

A week before we were to leave for Tennessee and college, Madame Gray finally agreed to let Sonia go shopping with me at the mall in Amarillo — we wanted to buy matching bedspreads for our dorm room. Sonia knew what time I was coming to pick her up, and yet when I arrived and let myself into the house with the key from Frank the Frog, she was sitting on the couch in the living room with Will. They were so entranced with each other that they hadn't heard me come in, didn't see me standing there, and I was paralyzed by this and couldn't interrupt them. There was an air of tragedy about them. Will's cheeks were splotched red, and if he had not been crying, he had at least wanted to. He was going to school in Massachusetts, leaving the week after us.

Will lifted Sonia's arm and kissed the inside of her elbow. I backed out of the house as quietly as I could, a lump in my throat.

I circled Sonia's development in my hatchback a few times, passing the same three little boys on bicycles until they started to give me suspicious looks. A week suddenly seemed too long to wait for departure. I wished that we were leaving right then, that day. My parents were leaving, too. Our tour of duty was up.

I turned out of the development and pulled into a gas station, and as I stood at the pump I saw Madame Gray's car go by. I waved, but she didn't see me. When I went to pay, I reached inside my pocket and realized I still had the front-door key. That meant the front door was unlocked, that Madame Gray would walk right in without the warning Sonia probably expected.

I sped back fifteen miles an hour over the limit, as fast as I dared.

Madame Gray's car was parked in front of the closed garage, the trunk open, bags of groceries baking in the sun. The front door was open. In the foyer two plastic grocery bags spilled out on the floor. The coffee table was askew, and a dainty white bra was flung across the back of the couch. "Hello?" My voice was small. I tried again, louder this time.

Will appeared out of the hall bathroom. He was pale, with a strange cross-eyed look, one hand pressed to the side of his head. When he took his hand away I saw that there was blood on his fingers.

"Oh, it's you," he said. "I cracked my head on the coffee table."

I noticed Sonia's pink T-shirt on the floor and, without thinking, moved to pick it up.

"I can't decide whether to go out there," Will said, in an eerily conversational tone.

"Out where?"

"The backyard," he said. "She caught us . . ." He waved his bloody hand at the couch.

I ran from the room. From the kitchen I could hear the screaming — not even words, just this high-pitched animal sound — and my first thought was to hope that the neighbors had not called the police. I pushed through the screen door, and stopped.

Sonia was on the ground underneath the swing set. She was half-naked, curled in on herself, her hands cradling the top of her head. Above her stood her mother. In Madame Gray's hand was the chain that normally attached the swing to the bar, and as I watched, she whipped the chain across Sonia's bare shoulder, the swing's plastic seat beating against her side. Sonia's body jerked, but she didn't cry out or try to move. Her mother brought the chain back to strike another blow. But I was there. I had crossed the lawn without knowing it, and wrapped my hand around the chain.

Madame Gray rounded on me, and the rage in her face was like nothing I'd ever seen. I faltered, and she moved like she was going to hit me, too. All at once my rage equaled hers. I lifted my hand; it seemed to drop from a very great height, and as hard as I could, I slapped her across the face.

I lifted my hand again, but Madame Gray's face was already dissolving, like a child's, into tears, and even though Sonia never cried, she looked so much like Sonia that for a head-spinning moment I couldn't be sure which one of them she was. From somewhere in the distance I heard Sonia shouting my name.

Sonia got up off the ground and pulled her mother away from me. She put both hands on her mother's shoulders and looked her in the face. Madame Gray closed her eyes and shook her head. *"Maman, maman,"* Sonia said, her voice soothing. *"Ne pleure pas. Ce qui est fait est fait. Maman. Je t'aime. Ne t'inquiète pas. Je t'aime."* If Sonia remembered she was half-naked in the yard, she gave no indication. The Sonia of just moments before, curled up on the ground beneath a swinging chain, might have been my imagination.

I stood there shaking. Was I in the wrong? My palm still stung from the blow.

"*Ça va?*" Sonia said.

Madame Gray nodded. Sonia said, "Good." She took her mother's hand and led her back inside. "Go take care of Will," she said over her shoulder. She hadn't once looked at me.

I found Will sitting on the couch with his head in his hands. When I said his name he jerked like he'd been asleep. From the kitchen I fetched some ice and wrapped it in a dish towel. I sat beside Will and pressed the ice to the cut on his head, and when he reached up to hold the ice himself, his hand brushed mine, and I snatched mine away. "What happened?" he said.

"Did you pass out?"

"I don't know. I'm such a weakling."

I didn't contradict him. We sat there and listened to Sonia on the phone upstairs, telling her father not to worry, that everything was fine, but that her mother wasn't feeling well and he'd better come on home. Not feeling well. I couldn't believe this had happened now, when I was so close to taking Sonia away. Maybe my notion that I could rescue Sonia from Madame Gray was laughable. Maybe, no matter how far away I took her, she'd bring with her the memory of what had happened here today; she'd go on loving her mother, even if her mother never loved her back.

"What the hell happened?" Will said.

"Nothing," I said. *"Rien."* I hated him, and myself, for our inability to help or understand — both of us so tall, so capable and controlled, so large with failure.

15

I left the city for Gloucester on Route 1. As night came on I drove past restaurants that were like a series of illustrations mistakenly put in the same storybook. First, a gargantuan Chinese place built to look like a temple, the corners of its roof rocketing into the sky, huge Tiki faces grimacing outside. Then a seafood restaurant shaped like a ship, so true to life it was as though some great wave had marooned it there centuries before. Then a steak house in the green, glowing shadow of a giant neon cactus.

The postcard sat atop the package in the passenger seat, and I wondered if it meant anything that the picture was of a place where Sonia and I had traveled together. Searching for lunch late in the day, in a town that seemed nearly deserted, we had wandered into the lobby of a once-grand hotel. There we found tables of old people playing bridge, Benny Goodman on the speakers, and the remains of a fried-chicken buffet. At first, the sight gave us the giggles — two of the ladies had hair that approached a beehive — but as we sat at a table in the corner eating red Jell-O with cocktail fruit, we were hushed into silence by the way no one took notice of us, as if they were ghosts, or we were. That feeling of unreality persisted everywhere we went. Hot Springs had once been a resort town, and the pictures in the old bathhouses were of fine ladies and their gentlemen arriving in carriages to take the baths. I couldn't shake the feeling, as we passed through, that we would turn a corner and find ourselves in period clothes, attendants brushing past, voices ringing off the stone walls. I could tell by Sonia's face that this was a feeling we shared, and that communion made it seem all the more possible that everything was about to change. How strange it was to emerge from that still, cool place into the sun-bright afternoon.

Now I thought of wild, implausible things — that she had deliberately left this postcard to lead me somewhere. "Stupid," I said out loud. Oliver was right — I was too much alone. My life was becoming a story I was telling myself. If I went to the address on the card, I would probably find nothing more spectacular than an art gallery. A restaurant she liked. A shop full of architecture magazines. I came up with a long list of prosaic things I might find in Gloucester, Massachusetts, but I believed in none of them. What I did believe in I wasn't quite sure — that I would turn a corner and find myself in a long-ago world.

I merged onto 128 toward Gloucester. The concrete and strip malls receded. I reached the woods, and everything began to seem beautiful and ominous, the lighted windows of houses glimpsed through trees. I passed the exit for the beach, and then turned off onto a tree-lined road. I passed a convenience store like a block of cement, then a fruit-and-vegetable stand, closed for the night. The moon was bright, and the light bounced off the little bodies of water that appeared, gleaming, around certain bends. I slowed to fifteen miles an hour. There were no streetlights. Long, weird shadows fell across the road, distorting its shape so that every curve caught me off guard. At a gravel drive marked by a looming boulder, I saw a sign with the house number painted on it. As I turned in, I passed a CHILDREN SLOW sign that a tree had nearly swallowed, its bottom half overgrown with bark.

When I came to a fork in the drive, I

hesitated, the car idling, and then turned right, onto a dirt road. It led up a steep incline to a flat space with at least ten rusting vehicles parked askew, among them a milk truck, a fire truck, an ice-cream truck, and an old school bus, as though the service people of this town had driven here one day, gotten out, and vanished into the trees. I thought of abandoning my own car — I could imagine leaving it here, with all my things inside, and stepping into the woods. When I imagined it I saw myself from the outside, a tall figure disappearing among the trees.

I turned around and went back to the gravel drive. At the end was a house set back in the wood, with a porch that ran across its entire front. I turned off the car. There was a light in the house's front window. I took the postcard from my bag, studied the picture, and then turned it over and read the address again. I picked up the package. I thought of Sonia squeezing my hand at the edge of the swimming pool. "On the count of three," she said. I crossed the lawn and walked up the porch steps. I rang the doorbell and held my breath.

Will Barrett opened the door.

On the first weekend in April of our

freshman year in college, Will came to visit. In the fall semester I'd endured several of his visits, lying awake in the bed across the room while Sonia slept beside him. It was a relief to me to find that once I began dating Owen, just after Christmas, my feelings for Will receded to the point that I believed I was finally over him.

He arrived on a Friday, and we went out to dinner — Will and Sonia and Owen and I — and everything seemed normal, Sonia laughing and frequently touching Will's head or arm, and Will looking at her in a way that suggested the passion that lay behind his public reserve. This was only the second time Owen and Will had met, but they seemed to like each other. They spent much of dinner discussing with great seriousness the prospects for Paul Westerberg's career after The Replacements. In some ways they reminded me of each other. Like Will, Owen could be moody, withdrawing from company with a shadow over his face, and on occasion I was baffled by what made him lose his temper. Once, when I made fun of a sportscaster's hair, he shouted, "Oh, and you're so perfect!" and stormed out of the room. But I would've found him less appealing without those fluctuations in mood. I'd always been

245

suspicious of unrelenting sunniness, what it must be working so hard to conceal. If I'd never seen Owen displeased, the obvious pleasure he took in my company would have lost some of its value. I knew I made him happy. It was also nice — though I tried to repress this feeling — to at last be preferred to Sonia. Unlike Will, Owen was mine. What a relief to be free to love him as much as I wanted to.

That night, after dinner, I went back to Owen's to give Sonia and Will some privacy. When I returned to our room late the next afternoon, the blinds were down and the room was dark. I flipped on the light, and Sonia said, "Don't."

She lay in bed on her back, one arm flung across her face. I flipped the light off again, and she became a dim, frozen figure in the partial light, like a statue or an engraving on a tomb.

I knew the news was bad, but it didn't occur to me that she and Will had fought. My first thought was that someone had died; my more moderating second thought was that Sonia's mother had called and upset her. "Where's Will?" I said.

"Gone," she said flatly.

"What do you mean, gone?"

"I mean gone." Her voice sharpened.

"How many meanings does it have?"

"He's gone where?" I was still confused. Even in the worst days of my crush on Will, I'd never imagined the two of them breaking up — or more precisely, I'd never believed that it would actually happen, even if I had from time to time been unable to prevent myself from imagining it.

"He's at the airport," she said. "We broke up. He changed his flight."

"Oh, no," I said. I meant only to express sympathy, but Sonia heard it differently.

"You could run to the airport and say good-bye," she snapped. "If you hurry you'll catch him."

For a moment I wondered if she knew, had always known, about my feelings for Will, and was only now, in the stress of losing him, being careless enough to reveal it. "That's over now," I wanted to explain. "I have Owen. I love him." I moved closer to the bed and asked if she was all right.

But then she said, her voice gentle again, "Cameron, I'm sorry. I really just want to be alone."

When I left the room, I had no intention of going after Will, but the suggestion had entered my subconscious. I found myself outside with no clear idea of where to go, thinking that if this breakup was final I really might never see Will again, and that that would be a shame, because we were friends, after all. It was amazing how quickly a person you've liked could go out of your life at someone else's discretion.

I jogged to the parking lot, got in my car, and drove. I hadn't even reached the interstate before I started to second-guess myself. What if he found my sudden appearance melodramatic, out of proportion to the level of our friendship? What if all he showed was his disappointment that I was not Sonia, come to reconcile? At some point I kept driving mostly because I was more than halfway there.

Inside the airport I realized I had no idea what flight Will was on. There was one to Boston leaving in twenty minutes — that had to be my first guess. In the line for security I danced up and down on my toes, feeling the minutes tick by as if there were a clock at my ear. As soon as I passed through the metal detector, I broke into a run, slowing to a walk when I got close to the gate.

People were already boarding, the line short enough that more than half of them must have been on the plane already. Will wasn't in the line. I stopped walking and turned to look up at the monitors to see if another flight was leaving soon, sure all the time that he was on this one.

But then I saw him. He was sitting in the row of chairs on the other side of the monitors, close to the gate door. He hadn't seen me. He was staring at the ticket in his hands, head down, elbows propped on his knees, carryon suitcase tipped over carelessly at his feet. He was the picture of stunned misery.

I walked over to him, suddenly out of breath from the run. My heart beat uncomfortably. How easy it would be to slip away unnoticed. But how terrible for him to look up and see me walking away. I stopped in front of him, and after a moment he raised his head.

"Cameron?" he said. He didn't look surprised. Perhaps his unhappiness was too great for any other emotion to intrude. His eyes were dark, and I had to fight a physical impulse to look away, every bit as nervous as he used to make me feel. "I came to say good-bye," I said.

"Why?" he asked, his voice tight.

"I don't know if I'll ever see you again," I said. "I'll miss you." I would never have been able to show him this much emotion in the past, but now Owen stood between us like a bodyguard.

He gave me a grateful smile, then rose to his feet. To my surprise, he took my hand and squeezed it. I had the impression that in a more formal era he might have raised it to his lips. The gate attendant announced the last call for boarding. She looked at Will. "Sir?"

"Coming," he said. He turned back to me, and I was nervous again, not sure what to say now. And then I thought — no, I was certain — that he was leaning toward me at the same moment I leaned toward him. We kissed. A chaste kiss, just a quick pressing together of our closed mouths.

"I'll miss you, too," he said, and released my hand. He turned. Without a look back, he was through the gate and gone.

I told both Owen and Sonia that I had gone to the airport and caught Will in time to say good-bye, because I would have felt guilty keeping it a secret. Sonia asked how Will had looked, and I told her, "Sad." After she fell asleep, I turned out the light and left to spend the night at Owen's. I was glad to be snug in his twin bed with his arm around me. I loved Owen — my love for him was no less just because it couldn't conquer every other feeling I had ever had.

Some memories are kept not in the mind but in the body. That night, and for years afterward, I could summon the sensation of that brief kiss, the instant when Will's warm lips touched mine.

Now Will stood in front of me again, a book in his hand. He looked from me to the book and back, as if I had just stepped from its pages. He had a small scar — new, I thought — that cut his left eyebrow in two. I asked, "What happened?"

"What?" He had a freckle on his right earlobe. Had I ever noticed that before? I pointed at the scar.

"Oh." His free hand flew to it. "Basketball," he said. "I caught an elbow."

"When?" It seemed important to confirm that I hadn't seen this scar before.

"A couple years ago, in a pickup game at the gym." He gave his head a determined shake, as though to throw off this non sequitur of a conversation. "Cameron?" he said.

"Surprised?" Before he could answer I said, "Me, too. I wasn't expecting to see you here."

He looked perplexed. "I live here."

"Yes, but I didn't know that." I wanted to offer him a quick explanation — I was beginning to be afraid he would think me a stalker, arriving on his doorstep at night —

but I couldn't think of how to frame it. "It's a long story," I said.

"You'd better come in." He stepped back and waved me down the hall with his book. I didn't risk a glance back as he followed me in silence. My heartbeat was rapid. I felt slightly breathless — I felt like a girl again, and I didn't know whether there was more pleasure or distress in seeing Will this way. He and Sonia had to be friends — why else would she have his address on a postcard in her office? — but they couldn't be a couple, because of Martin, and she couldn't be hiding out here, or Will would have seemed guilty, rather than surprised, when he opened the door.

The hall opened into an enormous, even cavernous, room, with a small kitchen on the left, an arrangement of couches on the right, a doorway at the back next to a tall shelf full of record albums, and a winding metal staircase in the far-left corner. On the walls were pictures of animals — an old sign for a dairy featuring a large painting of a cow, a black-and-white print of a dog in motion beside a pond. No people any-where. Asleep on one of the couches, chin on paws, was a large, pointy-eared dog. A gray cat watched me from the top of the television with a regal but suspicious air.

Will came up beside me and looked at the room as though he, too, were seeing it for the first time. "This used to be a Montessori school," he said. "Then they converted it. This was the main classroom."

"You know, I saw you today," I said. "In Porter Square. You were getting on the T."

"I didn't see you," he said. "Why didn't you say something?"

"I wasn't sure it was you." I looked at him now. "I mean, it seemed crazy that it would be you."

He looked baffled.

"I wasn't expecting to see you here," I said again. I was sounding ever more like a stalker, insisting all our encounters were by accident. I moved away from him and pretended interest in the bowl of apples on his kitchen counter.

"Do you live here now?" he asked.

I said no. He frowned. I could see him trying to put the pieces together. "I'm a nomad," I said. "Everything I own is in the car."

"Really? You don't live anywhere?"

"I'm between homes. It's a boring subject."

"Okay." He frowned. "Well, what's in that package?"

"I don't know," I said. "It's for Sonia."

At the mention of her name his expression became guarded. "Is that why you're here?"

"Sort of." In a rush, I said, "I've been living in Mississippi, in Oxford. I was supposed to help Oliver Doucet with his memoirs. He's a historian. His daughter, Ruth . . ." In the way Will kept his eyes trained on my face I saw an effort to conquer impatience. I was beginning the story too far back. I said, "Oliver wanted me to bring this package to Sonia. Obviously, she's not here, so I guess I should go." I turned back toward the door.

"Wait, wait a minute," Will said. He reached out like he was going to touch my arm, then let his hand fall. "Don't you at least want a beer or something?" He was headed to the refrigerator before the *yes* was out of my mouth.

I sat on one of the couches, and Will shifted his dog so he could sit on the other. The dog yawned hugely and resettled with its head on Will's leg. "So," Will said, "tell me why you're here."

I told him. He had no idea why his address was on that postcard. He'd been in touch with Sonia on and off ever since he moved to Gloucester, about a year ago, and had seen a lot of her lately. He said this in a casual way that put to rest any lingering doubt I had about whether there was something between them. He said he didn't know where she was. After that there was a long silence before I thought to ask him about himself. He was a veterinarian. He'd gone to vet school at Tufts, and then moved to California with his girlfriend. But he didn't like it there, and so he came back to Massachusetts. I wanted to ask, but didn't, what had happened to the girlfriend. I thought of him saying, when he was a boy, that he was unlucky in love.

"I should've known you'd be a vet," I said.

"Because of that day with the dog?"

I nodded, pleased that he'd known immediately what I was talking about.

"I felt so helpless handing him over to that woman," he said. "And then I made a fool of myself in front of you, kicking that tree and crying like a baby."

I shook my head. "I was just worried you'd hurt yourself."

He laughed. "I did. My foot was killing me."

"You didn't show it."

"I was trying to be a tough guy," he said. "And failing. You had a knack for catching me in vulnerable moments."

"Yeah, but that was why I . . ." I swallowed back the word *loved*. Our eyes met and held too long. "Liked you," I finished, looking away. There was a silence. My mind raced, looking for another subject, and then to my relief Will spoke.

"So what do you think is in it?" Will asked, pointing at the package.

"I don't know. Maybe nothing. Maybe it's just Oliver's way of giving me something to do."

"To get over his death?"

"Maybe," I said, although I thought with some surprise that this was one motive I hadn't considered.

Will looked at his watch. "It's late," he said. "And I've been up since five."

"Oh, I'm sorry," I said, sliding forward on the couch. "I'll go."

"No, stay. It's a long drive."

"I don't want to impose."

"Just stay," he said. "If she's really left town she's not going to come back on the weekend, so there's no use waiting at her place. I've got plenty of room. There's a futon in there." He pointed at the back of the room, where a door opened into darkness. "I'll show you the beach in the morning. The water's too cold for swimming, but it's pretty."

Though I felt that I shouldn't stay, there was no reason not to. It was hard to let go of the habits of avoidance and restraint I had always practiced in his presence. "Okay." I glanced at him and then away. "Thanks."

"No problem," he said.

The room in the back was small and seemed to be a repository for all the things Will no longer used. The built-in bookshelves along one wall were full of college and vet-school textbooks, *The Lord of the Rings* and other books he must have read as a boy, and a set of encyclopedias from 1983. There was a small futon with a white mattress that had a few holes in the fabric, and a sturdy but awkward-looking table beside it, painted three shades of green. His guitar was on a stand in the corner.

"God, that looks awful, doesn't it?" he said. He was looking at the futon mattress.

"You don't play anymore?"

He shot me a look of confusion, and I pointed at the guitar. "Oh, every once in a while." He shook his head. "I never got good enough."

He left the room. I heard his footsteps clanging on the metal staircase. I walked over and touched the guitar. Two of the strings were broken.

I heard Will's footsteps again and moved away from the guitar. He came in with an armload of bedding, and we unfolded the futon and put on the sheets. "I think your feet will hang off it," he said. "Mine always did." He flipped open a blanket and smoothed it down. He seemed in a hurry, and his rapid movements were making me more and more tired. "Okay, good night," he said.

I said good night. He closed the door behind him, and I felt both relieved and bereft. I changed into a T-shirt and boxer shorts, and then there was a knock at the door. I opened it, hyperconscious of the way my breasts now swung loose and heavy beneath my shirt.

"Pillow," Will said. He thrust one at me, and I took it, hugging it to my chest. We stood like that a moment. Each of us seemed to be waiting for the other to speak. Will's eyes darted to my mouth and back up again, and for a moment I wondered if he was going to kiss me.

"Good night," he said again. And then he pulled the door shut.

He had been right about my feet. On my back, I let them dangle off the futon, and then curled onto my side. Many times I had imagined spending the night with

Will. I had never imagined it like this. Perhaps I had been wrong about his desire to kiss me, or perhaps that girlfriend was still a presence in his life. Several months after Sonia and Will broke up, Sonia showed me a letter he'd sent, in which he said he still thought about her, that he hadn't really dated anybody else. She'd said, "What does 'really' mean?" I supposed he had dated other girls, but hadn't fallen for any of them. I pictured him lying in a single bed in a dorm room, a snowdrift against a solitary window, dreaming of Sonia while the phone rang and rang, some girl he couldn't love on the other end of the line. There was no way of knowing what would happen if I went upstairs.

I heard him moving around up there, water running through the pipes. There was a creak as he got into bed. A click as he turned out the light. I lay awake for a long time, listening to the bed groan beneath his restless weight. I wanted to believe that I was the reason why he couldn't sleep.

16

Over coffee the next morning I said that I should be getting back to Boston, but Will argued that in all likelihood Sonia still wasn't home, and that as long as I was in Gloucester, I should let him show me around. To prove there was no reason for me to go, he called Sonia and left a message on her answering machine. I noted without comment the way he said, "Hey, it's me," the fact that he had her number memorized.

The morning was overcast and windswept, but we went to the beach anyway, and Will fell silent at the sight of the white spray against the rocks. He was one of those hosts who, in showing a place to a visitor, seems struck anew by its pleasures himself. This was not one of the mild, welcoming southern beaches I was used to, but an imposing one, where you seemed more likely to drown than dog-paddle. The scene was nearly monochromatic, like a black-and-white photo, the sky light gray with a hint of blue, the clouds etched in darker gray, the water a matte silver-gray rolling with white. We stood on the sand, looking out at two blurred outcroppings, one supporting houses, the other a light-house. On our right were huge rocks — "Mostly granite," Will shouted over the wind. After a moment he moved away from me toward the water. I stayed where I was, studying his profile against the dark, enormous rocks.

With his hair blowing in the wind, that intense, unreadable expression on his face, it was a little too easy to picture Will as Heathcliff gazing across the moors. In high school I read *Wuthering Heights* and *Pride and Prejudice* over and over, torn between the murderous, consuming desire of Heathcliff and the secret, reluctant love of Mr. Darcy. On the whole I preferred Mr. Darcy, but when Heathcliff beat his head against a tree and cried that he could not live without his soul, I longed to be caught in the grip of a strange and violent passion. I thought with some amusement that with those two for ideals of romance it was no wonder I had so long harbored feelings for a man as remote and changeable as Will. I felt a little ridiculous, because it was clear to me that morning that I was still as enamored of him as I had been at sixteen.

Will turned and caught my eyes on his face. "What?" he shouted.

"You could be the hero of a tragedy," I said, but he didn't hear me. He came closer, and I had to repeat myself at a louder volume, with greater embarrassment.

"God, I hope not," he said.

"I meant it in a good way."

"How can you mean that in a good way?" he asked. I couldn't tell if he was amused or offended. I shrugged. "Come on," he said, jerking his head toward the rocks.

I clambered up behind him, wary of the sharp barnacles, and stood on the rocks, droplets of ocean water hitting my face, my hair tangling in the wind. I hadn't dressed appropriately — I was wearing a T-shirt — and all the hairs on my arms stood up. I tasted salt on my lips and glanced over at Will.

"Want to go for a swim?" he said.

"You first."

"You're really cold, aren't you?"

"I'm okay."

"You're shivering." He moved like he was going to put his arm around me, and then he hesitated. "Let's get out of here," he said instead. "Let's go eat."

We ate lunch in town, and then spent an hour browsing through an enormous used-record shop. Will seemed to know the guy behind the counter, a kid with a seventies-era Rod Stewart haircut, but he didn't introduce me. I wandered by, heard them talking about a band I'd never heard of, and moved on. Will bought a stack of records, and as we walked outside — the sun was out now, the sky blue — he showed me one of them and explained why it was a good find.

"Now what?" he said, looking up and down the sidewalk. He seemed alert, almost excited. "How about a walk?"

We followed the boulevard past the statue of a fisherman, then backed up at Will's insistence to read the inscription — *THEY THAT GO DOWN TO THE SEA IN SHIPS 1623–1923*. "It's touristy, I know," Will said. "But it still makes me . . ." He shook his head.

"Sad?" I suggested.

"Yeah, thanks, wordsmith," he said. "I was going to say it gave me a thrill of sorrow, or something poetic like that."

"That would indeed have been poetic," I said.

"Are you making fun of me?"

"I'll leave that to your judgment."

He laughed. "Come on," he said. We walked down to the water, which looked prettier now under sunny skies. Will pointed to a contraption about two hundred feet out that looked like an enormous high chair and explained that during the St. Peter's festival a greasy-pole contest took place out there, in which competitors — all men — walked an enormous, slick telephone pole to capture a red flag, most of them coming away with bruises or broken ribs instead. "I'm entering this year," he said.

I stared at him. "You are?"

He nodded. "There's a log in my backyard I've been greasing up to practice."

"Really?"

"Every day after work," he said. "That's what I do with my solitary life." He looked solemn, but now I understood he was teasing me.

"You'd think I'd know better by now," I said. "I believed you."

"That's sad." He shook his head. "That gives me a thrill of sorrow."

He took me to the lighthouse we had seen that morning from the beach, promising me a view of Boston. As we walked out the narrow point, the weather began to change again, and by the time we reached the lighthouse the breakwater was high, and the wind whipped away all sound and made my hair fly around my face. We looked out across the water. Boston was ghostly through the fog. Will turned to me and shrugged. He sat on the ground, and I sat beside him, my shoulder brushing his. We looked at each other. He gave me a quick smile and then gazed out toward Boston again.

As we walked back down the point, our steps fell into a left-right, left-right rhythm, my stride as long as his. "Where do you think Sonia is?" I asked him.

He shrugged. "Have you talked to Suzette?"

I shook my head. "I couldn't find her number. Did she get married or something?"

"She is married," he said. "I don't know her new last name. Her husband's first name is Chris. He's an investment banker or something."

"You met him?"

"I went to a party there once."

"So you know where they live?"

"I don't know the address," he said.

"You could draw me a map."

We walked in silence a moment. "Okay," he said. "Before you go back tomorrow I will."

"Great," I said, but I wasn't thinking about Suzette, or Sonia, anymore. I was thinking about the fact that he wanted me to stay another night.

For dinner we went to a seafood restaurant, a warm place where the light was dim and the wooden walls were a rosy brown. We sat in a booth in the back, drinking Ipswich Ale, and ordered fish that arrived wrapped in tinfoil. We were still sitting there long after the food was gone. I was content, full and tipsy, feeling the sort of pleasant weariness that comes after a leisurely day spent mostly outdoors. Neither of us had spoken for a minute or two. I was studying the artwork and rudders hung high on the walls — I had already looked at the framed photos of actors and what Will called "famous fleet people" behind the bar.

Will said, "Where will you go after this?"

I laughed. "Home to pass out." I caught myself and flushed. "Not that your place is . . ."

He dismissed this with an impatient gesture. "No, I mean after you find her. What's home?"

What was home? The tree-lined streets of Oxford. The Nashville skyline. The red mountains of New Mexico. Yucca and brown grass. A white silo. Grit kicked up by a wind. All of it. None of it. The highway went everywhere.

"Let's talk about something else," I said.

"Okay," he said. "I like your ring."

"What?" Without knowing it I'd been tapping my ring against the glass. It was the antique, set with five small opals, that Oliver had given me. "Oh, thanks. It belonged to Oliver's aunt. He always said I reminded him of her."

"Why?"

"Because she was wicked, and according to Oliver, so am I." Thinking of this, I felt amusement and affection, only slightly tinged with loss, and I thought maybe this was how I could look forward to feeling about Oliver in the future.

"Are you?" Will asked me, his voice low and flirtatious. But before I could answer, he said, business-like, "What are the stones?"

"Opal. Really I'm not supposed to be wearing them. It's not my birthstone, so it's supposed to be bad luck." Perhaps I had imagined that flirtatious tone. I almost hoped, my stomach still fluttering with nerves, that I had. Strange how uneasy I was at the thought of actually getting what I wanted. Maybe I was afraid of exchanging desire for disillusionment. I said, "You're only supposed to wear them if your birthday's in October."

"My birthday's in October."

"Well, maybe you should wear it." I took off the ring and presented it to him with a flourish. He put it on his ring finger.

"A perfect fit," he said. "How embarrassing."

"Why? We're practically the same height. I've got big hands." I held my hand up, palm toward him, and he pressed his hand against it. "Same size," I said.

"No, you're cheating." With his other hand he repositioned mine so that the heels of our hands were aligned. Now his fingers extended a little past mine.

"Your fingers are longer but thinner." I smiled. "They're slender and tapering."

Will frowned. "I hate my hands. I look like I've never worked a day in my life."

"Don't be ridiculous," I said. "I've always thought you had beautiful hands."

He looked at me a second — we were still palm to palm — and then he said, gruffly, "Thanks," and withdrew his hand. He made a fist and cupped it, paper smothering rock.

I blushed so deeply I was certain even the dim lights couldn't hide my embarrassment. Why had I used those words *always* and *beautiful?* I might as well have told him I'd been in love with him for years. I wanted to shout, "You're stupid!" and run from the room. Instead I caught our waitress's eye and mouthed, "Check, please."

Will stared at the table, his hands hidden beneath it, and now I worried that he thought I had asked for the check because I was desperate to get him home and into bed. There was nothing I could do or say that couldn't be misread. So I sat quietly until the check came, and then insisted, despite his protests, that I pay for my half.

We drove back to his house in silence. He unlocked the door and went inside without a backward glance at me. I followed him, trying to decide if it would be too dramatic a response to pack my things and go. He went to drop his keys on the kitchen counter, and then he stood there a moment with his back to me.

"So." I swallowed. "I guess I should go."

He turned. "Go? What are you talking about?"

"You just seem like you . . ." To my dismay, my voice sounded tearful. I wished

I'd never come to Gloucester — it was unbearable to be around him — I wished I had never met him at all.

"I don't want you to go," he said, as though the admission pained him.

"Why not?"

In two long strides he reached me. He reached out like a man hypnotized and ran the tips of his first two fingers along my collarbone. My breath caught in my throat.

"Because," he said. He touched my cheek, ran his hand down the side of my neck to let it rest on my shoulder. Then he kissed me.

The beauties of his body, its hollows, its muscles, skin and bone. The valley above his pelvis, large enough for my hand, laid flat. The fine clear lines of the tendons in his neck. The thick veins rising from his forearms to spread across the backs of his hands. The grace of the small of his back. The heat that lived in his belly. To touch him was better than anything I could have imagined. I felt like I was getting what I wanted for the first time in my life, and this was both terrifying and exhilarating, a free fall. I hoped he couldn't tell how badly I was trembling. Or was he the one trembling? I couldn't tell, I didn't care, it was us both.

★ ★ ★

I woke in a panic, found myself alone in Will's bed, and sat up. It was not just dark but black in the room. I must have had a nightmare. It had faded from my mind, but my body was still cold, my breathing shaky — the aftereffects of adrenaline. Will was gone. I imagined he'd woken with regrets, and had gone to sleep the rest of the night downstairs. My throat began to close.

Then I heard the bathroom door open. At this evidence of Will's presence, instead of a flood of happiness, my panic returned. I rolled over on my side, away from the door, and as I heard him approach I tried to breathe like I was asleep. The bed bounced under his weight as he eased back under the covers. I could feel him there behind me, on his side and propped on his elbow, looking at me. I thought, If he touches me I'll know he's not sorry.

I felt him bend over me, felt him brush his lips against the place where my throat joined the hollow above my collarbone. I sighed with pleasure and relief. He put a line of kisses down my bare shoulder, and as I rolled toward him I thought again of dancing with him at the senior prom. I had never danced with a boy so exactly the right height. We seemed to fit together, in a way that suggested nothing had ever quite fit before.

When we woke again in early afternoon Will brought two mugs of coffee upstairs, and we sat propped up in bed and drank them, my leg thrown over his. Will had opened the windows, and a breeze lifted the white curtains. I imagined I could taste salt on the air. I said, "Gloucester seems like a nice place to live."

"I like it," he said. He set his coffee down and laid his palm flat on my bare stomach. "Maybe you should stay right here," he said.

I laughed. "In bed?"

"Exactly," he said. "This bed is a nice place to live."

"Won't my muscles atrophy?"

He grinned. "No," he said. He moved closer and said into my ear, "Is it crazy if I want you to stay?" He took my earlobe into his mouth.

"I like crazy," I said. "Crazy's good."

"Well, then," he said. "Stay." He kissed the side of my neck. "Everything you own is in the car."

"That's true."

"We could move you right in."

"I could sleep in that back room. With my feet hanging off the futon."

"I don't know. I was thinking you could sleep with Jessie on the dog bed."

I laughed. "I'm not sure how to take that."

He stroked the inside of my thigh. "I want you to stay," he said.

"Okay," I said. "I just have to go back to the city first."

Will tensed. He sat up straight. "You really don't," he said.

"But I've got to find Sonia. It's my job."

"Your job's over."

I flinched. I swirled the coffee in my cup and took a sip. "Oliver left me instructions," I said.

"But he's . . ." He stopped. "I just don't think you're going to find her if she doesn't want you to."

"How do you know?"

"What are you going to do? Hire a private eye?"

"Suzette," I said. "I'll start with Suzette."

"And if she doesn't know?"

"Then I'll find this Martin guy. He's her fiancé. He must know something."

Will looked at the clock on his nightstand. "It's late," he said. "I guess we'd better get dressed."

I watched as he got out of bed and disappeared into the bathroom. When I heard the shower go on, I followed him. He was standing with both hands on the sink, staring at himself in the mirror. He turned as I came in. I touched his arm. "What's the matter?"

He pulled me close, holding me tight. "I'm afraid if you go you won't come back."

"That's silly," I said. "Why wouldn't I?"

I found Sonia's apartment empty and dark. This was no surprise — at Will's insistence, I'd called her before I left and gotten the machine. I sat on the couch with my feet propped on the coffee table and looked at the map Will had drawn to Suzette's apartment. First thing in the morning I'd go there. In the meantime here I was, alone again in someone else's home. I'd felt sure of my purpose when I'd parted from Will, and sure, too, of the happiness that awaited my return, but suddenly, as I sat there in silence, some uncertainty began to creep in. Everything had happened so fast — maybe I couldn't trust Will when he said he wanted to be mine. My memory of the last two days seemed like a story someone else had told me, as though I hadn't been living my own life but some shadow version of Sonia's. Will had always belonged to her, after all — what if our relationship could exist only in her absence, and was just an echo of theirs? I'd slept with her boyfriend, slept in her bed, and considered working at her office, and now I was tracking down her friends. Oliver had accused me of wanting to lead his life — maybe that was what I was doing with Sonia, moving in like a magpie, trying to take back the life that, eight years before, she'd taken from me.

After college graduation, Sonia and I drove west together, on a trip she kept calling our farewell tour. It had been almost a year since her father died of a heart attack, walking between his office and his car. In the last few weeks, as we planned the trip, Sonia had started to seem more like Sonia, instead of the remote, brittle person who had been inhabiting my room, staring out the window at the parking lot, drinking bottles of white wine. She had let a junior take over most of her duties at the paper, and she'd all but dropped out of her sorority after they called her before the comportment committee for public drunkenness.

When Mr. Gray died, I was in Korea,

where my father had been transferred, and it was days before Sonia found me to tell me the news. I missed the funeral. When she first heard, Sonia was in Nashville, in the summer sublet we had rented with Owen and two of his friends, and Owen was the one to take the phone from her hand after her mother called, screaming as if Sonia herself had killed him. Owen was the one who packed her bag and booked her a ticket home. They had seemed irritated with each other ever since, and I thought perhaps Owen couldn't cope with Sonia's grief and need, and Sonia couldn't cope with his having witnessed them.

After refusing for months to think about the future, Sonia decided a week before graduation to move to Boston with Suzette. She said she would find a job and try becoming a Yankee. There was no reason to stay in Nashville, and certainly no reason to go home. I was headed to the University of Michigan to start a doctoral program in literature. Owen had decided, in the last month, that he wanted to come with me. We had gone up to Ann Arbor and picked out an apartment, and I'd spent the entire weekend clinging to his hand like a new bride. For years he had talked of moving to Memphis with a friend to start a record label. Now all he wanted was to be with me.

Sonia and I planned to spend two weeks exploring Texas and New Mexico. Then together we'd pay a brief visit to her mother before I went back to Tennessee to pick up Owen for our move. As we headed west, the trees grew more and more sparse, until finally we were back in the flat, brown lands of our adolescence. "Ah," Sonia said, waking up from a nap as we sped across the plains of Texas. "Don't you feel like you can breathe?"

In preparation for this trip I'd bought all manner of guidebooks, but Sonia refused to be drawn into planning our route. She said that, for once in my life, I needed to just let a thing unfold. She said, "Every night, in whatever seedy motel room we're in, we'll study the map and pick where we want to go the next day." I let her talk me into this, and later, when we lost many hours of driving by doubling back to see something we'd missed, I tried unsuccessfully not to say I told you so. Sonia said, "The drive is the point, Camazon. Say it with me now: 'The journey, not the destination.' "

In Santa Fe, we bought each other turquoise earrings. We went to Bandolier and took pictures of the holes in the cliffsides where people, unbelievably, used to make a life. We went to Taos, where, sick of crappy motels, we splurged on a room in a bed-and-breakfast. There was a tray in the room upon which were an ice bucket and champagne flutes. There was a fireplace, with logs, kindling, and matches provided. We used up all the fire starter but still we couldn't get the fire lighted. In the morning the kindly couple who owned the place spent half an hour describing a lesbian commitment ceremony that had been held in the inn the month before. We listened politely. In the car on the way out of town, Sonia said, "God, that was a long story. Why did they tell us that?"

"Oh," I said. "Wait a minute . . ."

"Champagne flutes in the room," Sonia said. "That was the honeymoon suite, wasn't it?"

We laughed so hard that tears came into our eyes, but I could understand the innkeepers' mistake. I thought, but didn't say, that there were ways in which a friendship like ours was like a love affair. Hadn't I been jealous of Sonia's bond with Suzette? Hadn't she accused me, once, of spending more time with Owen than with her? Hadn't we spent four years living together, fighting and making up, cooking each other dinner?

One afternoon we stopped in Roswell, where we had driven many times for high-school football games. Since then, the town had embraced its science-fiction past. Fast-food restaurants welcomed alien invaders, and signs told us where we could park our spaceship. We wandered around the UFO museum together, marveling at the framed documents, the photos, the vast and fantastic paintings of space donated by amateur artists from around the world. Sonia pointed at a picture of Pegasus flying over the moon. "Who looks at the sky and sees this?" she asked.

"Oh, I do," I said. "All that and more."

"This place is demented," she said. "Everything about it is completely insane."

I was more credulous than she was. We watched a documentary about alien abductions, and Sonia cracked jokes about the abductees until a fat man in a baseball cap turned around and shushed her. After that she satisfied herself with sighing. I couldn't take my eyes off these people, these plump and twitchy intergalactic travelers. I found myself half-persuaded by their crazed conviction. What if all of it were true? What would it be like to go so far?

"I just had no idea," Sonia said in the gift shop. She was looking at "Believe" key chains. "All those times we were here. I just thought of Roswell as a rival football team."

I picked up a green lollipop shaped like an alien's head. "I took the SATs here," I said. "At New Mexico Military Institute. I was trying to do math, and they were playing the trumpet and marching outside. It was damn hard to concentrate."

"This place is part of a myth." Sonia picked up a red alien lollipop. "For me it was just another crappy town." She unwrapped the candy and popped it in her mouth. "Life is funny," she said.

That night a guy who hit on Sonia in the hotel bar told her she hadn't lived unless she'd seen Big Bend, so the next morning we headed back into Texas and down to the park. We spent the day hiking, amazed by the strange, almost lunar landscape, and then rented a room at the seventies-era park motel, an odd, ugly building lodged among the startling and austere mountains like something washed ashore. We sat out on the balcony and watched it get dark, passing the joint the guy in the bar had given Sonia. It was so quiet, the landscape around us so beautiful and unforgiving and large. Sitting there I felt as though I had stopped to think for the first time in months. I had made my plans with such methodical confidence that even I had failed to notice the depth of my uncertainty.

"You want to know something?" I said.

"What?" she said.

"I don't know what the fuck I'm doing."

"What do you mean? You're sitting on a balcony in Big Bend. With me."

"No. With my life."

"Cameron, you always know what you're doing."

"Thanks," I said. "I'm glad it looks that way."

"You're going to grad school, like you wanted."

"Yeah, but is that what I wanted? Or what I thought I wanted? Or what I thought someone else wanted for me? I mean, how do we make decisions, anyway? How do we know we're right?"

"I don't know." She laughed. "Are you asking me for the meaning of life?"

"Yeah," I said. "Have you got it with you?"

"In my pocket," she said.

The moon was a white crescent, the stars so plentiful they seemed to multiply as I watched. I could see all the shades of darkness. The silhouette of a tree was the deepest dark, but the sky looked as though it had once contained light, and would again. I knew that the sky was space, the stars light that had traveled across the universe to be here, but I also believed the sky was nothing but a black curtain, the stars just holes in the fabric, poked with a steady hand and a straight pin. Everything was at the same time real and imaginary, true and false, beginning and ending. I wondered if the sky would ever look this beautiful again, and if so, when that would be and who I would be with.

"I'm just glad Owen is going with me," I said. "I'm really glad. I think I might marry him."

Sonia gazed up at the sky. "Good," she said.

That night, as I lay in bed and listened to Sonia breathe, I was both in that motel room and back in the dorm on our very first night at school. That first night, lying in my new bed with the lights out, I'd listened to Sonia's breathing, so familiar, but also foreign in a way it had never been at home, and it struck me that it could have been a stranger I heard, that I might have lain there, unable to sleep, and listened as a person I didn't know whimpered and rolled over in bed. The girls in our hall had been moved in by parents and younger siblings. The parents shook hands and rented dorm refrigerators from the tent on the lawn and hoisted beds up on cinder blocks, and then parted from their children with tears or warnings or jokes, and the girls sighed with relief and regret when their parents were finally gone. Sonia and I were without our families. I thought, with some amazement, of the long way we had come.

Now I realized just how completely this part of my life was going to end. For years I had listened to the sounds of Sonia sleeping, the deepening of her breath as she drifted off, the inscrutable things she murmured in her sleep, messages from the dream world. I wouldn't hear those things anymore. I wouldn't hear her.

When I woke, minutes or hours later, Sonia wasn't in the bed beside mine. It took me a moment to process this. Then I heard the sound that must have awakened me, high-pitched and airy, like a ghost drawing breath. "Sonia?" I said. No answer. I got out of bed and saw that the bathroom door was closed. Confused, I opened it.

Sonia was in there in the dark. She was

crying. I turned on the light, and we blinked at each other. She was sitting on the closed toilet, her arms wrapped around her stomach, and as she looked at me her throat convulsed. Tears filled her eyes and rolled down her cheeks.

"Sonia?" I said. I'd never seen her cry, not even after her father died.

"I'm sorry," she said. She began to rock back and forth. She lifted her hands to her face.

"What's the matter?" I was bewildered. Nothing in our day had called for this. My first coherent thought was that something must have triggered a memory of her father. Perhaps she'd dreamed of him.

"I didn't mean to do it," she said, as though I knew what she was talking about.

"Do what?"

She stopped rocking, but she kept her face in her hands. "Sleep with Owen," she said.

I put a hand on the doorframe. I didn't seem to be dreaming, so maybe she was. "You didn't sleep with Owen," I said, in a voice you'd use to reassure a silly, frightened child.

Now she looked at me. "Yes, I did," she said.

I didn't understand. She'd never wanted

Owen. Will had been hers. Owen was mine. "Are you in love with him?"

She sighed, almost as if she were exasperated with me. "No, of course not."

I felt a numbness spreading through my body. "When?" I asked.

"After I found out my father died. That night." She sniffed hard.

"That night?" I repeated.

"I was freaking out," she said.

I nodded. "You needed comfort."

"Yes," she said. She looked at me with some hope.

"Was that the only time?"

She said nothing. She began to rock again.

"Just tell me the truth." I noted with detachment how calm my voice sounded. "I just want to know that you're telling me the truth."

"Christmas break, the night before you came back from Korea," she said. "It happened again. We got drunk."

"So two times," I said. "Twice. That's all."

She nodded. She opened her mouth to speak but managed only a tiny, helpless squeak.

"That's all," I repeated. "That's all."

"I'm a bad person," she said. "My

mother was right."

I just stared at her.

"Please don't tell Owen I told you. I promised him I wouldn't tell you. Please don't tell him."

The first wave of fury swept over me. "How can you ask me that?" I said.

She put her hands to her face again, rocking and rocking. I looked at her soft hair falling forward and wanted to put both my hands on it and pull. Never in my life had I had such an urge to be cruel. I could have hit her. I could have asked her whether her father would be proud of her now. I didn't do it, but I thought of it just the same.

I took a step back. She looked up. "Please, Cameron," she choked out. "He loves you." I shut the door, gently, in her face.

For the rest of the night I pretended to sleep. She came out of the bathroom as the sky began to lighten. She stood beside me and said my name. I kept my eyes closed. She got into her bed and cried until she fell asleep.

I got up, dressed, and packed my things. I went outside and watched the sun come up. I'd been replaying the last year, the strange behavior of Sonia and Owen that I had taken, in my naïveté, for grief and irritation and mutual dislike. I wondered about the conversations that must have ended when I walked into the room. I still felt numb, my movements automatic, but I could tell that that numbness was a scrim, and that on the other side was rage. How ridiculous that I'd ever felt guilty about Will, about things that I'd wanted to do but had never done. This was how she repaid me for all those years of putting her first, by fucking my boyfriend, a man she didn't even love. There was nobody you could trust with your heart. I saw now that I'd be going to Ann Arbor alone, that in one fell swoop she'd robbed me of best friend and boyfriend. I thought, with a strange dispassion, that she had made a lie of my existence, when all this time I'd considered her part of what made it real.

I woke Sonia up when I was ready to go. I barely recognized her. She seemed like a stranger, the sort of familiar-looking stranger you cross the street to talk to, only to find, when you get close enough, that she's no one you ever knew. "Get in the car," I said, and then I went outside and waited in the driver's seat until she did. I didn't even look at her. I hit the gas before she had the door closed. I heard her intake of breath, but she said nothing, just yanked the door shut. We'd planned the night before to head next to White Sands, but that morning I'd studied the map and found the fastest route to Clovis.

I didn't know if Sonia noticed when I took us due north instead of northwest. She didn't say a word, and neither did I, for nearly three hours. Her eyes were closed, but she wasn't asleep. I drove twenty miles over the speed limit, certain that no cop would stop me. I kept my eye on the odometer, ticking off each mile. We'd gone about two hundred miles, not quite halfway, when Sonia said, "I really have to pee," in a small, timid voice, like she was afraid of attracting my attention, afraid that if she did I might hit her. I swerved into the right lane to catch the next exit. A car blared its horn, but I didn't turn around. Off the ramp was a rundown gas station, with a metal door around the back with LADIES scrawled across it.

I got out of the car when she did and watched her walk to the door and open it. "Oh, disgusting," she said, hesitating there. She shot a look back in my direction. I could tell she was tempted to wait and find another bathroom, but afraid to ask me to drive on farther and stop again. She took a deep breath and went inside.

While she was in the bathroom I opened the trunk of the car. I took out everything that belonged to her and piled those belongings outside the bathroom door. I was setting down the last bag when I heard the toilet flush. I hurried back to the car, locked the doors, and turned the key. Out of the corner of my eye I saw the bathroom door begin to open. I stepped on the gas, and the car squealed into motion. I looked into my rearview mirror and saw her mouth open in shock and dismay. She ran after me, shouting my name, but when I hit the highway she stopped.

As she disappeared I thought about driving the farm roads outside of Clovis, cutting straight lines through the fields, "Take It to the Limit" on the radio, Sonia shouting "Drive, Camazon, drive!" clouds of dust behind us, the sky big enough to swallow us whole. Me pressing the pedal down, wanting to see how fast we could get the car to go.

I looked for her in the mirror long past the point when it was still possible to see her there.

Eight years later, I relived all this — involuntary time travel, as Oliver had called it. It wasn't just what Sonia had done I hadn't wanted to remember. It was what I had done. I didn't abandon her impulsively. I planned to do it. I wanted to leave her somewhere so isolated she'd have no choice but to call her mother to come get her, far enough from Clovis that they'd have hours in the car together, hours for her mother to tell her again and again what a bad person she was. It was the worst thing I could think of to do to her, to give her up to her mother for punishment. Even after all those years of friendship, when she hurt me I did the worst thing I could think of to do. That was the kind of person I was. I wanted to break her heart, I wanted her to cry. I wanted us both to be alone, but her aloneness was to be desolation, mine was to be freedom. I lay awake all night imagining it.

Three

17

At the end of our freshman year, Sonia comes home drunk from a frat party at two in the morning. I hear her key in the door, but I don't really wake up until the lights come on. Then I sit up, blinking. A blond girl is holding Sonia by the arm. Even with the support Sonia is listing to the side, and her mouth is covered with blood. She waves a bloody tissue at me. "Cameron," she says loudly, although I'm already sitting. "Wake up!"

"What happened?" I ask, but before they can answer I get out of bed and go to the bathroom for a damp washcloth. Sonia winces when I press it to her mouth.

"She fell and knocked out a tooth," the other girl says. "I'm Suzette. We still have the tooth."

"It's in her pocket," Sonia says.

"Why didn't you go to the emergency room?" I ask.

"She wouldn't go without you," Suzette

says. "She insisted we come wake you up."

I can tell she's annoyed by this. As for me, I feel a strange mixture of irritation and pride.

"That's right," Sonia says. "I wouldn't go without you. So let's go, Cameronia, Camazon. You can drive."

In the waiting room Suzette and I sit on either side of Sonia. Sonia has another tissue pressed to her mouth, blood seeping through it. I hold her free hand while Suzette pats her leg.

I've been hearing about Suzette the last few months, but this is the first time I've met her. She's Sonia's closest friend in her sorority, but I haven't taken their friendship any more seriously than I take the sorority. The stories Sonia's told me — of boring meetings, of vain and malicious girls — have convinced me I was right to refuse when she wanted me to rush with her. When we got to campus, she'd never even heard of rush, but once she knew about it she was obsessed — it was like she was trying out for cheerleading again; she had to know the right routines. We already belonged so thoroughly to the newspaper, I couldn't understand her desire to belong to something else. And I couldn't bear the thought of standing in a group of freshman girls, smiling and making small talk about our hometowns, when really all we wanted to say was, *Please, like me. Please, like me. Please.* Sonia doesn't take the sorority seriously either — she's told me all their secrets, the handshake and the songs.

Now Sonia keeps slumping like she's going to pass out, and when she does I squeeze her hand to wake her, and whisper, "Show no weakness." After a while I realize that on the other side of her Suzette is whispering something, too. Maybe she's singing one of those songs. Maybe she and Sonia have their own motto I don't know about, a secret Sonia's kept after all. I listen hard but I can't hear what Suzette is saying. Sonia nods, yes, yes, when she speaks, and in that nod I see a history I don't share.

All at once it strikes me that as well as I know Sonia, I know only one version of her — that all you know of a life are the places where it touches your own. Under the fluorescent lights of the waiting room I'm catching a glimpse of the places where I don't exist. It's strange and diminishing, like looking through a telescope at the stars.

The next day Sonia stays in bed, nursing a hangover and mouth pain. I bring her chocolate pudding, water she sips gingerly through a straw. I ask her so many questions about Suzette she finally says, "Don't be jealous. I still love you best."

"I'm not jealous," I say, standing up from my perch on the edge of her bed. "I'm just curious."

She grins at me, then winces, her hand going to her mouth. "She's just a normal girl," she says.

"What does normal mean?"

Sonia shrugs. "You know. She's not that quirky. She likes mainstream movies. Romance. Action-adventure. She's not into inner turmoil. She's one of the most practical people I've ever met. It's like, life is a job. She's a realist."

For some reason I feel slightly affronted. I say, "I'm a realist."

Sonia laughs. "You're not a realist," she says. "You're a dreamer who doesn't believe in the dream."

18

Will's map to Suzette's apartment was like a treasure map. It began with a bakery in Inman Square, and then a series of rather puzzling dotted lines led to a rectangle labeled *park,* across from it a large *X* marking the spot where I'd find Suzette. From the T stop in Central Square, I walked into Inman and found the bakery, and then I stood on the sidewalk and turned the map until everything lined up.

Oliver's package looked tattered. The jagged pieces of paper he'd left sticking out were beginning to tear. There wasn't much I could do about that, other than unwrap the package and start over. I tied the dangling ends of the red yarn into a neat little bow.

I crossed the street and rang the bell for number 26. A dog barked inside, and then there was a bang as it hit the door. A woman's voice scolded, "Milton." I heard heavy footsteps, and then just on the other side of the door her voice saying, "Be good, now." The dog continued to bark, but for a moment nothing else happened. I supposed Suzette was looking at me through the peephole. Maybe she was trying to remember who I was. Maybe she knew, and was trying to decide whether to let me in.

Finally the door swung open, and there was Suzette, smiling a welcome. I wouldn't have recognized her on the street. She was a brunette now, with her hair in a news-anchor bob, and she was enormously pregnant, at that stage when an expectant mother looks less like a person than a monument to womanhood. She was trying, unsuccessfully, to hold back her dog with her foot. The dog, a beagle, whimpered and wagged its tail, anxious to greet me. "Well, hey," Suzette said. She hadn't lost her Louisiana drawl. "It's Cameron."

Suzette didn't know where Sonia was. She confirmed this as we stood on her doorstep, then invited me in anyway, as unfailingly polite as she'd ever been. In college, whenever we ran into each other, she always asked about Owen, my classes, the newspaper, even though I was certain she disliked me as much as I did her. This pretense at interest was one of the reasons she drove me crazy. I'd say to Sonia, "Why does she ask me so many questions?" and Sonia would shrug and say, "Good manners are like a religion to her."

At the top of the stairs was a small kitchen with shiny fixtures. Sunlight sparkled on the pots and pans hanging from a ceiling rack. On the counter, a little message board on an easel read *I love you, C.* Suzette paused, her hand braced on the wall, and took a deep breath before she went into the living room. This room had a wood stove, built-in bookshelves, a glass door opening onto a small deck. Suzette sank back into the oversize couch. I could have sworn the coffee table was identical to Sonia's. It used to irritate me in college when the two of them went shopping together and came back wearing the same pair of shoes, something narrow and high-heeled that would never be available in the size eleven I wore.

Being alone with Suzette made Sonia's absence all the more conspicuous, a ghost in the room. I perched on the edge of a chair across from Suzette and admired the apartment. Suzette told me about the projects she and her husband had done themselves — they'd painted, built the bookshelves, retiled the kitchen floor. Then I asked about her pregnancy — she was having a girl, and yesterday had been her due date. "I'm tired of being pregnant," she said. "I miss caffeine. And wine. I really miss wine."

"I thought you could have a glass a day," I said.

"Some people say that. I'm being extra cautious. Besides," she said with a smile, "it's so hard to stop at just one."

Sonia always said that, when drunk, Suzette told the most hilarious stories, but I'd never heard one. Now she began to chat with me like we were old friends. She was on maternity leave from her job as an architect for a firm that did mostly office buildings, schools, hospitals. "Useful buildings," she said, with some satisfaction. She described her theories of architecture, and I wondered about the magazines on Sonia's coffee table. Had Sonia bought them in an effort to share Suzette's interest? Did she have to work that hard to have something in common with her?

From her own job, Suzette moved to talking about Sonia's, and I learned how long she'd been working at the magazine — a year — and heard again how she was the only one who really got along with Avery, the boss, because they were both photographers. Suzette said Sonia kept turning down Avery's offers to help her get gallery shows.

"Why?" I asked.

"I just don't think she's ready to take the risk," Suzette said. "She thinks private praise is better than public criticism."

"That makes sense."

Suzette made a face that suggested she wasn't so sure. "Nothing ventured, nothing gained," she said, and I wondered how many times she'd said that to Sonia, how much it frustrated her to have her advice ignored.

"Maybe it's because of her mother." I was conscious of testing her, wondering if she knew how Sonia's mother belittled her talents, if she'd seen the photographs of Madame Gray. I didn't know what it meant that all these years later I still wanted to know Sonia better than Suzette did, to lay claim to some little part of her she'd never otherwise shared.

"Maybe," Suzette said, her tone and expression as noncommittal as the word. If she knew Sonia's secrets, she wasn't going to tell me. I felt uncomfortable, like I'd broken a rule, so I changed the subject and asked about Sonia's engagement, her fiancé.

Martin worked for a creative-arts after-school program for high-school kids. He and Sonia had been dating for nearly five years. He'd proposed to her in the first six months, but she thought it was too soon. Three years later, when she started to want to get married, he was the one dragging his heels. Finally, after months of arguing — "He was doing that typical, why-mess-with-a-good-thing routine," Suzette said — Sonia broke up with him. Two months later, he showed up at her apartment with a ring.

I resisted the urge to ask how Suzette coped with all of that inner turmoil. She was the sort of person whose solution for a breakup was ice cream. After Sonia's father died, Suzette gave her a teddy bear. But Sonia had decided she hated stuffed animals — she found them creepy — so she hid the bear under her bed. If Suzette ever asked where it was, Sonia planned to pretend it had just fallen under there.

"I'm glad they're back together," Suzette said. "She was strange when they were broken up."

"Strange how?"

"She became sort of unreachable. I

mean, I hardly saw her, and even when I did she wasn't all there. You know the way girls are when they get a new boyfriend?"

"You think she was seeing someone else?"

Suzette shifted position and grimaced. She rubbed a small circle on her belly. "I don't know," she said. "I asked her once, and she said no, but you know that thing she does when her eyes dart back and forth?"

I nodded. "Why wouldn't she have told you?"

"You know how she is."

"I don't know if I do," I said.

"She likes to add mystery to her life. She's the mistress of the pointless secret."

"She doesn't tell you everything?" I cringed, as soon as the question was out of my mouth, at the combination of surprise and judgment in my voice. I sounded as immature as a fifteen-year-old.

Suzette gave me a rueful smile. "How would I know?"

I thought of Sonia saying, "I've decided to tell you everything," how I believed she meant not just then but always, how I believed it would always be easy to tell her everything in return. "Did she tell you she wrote to me a couple months ago?"

Suzette nodded. "Two or three weeks ago we went out for Martin's birthday, and Sonia got really drunk. I haven't seen her that drunk since college — remember how she used to upend a bottle of vodka like it was water? Anyway, that's when she told me. She said you'd never written her back. She said maybe you didn't really exist, that you'd just been her imaginary friend, but I said no, because I remembered you. She said she might as well have written to Santa Claus. Then she started talking about how you'd never forgive her. She said sometimes she understood that and sometimes she didn't."

I bristled at the thought that there might be criticism in Suzette's voice. "Did you know what she was talking about?"

Suzette shook her head. "That's the first I'd heard of any drama between you. After college she just told me you two fell out of touch. But I assume it had something to do with a boy."

"It did," I said. "What else did she say?"

"She wanted to know if there were things I'd never forgive her for. I said, sure, there were probably lots of things, and then she wanted to know what. She kept saying, 'Would you forgive me for being stupid? Would you forgive me for that?' "

Suzette sighed. "She said, 'Isn't there love that could survive anything?' I said no, probably not. She said yes, there was, that her father had loved her like that."

"He did," I said.

"She was lucky, then," Suzette said. For a moment our eyes met and locked. I had a feeling I couldn't explain, that Suzette and I were more alike than I knew. Then Suzette looked down at her belly, both hands going to it now. "That night she was so drunk Martin had to practically carry her out of there. She kept saying, 'Forgive me, forgive me,' as he dragged her out. I don't know who she was talking to."

I could picture this so vividly it was like I had a memory of it, Martin carrying her away while she shouted "Forgive me" at no one in particular. I was surprised by how sad the image made me. "What did you say you wouldn't forgive her for?"

"I didn't. I don't like hypotheticals." She toyed with the tassel on a throw pillow. "Actually, I'm angry at her now. We had a fight when she called to say she was going out of town. I lost my temper. She'd promised she'd be here to help with the baby. That's what friends do."

I nodded.

"That's why I don't know where she is,"

305

Suzette said. "I didn't ask. She said, 'I'm having a hard time,' and I said, 'I'm having a baby,' and then I hung up on her."

"What kind of hard time?"

"I don't know," Suzette said. "Maybe something to do with the guy she was seeing, whoever he was."

The guy she was seeing. I had a vision of Will leaving a message on Sonia's answering machine, saying only, "It's me." I thought of him leaning over to plant a kiss on the rise of her breast. "Does she ever talk about Will Barrett?"

"Her ex? Yeah, she brought him to a party we had like a year ago."

I stared at her. It's okay, I thought. He told you that. "But it wasn't a date," I said.

"I hope not. She was with Martin then."

"You don't think he was the guy?"

Suzette shook her head. "I doubt it. She said seeing him was really awkward. Why?" The last word disappeared into a gasp. I froze. After a moment she smiled again. "I'm a little uncomfortable," she said.

"Can I get you anything?" I said. "Should I boil some water?"

She laughed. "What's that boiling water for, anyway? I've never understood that."

"You're not going into labor, are you?"

"No, more's the pity. The baby's just

moving around. I am so ready to deliver, I can't even tell you." She frowned. "I'm just so angry at Sonia for not being here."

"Maybe she'll be back in time."

"I don't know," she said. "And even if she is . . . I mean, if you can't count on someone to be there when you need them . . . I wonder if we should even be friends anymore."

I'd ended my friendship with Sonia by deserting her in the middle of nowhere, my tires kicking up a cloud of dust. Suzette sounded like she'd end hers with a memo. She went on to say that her anger might be the hormones talking, that she'd no doubt feel much less angry at Sonia after the baby was born, or would, at any rate, be too preoccupied to think about it. But as I walked away from Suzette's apartment, I couldn't stop thinking about the calm with which she'd suggested bringing their relationship to a close, as though that would erase all the time and affection between them, as a house fire destroys your photographs, leaving you to start over without any record of where you've been.

After we'd been friends for five years, Sonia gave me what she called an anniversary card. On the front she'd drawn our old logo, the C and the S intertwined, and inside she'd written a list. *One hundred pounds of chocolate, three thousand Cokes, three cavities, one cross-country drive, thirty trips to the Amarillo mall, one trip to Graceland, thirty-six pairs of sandals, five frat parties, seventy-five late nights at the paper, eighty-three prints I would've measured wrong, one first kiss, twenty-three viewings of Dirty Dancing, seven hundred and two fights with my mother, eight hundred talks about love, one friend for whom I would write all these numbers down.*

At the time I found it amusing that a person who struggled so with numbers would see a friendship as a kind of math. Now I thought it made sense. I remembered Sonia saying, "Numbers are everywhere," and I thought that because numbers were difficult for her she was forever aware of their presence. A relationship was a series of additions and subtractions, and maybe she couldn't understand why I couldn't forgive her because, while sleeping with Owen was a big minus, the balance remained in her favor.

But for me a relationship was a story. It was made up of individual moments, of snapshots: I could see Sonia standing on her bed, singing "Climb Every Mountain" at the top of her lungs, or baking a cake at midnight, making the frosting from scratch, the two of us eating the cake with our fingers straight from the pan. I could remember a night, two weeks after I learned about my parents' separation, when I lay awake in our dorm room, crying so quietly Sonia couldn't possibly have heard me, but she rose to comfort me anyway. Even in her sleep she knew she was needed. But when I thought of these things, I couldn't keep the memories discrete, just as when I looked at the old photographs in Oliver's attic, I'd never been content with the single image each picture contained. I'd always had to imagine what happened next.

Someone who found my album from the last trip I took with Sonia might look at that final photograph, of Sonia laughing in a beauty mask, and from that image extrapolate a happier tale. But when I looked at it I saw not the laughter but the mask. Once you know the end of the story, every part of the story contains that end, and is only a way of reaching it. Sonia disappearing in the rearview mirror.

Oliver sprawled out at the bottom of the stairs.

19

Martin Linklater worked downtown, in the basement of an enormous performing-arts complex. I made a wrong turn looking for the stairs and found myself beneath the high-domed ceiling of an empty theater — rows of red-velvet seats, chandeliers, gilt trim, a blank and waiting stage. A security guard materialized to shoo me out. He pointed me to the stairs, but the basement was a labyrinth. There were people in various stages of costuming scurrying through the halls. I opened one door, and a group of dancers turned their heads — one choreographed movement — to look at me. The office, when I found it, was a comforting return to normalcy, with institutional gray carpeting and plain wooden desks. But Martin wasn't in it. A girl who appeared to have paid a great deal of money to look frumpy — she wore a shapeless dress and a loose brown scarf in expensive fabrics, plus a pair of black horn-rimmed glasses — directed me to a bench by a pond in the Public Garden, where she said I was sure to find him.

"So you want me to just walk into the park and look for a bench by a pond," I said.

She sighed. She pulled out the sort of map given to tourists, full of bright drawings and ads for restaurants, and showed me exactly where to go. I must have still looked skeptical, because she said, "I swear you'll find him. He'll be sitting on the bench beside a tree with a plaque that says white ash. He's a creature of habit. He eats his lunch there at the same time every single day."

I couldn't ask her what he looked like, because I had lied and said we were old friends, and so of course she thought I already knew.

It took only a few minutes to walk from the busy city street to the gardens, pretty as a fairy tale, where sunlight shimmered on the water and brightened the green of the trees. I crossed a white bridge that looked like a spot where a lady with a parasol might linger to have her portrait painted. The pond was ringed with majestic trees trailing leaves down to the water, and everywhere there were ducks and Canada geese and people tossing them the crumbs from their lunches. A boat shaped like a swan glided past, dwarfing the real goose that paddled beside it. The scene had the casual incongruity of a dream.

Someone tapped me on the shoulder. I turned to see a man, just slightly shorter than I. He was attractive in a rumpled, boyish way, with wrinkles in his shirt, his hair in messy curls. "I was right," he said. "You're Camazon."

I stared at him. In a dream, strangers are not strangers, but people who know your mind.

"I'm Martin," he said. "I recognize you from Sonia's pictures."

"Oh," I said. "Hi." His explanation didn't make the moment any less strange. It was odd to be recognized by someone who knew me only through Sonia's descriptions. What pictures had she shown him? What stories had she told? What did he know about me, when I knew so little about him? All at once it bothered me that Sonia was marrying a man I'd never even met. I found myself examining him like he'd been submitted for my approval. He had a sweet, almost pretty, face — big blue eyes, a full bottom lip — made masculine by a square jaw. He was slender but broad-shouldered, and I had the feeling that if I squeezed his arm I'd find his bicep firm. He gave an impression of easy confidence, and he looked at me now with frank curiosity, waiting for me to finish looking at him.

"What do you think?" he asked.

"Of what?"

He grinned. "Of me."

I couldn't help grinning back, impressed by the way he'd managed to ask for my opinion without any appearance of aggression or insecurity. "You seem like a nice guy," I said.

"Good," he said. He looked me over again. "This is so weird. Sonia's been talking about you a lot lately. But she never said you were coming here."

I explained, one more time, about the package, how I couldn't find Sonia, how no one seemed to know where she was.

"Really?" Martin said. "She's in New York."

I was so surprised to at last get an answer that I just stared at him.

"She's at a conference for work," he said. "Going to seminars on black-and-white versus color, I guess."

"What?" I said. "For work? But Daisy

. . ." I stopped. I was not going to be the one to tell this man his fiancée was a liar. A liar and a cheat, if Suzette was right, and she must have been right — I could think of no reason for Sonia to lie to Martin about her whereabouts if she wasn't with another man. He was looking at me now with a worried, doubtful expression. "Okay, it all makes sense now," I said. "I misunderstood."

Martin still looked uncertain. "Daisy said she didn't know where Sonia was?"

"Yeah, but that's because Avery's the one who sent her to the conference," I said. "He didn't want Daisy to know. I just got the dates mixed up. I thought she was already supposed to be back from that."

"Oh," Martin said. "No, she's still there." He grinned at me, doubt banished, and I felt furious at Sonia, and at myself, for aiding her in her deceit, just like I'd always done. Before I'd left Suzette, I'd asked her if Sonia had changed. She'd thought about it a moment before saying no, she hadn't. She was certainly right about that. "That place is so dysfunctional, isn't it?" Martin said. "I mean, why wouldn't he want Daisy to know?"

"I don't know," I said. "I guess he's totally fucked up."

I must have spoken with more fervor than I intended, because Martin looked taken aback. "So," I said, trying to smile, "what has Sonia been telling you about me?"

Sonia had told him about a night she slept over when my parents were out, and we heard on the news that a tornado had been spotted eight miles west of town. We could already see bolts of lightning touching down on the golf course behind my house, and Sonia was terrified. We gathered supplies and made for the hall bathroom, the only windowless room. We'd forgotten the flashlight, so I ran back down the hall to retrieve it. We had turned off all the lamps, and when the lightning flashed outside it was startling and beautiful, an invasion of light. I heard a gust whip around the house and pictured us in the funnel of a tornado, balanced on the wind. In the bathroom Sonia greeted me as though I had braved enemy fire to make it back to the foxhole.

"She said you were really brave," Martin said. "Even though it turned out to be nothing. She said your parents laughed and laughed when they got home."

I hated to be laughed at, and in the living room I'd sat on the couch with my arms folded while my father put *Rumours* on the stereo and began to sing along to "Second Hand News." He had a good, clear, tenor voice. I liked to hear him sing. But I was still angry. "Come on, Camazon," my father said. He took my hands, pulled me up, and swung me around.

"You're my Camazon, you're my Camazon news," Sonia harmonized. That was when she adopted my father's nickname for me, made it seem affectionate instead of mocking. She grabbed my mother's hands and spun her once, and after a startled moment my mother relaxed and let herself be spun again. Everybody danced.

Sonia hadn't told Martin that part of the story, the part I most liked to remember.

While Martin talked, we walked along the edge of the pond. Martin had a plastic bag full of stale sandwich bread to feed the birds. He offered me a piece. Soon we had a crowd of ducks and geese around us, heads darting, beaks working, wings flapping in an irritated way as they nudged each other aside. I was in a state of confusion. My feelings about Sonia seemed to change every minute. Why had she told that story to Martin, a story that cast me in the best possible light? Was that the first thing her memory offered her when she thought of me, instead of the sight of my disappearing car? Wasn't she angry with me at all?

"Watch your hands," Martin said. "These birds are aggressive." He ripped off some large chunks of bread and heaved them toward the water, drawing off some of the crowd.

"So when's your wedding?" I asked.

"Three months," he said. "Are you going to come?"

"I don't know." To change the subject, I asked, "Are you excited?"

"Yeah." He smiled as if he were just realizing this. "I really am. It took us a while to get to this point, but now that we're doing it, I don't know why we waited so long."

"Why did you?"

He hesitated, staring out at the water, where one duck chased another with a great flapping of wings. "You might understand this, actually," he said. "I mean, understand Sonia. Maybe not me."

I waited.

"I've never met her mother." He glanced at me.

"Really?"

"Yeah, and I've tried. The very first year we were together, I wanted to go home

317

with her for Christmas. She's never let me. But she knows my whole family. She knows my second cousins, for Christ's sake. I've never met a single person she's related to. In fact, you're the first person I've ever heard her talk about from her childhood, and then actually met." He smiled. "So you can confirm she's not an alien, or an android, or a spy."

"As far as I know," I said.

"Anyway. That may sound like a weird reason. But at first it made me feel like she didn't take our relationship seriously. She didn't think of me as permanent, so why should I meet her family? And then later, when I picked up on certain things about her mother, I started to feel like it was something out of . . . what's the book where the man is tricked into marrying the girl that's going to go crazy, because they never let him meet her crazy mother?"

"*Jane Eyre.*"

"That's right," he said. "Not that I thought she was going to go crazy. Just that I started to feel like she was hiding this huge part of herself from me."

"I understand that," I said. "She was."

"Yeah." He took out the last piece of bread, ripped it in two, and gave half to me. Then he wadded up the bag and stuffed it in his pocket.

"And you don't care anymore?" I asked.

He shook his head. "You never have all of a person, right? So what I have of her is enough. I mean, she's mine, you know? She's still mine."

I thought of Will's mouth moving down my neck. I thought of him asking me to stay. I thought of Owen telling me he loved me after he'd been inside the naked body of my best friend. I let my hand drop and a goose nipped it. I brought my fingers to my mouth.

"I'm going to marry her," Martin said.

On the train I stared at my reflection in the dark window and tried not to picture Martin's trusting face. But I couldn't keep myself from identifying with him, from imagining again and again what he would feel when he found that trust betrayed. I tried to convince myself that maybe I'd been telling the truth about Avery — maybe he had sent Sonia to a conference neither of them had told Daisy about. It was possible, but I didn't believe it. Martin didn't know where Sonia was staying in New York, and for some reason, he said, she kept calling when he was out. I heard again the girl in his office telling me he was a creature of habit, that he did the same things at the same time every day.

There was only one explanation for Sonia's absence, for her lies, and that was another man. Either she was with him now or she'd been seeing him and had fled to nurse her guilt, to escape his desires, or her own. What if that other man was Will? I let my mind go too far in this direction, imagining that the whole time I'd been with him Sonia had been there, sequestered in a room I'd failed to see. I didn't believe in this picture, but still I couldn't banish it from my mind. After all, I hadn't believed Sonia would sleep with Owen, not even in the first few moments after she told me she did.

If only Suzette had known the other man's name. If only I'd found a note from him in Sonia's apartment, or a picture of a stranger in a hotel room. The train passed over a bridge; white sails dotted across the sparkling water below, and suddenly I remembered Sonia's photos, waiting at the shop in Harvard Square. Maybe, whoever he was, she had taken a picture of him.

The same clerk was behind the counter at the camera shop. He said he'd been wondering about Sonia, that she usually picked up her pictures the day he called to say they were ready. I said she was in New York, visiting galleries, and when I said it I tried to believe it. Sonia was there, walking hand in hand with some man who was not Will.

There were two rolls, one color, one black-and-white. I sat near the chess players outside the Au Bon Pain and looked at them. The color roll was taken right there in Harvard Square. Two teen-agers, a boy and a girl, sitting on the low brick wall near the newsstand. The girl was laughing, leaning forward, blurry, the boy looking at her like she was the only other person on earth. Two college students, heads together over a book. A white mother with her Asian baby. An old couple eating ice-cream cones. Two children — twins, it took me a moment to realize — staring directly into the camera. One smiled, one did not. Photo after photo of people I assumed were strangers, almost all of them in close-up.

Most of the black-and-white pictures were equally disappointing. I flipped through them quickly — trees in snow, bare twigs encased in ice. A few were in such close-up that the branches lost their meaning as things, became jagged black lines across a white background. The next two pictures were of Sonia. In both she was reflected in a three-way mirror. In the first she held the camera at her waist. Her two profiled reflections seemed to be staring, with disapproval, at the one facing out. Full on, her expression looked at once angry and hopeless. In the last photo she held the camera up so that the bright white flash obscured her face. It was as if she had studied her own face, and then decided to erase it.

And then, at last, there were two pictures of a man.

He was a good-looking, older man, probably in his sixties, with facial features so large and craggily handsome they made me think of Mount Rushmore. These photos were also close-ups, but I could see enough of the background to think they were taken in the same place as the tree pictures. I knew from something in the man's expression that he was not a stranger. I held one of the shots of him next to one of Sonia to make them a pair. Daisy had called Avery "Lord of the Jungle." I had a hunch that I was looking at him.

Suzette had talked about how much Avery liked Sonia. Daisy had said he found Sonia enchanting. Maybe she was gone because she'd fled an affair with her boss, a married man, or maybe she'd run away with him. I imagined her on a beach, wearing a bikini, while the man from the picture gave her an indulgent smile. I felt now that I didn't want to find her. I just wanted to know that she was really gone.

Daisy was in her office, listening to *Exile on Main Street* at a high volume. "Well, hey," she said, turning the music down.

I handed her the picture of Mount Rushmore man. "This is Avery," she said, surprised. "Did Sonia take this?"

I said she did.

"It looks like his house," Daisy said. "I was there once, for a fund-raiser, but that was before Sonia's time. I don't know why she would have been out there."

"You said he liked her."

"Well, sure," she said. "But they're not friends." She handed back the picture and swung from side to side in her chair, frowning. "He's got a book of photos coming out. Maybe he wanted her to take the jacket picture."

"Maybe he knows where she is."

Daisy let out a long breath. "I doubt it. Usually he doesn't concern himself with the doings of the little people. He's got bigger fish to fry. Hey, I forgot to tell you

323

the other day that he was a friend of your Oliver."

"Really? How did he know him?"

"I'm not sure. But that's why we did that article." She looked around and then pulled a magazine from the shelf behind her and handed it to me.

I looked at the cover. "The Past Is Memory: An Interview with Historian Oliver Doucet." I'd read the article before. I didn't want to read it again now. I asked Daisy if she thought Avery was at home.

"I know he is. I just got off the phone with him." She rolled her eyes. "Chewed my ass, as usual."

"Can you tell me how to get there?" I said.

Before I left, Daisy asked, "So what happened in Gloucester?"

My hand on Will's bare stomach. His fingers in my mouth. "A friend of Sonia's lives there," I said. "But he doesn't know where she is."

"I'm glad you found the right place," Daisy said. "After you left I realized I should've mentioned that the address could be wrong. I was worried about you driving all over a strange town at night. Thought you might end up in the sea."

"You know about that? Sonia and numbers?"

"Well, sure." She gave me a funny look. "Why wouldn't I?"

"That was her biggest secret, when I knew her."

"Oh, that's right," Daisy said. "She told me she used to hide it. I always thought, 'Honey, how could you hide something like that?' "

"I helped her," I said. "I was her accomplice. So what happened?"

"I don't know. She was a little shy about it at first. We thought it was kind of cute. It is kind of cute — you know, when she asks you what bills to give the pizza delivery guy." She eyed me. "You look stunned."

All that time, practicing so that my handwriting would be hers. The bad grades I took for her sake. Copying out my math homework for her, and then, in college, doing her homework outright. Making lists for her, with all her friends' phone numbers written out in words. The way she would summon me to the darkroom, saying, "Cameron, I want you to take a look at this," and then, once we were alone, she'd whisper, "I can't see the numbers today," and I'd line up the measurements so she could make a print. We'd look at the print together, alone under the red lights with everybody else shut out, and I'd say, "Perfect."

"Camazon," she'd say, "I don't know what I'd do without you."

That week when she wouldn't speak to me, when I stood there helpless in the hall, watching her walk away.

20

Avery lived in Wellesley, in a white house
with black shutters, set back in the shadow
of dark trees. A woman in workout clothes
opened the door. She had a taut, muscular
body — only the lines on her face suggested
that she was middle-aged. She wiped her
forehead with a towel slung over her shoulder and looked from the package under my
arm to me. She didn't speak, just waited.

I asked, in my most business-like manner, if Avery was at home.

Without a word, she stepped back and
waved me inside. There was a wide entryway with a red tiled floor, an enormous
vase full of white flowers on a table. I
stopped and waited for the woman to shut
the door. She mopped at her forehead
again, although I saw no sweat on her face.
She gave me a once-over, a kind of territo-
rial assessment that suggested — not jealousy, exactly, because she seemed too
confident for that. Her manner suggested

that she still saw Avery as a sexually viable man, even for someone my age. "Do you know Sonia Gray?" I asked her, just to see what effect Sonia's name would have.

"Of course," she said. There was no change in her expression. She walked past me, saying over her shoulder that Avery was out by the pool. Although she wore shorts and a jogging bra, she had an arrogant sashay to her walk. I followed her down a long hall lined with shelves, on which framed photographs leaned against the wall under art lighting. She led me through glass doors out to a patio. Beyond that, surrounded by ceramic tiles, was the pool — they even had a pool house — and beyond the pool was a rolling green lawn. The sun was bright, bouncing off the artificial blue water, and the woman shaded her eyes and pointed at a shadowy figure under a beach umbrella. "There he is," she said. Then she raised her voice. "Avery." The figure looked up. "There's a girl here to see you. I think she's from the magazine." She turned and went back inside.

I stood there a moment, looking out on this scene of man-made beauty, the blue water, the white tile, the green grass. I gathered my forces — purpose, pride — and then with my spine erect I crossed the patio and walked along the pool toward the man who watched me approach without a word.

He was sitting in a lawn chair beside a glass-topped table, his legs extended, his bare feet crossed at the ankles. Beside him on the table was a heavy square-cut glass of grapefruit juice with ice. He had what looked like a manuscript in his lap, a pen in the hand that rested atop the pages. He wore swimming trunks, though he looked dry, and a short-sleeve linen shirt that opened at the collar to reveal a white pelt of chest hair. Even in that outfit he managed to look imposing. It was something about the largeness of his head, the gravity with which he turned it to regard me. I stood over him so that he had to look up at me, but he wore sunglasses, so he didn't have to squint, and I couldn't see his eyes.

"Are you having an affair with Sonia Gray?" I said.

He laughed. "That's not what I expected you to say."

"Are you?"

He shook his head. "Sadly, no," he said.

I dropped into the chair across the table from him and pressed my fingertips so hard against my eyelids that when I opened my eyes I saw spots. "I believe you," I said.

"I'm so pleased," he said. "Do you want to tell me who you are? Or what you're doing here?"

"Not really."

"Do you work for me?"

"No," I said.

"Do you want to?" He asked this with mild curiosity. "Because this is a strange way to go about it."

"I work for Oliver Doucet," I said.

"Oh?" He took off his sunglasses. His eyes were a pale, sharp blue. "That's hard to believe."

"Why?"

"Oliver's dead." He said this like it had been a fact for years, like Oliver was a figure out of history instead of a man who'd been alive less than two weeks ago. It was an insult to Oliver to sound so calm. I wanted to shout at him.

"I thought you were friends," I said.

"We were." He put his sunglasses back on.

"How did you know him?"

"He taught at Harvard one year, when I was a graduate student. And you?" He picked up his glass and swirled it, ice clinking.

"I was his assistant. I was supposed to help him write his memoirs."

"That must have been fascinating work."

"It was hard," I said. "It was hard to get him to talk about himself."

"Even so. Just to be in his presence was an education. How did you get that job?"

"Luck," I said. "And a referral from an English professor."

"You must have been qualified. Oliver didn't suffer fools."

A single leaf floated in the pool. "No," I said. I watched the leaf turn in a slow circle, violating the careful order of the backyard.

Avery talked for a while about Oliver, and I heard again and again, like a bass beat, the word *was*. When I couldn't bear it anymore I interrupted him. "I'm looking for Sonia," I said. I explained about the package. "I thought you might know where she is."

"I didn't know she was missing." He shook his head. "Daisy hides things from me."

"Maybe she assumes you're not interested."

He looked at me like he was trying to decide whether to be amused or annoyed. "Perhaps," he said finally. "But I am interested in Sonia, whatever Daisy assumes."

"Then you'll want to know that no one knows where she is, not even her fiancé. In fact, she lied to him, told him the magazine had sent her to a conference in New York."

"Really. That doesn't bode well for her marriage."

"I have no idea where to look next," I said.

"Well, my dear, perhaps she went to New York, after all. Just not for a conference."

"Oh. I didn't think of that," I said, and then I remembered the question mark she'd written on the birth announcement from Owen. The time she'd disappeared, only to turn up in New York. Could she have gone to ask Owen for some kind of forgiveness when she couldn't get it from me? Might she even still be sleeping with him, now, when he had a wife and a new baby? "Maybe she went to see Owen," I said.

"Possibly," Avery said. "I don't know who that is."

I'd neither seen nor spoken to Owen since the day I packed my things to leave Tennessee. The first few months I was in Ann Arbor he wrote me countless letters and called many, many times. I never called him back, never replied. I lay in bed listening to his voice on the answering machine, and sometimes I thought about the first time we had sex, both of us virgins, how I'd reached up, touched his closed eyelid with one finger, and felt the delicate trembling. I'd wondered if Sonia had watched his face the way I did, if she waited with anticipation for the instant when he closed his eyes and his whole body tensed. Maybe she had. Maybe she still did. Funny that now that knowledge would come as a relief.

"I'm curious," Avery said. "What made you think we were lovers?"

"Her friend thought maybe she'd had an affair," I said. "And she'd taken pictures of you."

"Well," he said. "She's a lovely young woman. I'm flattered that another lovely young woman would imagine she might want to sleep with me." He raised his glass to me. "Unfortunately, I'm at the age when I'm more of a father figure than a romantic one."

"Oliver used to say he was my beau. He was much older than you."

"Was he your beau?"

I thought of Oliver pressing my hand to his cheek, kissing me goodnight. "In the most innocent possible way."

"Well, then. In that way I am Sonia's beau."

I felt a pang of longing. I wanted, just once more, to hear Oliver say, "That's my girl, all right."

In the car, I put the key in the ignition and then left it there to pick up the magazine Daisy had given me. I flipped it open to the interview with Oliver and read the first quote I saw: "Faulkner wrote, 'The past is never dead. It's not even past.' I interpret that to mean that the past is memory, which of course is a living thing. This is difficult to explain, but when I'm writing a book I come to feel not that I'm repeating the events I'm describing, as one repeats a story told by someone else, but that I'm remembering them. So I don't consider any of my books the definitive work on a subject. A history, like a life, is just what one person chooses to remember."

I knew this was not a message for me. Oliver had left no message for me, except the letter that had sent me here, which I'd read so many times, looking for it to say more than it did, that it didn't seem to mean anything anymore. But whatever I knew, I believed something else — I believed it was a message for me, just as some people believe that when lost you can open the Bible at random and find a passage that points the way.

One night, our junior year, Sonia and Owen and I abandoned studying for a History of Jazz exam to drive from Nashville to St. Louis at midnight. On the way there, whenever we crossed into a new state, we stopped to take pictures under the welcome sign, the three of us posing in combinations of two, Owen with his arm around Sonia, the bright camera flash. We weren't even sure how to get to St. Louis. We just followed the signs as they appeared out of the darkness. We arrived at six in the morning and circled the city until we found the arch. The sky behind it was a brilliant, overwhelming blue. I felt like Dorothy must have when she finally saw the Emerald City.

On the way back Owen slept with his arms folded across his chest, his head against the window. Sonia was curled up in the backseat. I was so tired the only way I could keep the car straight was to stare at the broken white line that divided the lanes. No one but me noticed when we crossed into a new state. An hour from Nashville they woke up and we took turns quizzing one another on Charlie Parker and bebop, all of us grumpy and sleepy and irritable, blaming each other for not putting a stop to this. Sonia said grimly, "We're going to fail this test."

Why was this what I chose to remember? We saw a sapphire city together, the three of us, a wash of brilliant blue. Why couldn't I believe it didn't matter what happened after that?

I opened the door to Sonia's building and stopped dead. Not three feet in front of me was Will. My heart leapt up like a puppy. I was so nervous I couldn't speak. He turned to me, apparently unsurprised, one hand bracing a piece of paper against the apartment door. "I was writing you a note." He seemed sorry that I'd interrupted him. He crumpled the piece of paper and shoved it into his pocket. He looked at the package in my hand. "No luck?"

I shook my head.

"I'm not going to attack you," he said. I stepped inside the foyer. The door shut behind me with a definitive click. Now we were trapped together in a space too small to contain us. "Do you know you haven't said a word?" Will said.

I stepped forward and kissed him fiercely. I felt him grip the back of my shirt, and I thought, It can't be him. It can't be.

I pulled away. He reached for me, but I moved around him to unlock the door. I gave him a look, then stepped inside. I thought of Avery's wife and walked with an arrogant sashay. In the living room I turned to see him hesitating, looking around Sonia's empty apartment, and so I went back to him, grabbed the waistband of his jeans, and tugged him over to the couch. I wanted to claim him, to brand him, so that every place I touched him I'd see not Sonia's imprint, but mine.

Afterward we went to the North End, which, Will explained in the car, was Boston's Little Italy. He was in a good mood. He told me the note he'd been writing had said, *Check this box if you like me.* At stoplights he leaned over to kiss me. As he drove he kept his hand on my thigh. It seemed funny to me now that I'd been so paranoid as to imagine he was sleeping with Sonia. I almost wanted to share the joke.

Will wanted to walk around the North End before dinner, so we went up the street to the Old North Church, and he told me that this was where Paul Revere hung his famous lantern. "One if by land, two if by sea," he said. "Only it wasn't really Paul Revere." He gazed up at the belfry like he was waiting for the signal. "It was some other guy." He shook his head. "That poor guy. Why did he get ignored?"

"Maybe his name didn't have a good rhyme," I said.

Will laughed. It gave me a little thrill of pleasure every time I made him laugh. "Lost to history for want of a rhyme," he said.

Strolling back down the street to his favorite restaurant, we came up with rhymes for our own names. "Poor Will Barrett," I said. "Lived in a garret."

"Leading a solitary life," he said.

"Along came a . . ." I stopped.

He waited. "What?"

"I don't know. Parrot? Carrot?"

He grinned. "Along came a you."

I said, "That doesn't rhyme."

The restaurant was hot and crowded, redolent with tomato sauce and garlic, and we had to wait so long for a table, drinking red wine at the bar, that I was drunk by the time the hostess called Will's name. Walking to the table, I held on to him to steady myself. When we reached our seats it was hard to make myself let go. During dinner I found myself thinking of Sonia again, as much as I wanted to banish her from my mind. I kept lapsing into silences. I'd look up to find Will watching me, a worried look on his face, and I'd try to smile. He kept asking me what was wrong. Again and again I said it was nothing, and each time I said it I was less sure it was true.

Over dessert, Will said, "What's going on?"

"What do you mean?"

"Something's on your mind."

I ate the last bite of tiramisu. "I've got a new theory about Sonia. I think she's in New York."

"Doing what?"

I told him how she'd lied to Martin about going there, about the birth announcement and the question mark that Sonia had written on it. "So maybe she's gone there to ask for forgiveness or something."

He frowned. "I don't get it. Forgiveness for what?"

"Oh." I stared at him. "You don't know?"

"Doesn't seem like it."

"She slept with Owen. In college. That's

why we broke up, he and I. That's why Sonia and I aren't friends anymore." It struck me, as I told him this, that for the first time it meant nothing to me. For the first time since Sonia told me what she'd done, I really didn't care. But Will looked like he cared. He sat back in his chair.

"I can't believe that," he said.

"Well, it's true." I waved my fork in the air.

"Jesus," he said.

"What?"

"I just can't believe it."

I was starting to get annoyed. I let my fork drop with a clatter onto the plate. "Why?" I said. "Because she's such a precious little angel?"

He ignored this. "I still don't see why she'd want his forgiveness."

"Well, she fucked up his life, too, didn't she? I mean, he and I were going to move in together."

"But why now? Why not eight years ago?"

"Who knows? She's having a crisis?" I shrugged, pretending nonchalance. "Anyway, that might not be why she went. Suzette said she thought she'd been seeing someone else. Maybe she's fucking Owen again."

"I doubt it," he said.

My stomach twisted. "Why would you doubt it?"

He looked at me.

"You would doubt it," I said slowly, "because you're the one fucking her. Of course. How stupid of me."

"I'm not," he said. "Not anymore."

I stood. I hardly knew what I was doing. I felt the chair wobble and right itself behind me. My eyes filled with tears. Show no weakness, I thought. I will kill you if you cry. A waitress passed by with a steaming plate of mussels. A man at the table next to ours ordered another bottle of wine. Talk and laughter swelled and receded, swelled again. For a moment Will and I stared at each other in a pocket of silence. Then he said, "Cameron. Please, let me explain. Please sit down."

I turned and walked out of the restaurant, and when I reached the sidewalk I ran.

It took me an hour to get back to Sonia's on the train, and by then I thought I was sober enough to drive. I got on the Mass. Pike, headed west, and drove fast, like speed could erase what Will had told me. I felt like I was twenty-one again, racing back to Nashville from the gas station where I'd left Sonia, wanting her to cease to exist, wanting the moment when I hit the gas to be the end. It had seemed to me then that if I got back to Owen fast enough it'd be like I had never gone, and nothing Sonia had said would be true. Outside Owen's house that day I'd sat in the car with both hands still on the wheel, staring out the windshield. The front door slammed and I turned to see Owen looking at the car as he walked down the steps. He approached cautiously, his hands out in front of him as if to show he was unarmed. I saw his face, the look of fear and guilt, and I knew Sonia had called to warn him. They were co-conspirators, unified against me, sharing secrets, sharing the memory of each other's touch. I had driven back to him as fast as my car would go, but still I couldn't outrun her. I turned to stare out the windshield again and, gripping the wheel so tightly it hurt, began to cry. Owen knocked on the window. He went around to the front of the car and put his hands flat on the windshield, begging me to open the door. His voice was muffled and meaningless. Didn't he understand? He was just scenery outside the window. I was already gone.

Now I drove for an hour or so before I caught myself letting the car wander into the next lane. I was still tipsy. In a motel room in Sturbridge, Connecticut, I sat in the middle of the king-size bed and started to open the package. I had the yarn off and one flap pulled up when I stopped. I couldn't do it, even though I hated Oliver for giving me this errand, for being so difficult to live with in the beginning, for making me love him and then leaving me. I put the package back together.

I was alone, and it was better that way, because this time I had chosen it. One way or another everybody left, and so life presented two options: You could be the one who got back on the road, or you could be the one left behind.

21

In the morning I woke and lay there for a few minutes, waiting for the knowledge of where I was to come to me. In that instant before it did, I had the familiar feeling, both magical and terrifying, that I'd been transported into another life while I slept. When I realized where I was, I wished I had been. I was hung over in a motel room in some in-between town, neither where I'd been nor where I was going.

Outside I could hear the housekeeper's cart trundling by. I imagined living a life where that was the first sound I heard every morning, where I ordered all my meals from room service and spent my days watching cable television, sometimes leaving to eat at a fast-food place or buy toiletries from a superstore. I could be any-place in America. It mattered to no one, not even me, where I was.

I called Sonia to see if she was back. Her machine answered, and I said, "Pick up if you're there," and waited, listening to a faint whirring on the other end of the line. "Okay," I said. "I guess I'll go to New York." I waited again, but she still didn't answer. "I don't know what else to do," I said, and then, embarrassed by how lost my voice sounded, I hung up.

When Sonia and I left Clovis for college, she was far more nervous than I. I'd lived enough places to make inhabiting the wider world seem not only possible but inevitable. Home was just a place where I happened to be. But Sonia had never been east of Dallas, west of the Grand Canyon, or north of Oklahoma City. She couldn't be sure that everything she knew about herself was portable. Now I was the one feeling that the more places I went, the more of myself I left behind.

Back on the road, I turned south on 91 and went straight through Hartford to the Connecticut coast. Just past Bridgeport, I called information for Owen's number and address. When I called him, his machine picked up, and at the familiar sound of his voice, I felt even more dislocated in time and space. "Hi," I said, and then, because I didn't know how to explain why I was calling, what I wanted, I hung up the phone. An hour later I was in Brooklyn, looking for a parking place on his street.

Owen's apartment was above a deli. I stood outside for a few minutes, looking at his last name beneath the buzzer, and then I lost my nerve and walked up the block. I hadn't been to New York in four years. I'd forgotten the feeling of being caught up in something that you could get just from walking down the street, all those people hustling with you and against you. It seemed to me you could walk the streets of New York and feel you'd lived an active life without ever doing anything at all. I moved like I was going somewhere, but the farther from Owen's door I got, the more I thought about Will's fingers tracing the lines of my ribcage, his warm breath against my skin, and then the time I saw him bend to place a kiss on the rise of Sonia's breast.

I walked back, and when I was still some distance away I spotted Owen, standing on the corner outside the deli. He hadn't seen me yet. He stood with both hands on his lower back, elbows splayed. It was the position he assumed when he was thinking hard about something. Suddenly he looked up and saw me. He did a double take, lifted a hand in greeting, and jogged toward me across the street.

His face had never been full, but it seemed to have lost a certain softness. Other than that he looked exactly the same. He was wearing a Paul Westerberg concert tee and a pair of jeans that were beginning to fray at the ankles. "Cameron?" he said. "Holy shit."

"Hi," I said.

Right there on the street he pulled me into a hug. He held me tight for a moment — I fought a surprising urge to cry — and then he stepped back and smiled. "What are you doing here?" he said.

"I'm looking for Sonia," I said.

He looked puzzled. "Sonia?"

I nodded. Looking past him, I said, "Did you order a pizza?" A man was shifting a pizza box from one arm to the other to ring the buzzer at Owen's door.

"Oh, shit, hang on," Owen said, and ran, yelling, "Wait, wait!"

When I caught up with him he was standing there with the pizza box, grinning sheepishly. "I didn't want him to wake the baby," he said. "Did you know I had a baby?" When I nodded, he said, "I didn't realize my whole world would revolve around getting him to sleep." He studied me. "Wow," he said. "Cameron. Do you want to come in?"

It was a small, sunny apartment — one bedroom, galley kitchen, bathroom, narrow living room, and a tiny alcove with floor-to-ceiling shelves of CDs. The living room was full of baby paraphernalia. Stuffed animals lined the mantelpiece. The baby himself, a tiny pink creature, was asleep in his carrier, nothing visible but his face and one balled-up hand.

Owen's wife was named Anna. She was a pixie of a woman, with a small frame and a sprightly air. She wore her fine blond hair cut short, and I could have sworn her ears were slightly pointed. When Owen introduced us, she hugged me. I patted her gently on the back, feeling like a giant who'd been handed a piece of delicate china.

After I'd admired the apartment and the baby, Anna asked what I was doing in New York, and I repeated that I was looking for Sonia. They hadn't seen her lately, though she'd stayed a night with them a couple months ago. I told the story about the package and summarized my search for her, though I lied about why I'd thought she might be there. I said I'd seen the birth announcement and surmised she'd come to see the baby. I wondered how much Anna knew about Sonia and about why

Owen had broken up with me. Or rather, why I had broken up with him. I supposed I had been the one to end our relationship. Funny how I tended to think of it the other way around. If Owen had told her, he must have offered some explanation, to assure her that nothing of the kind would ever happen to her. I wondered if that explanation had been "I was young, I was drunk," or if it had been something better, something that would be worth hearing now.

Anna and I sat on the futon while Owen fetched glasses of water from the kitchen. I admired the baby again. "He looks just like Owen, don't you think?" Anna said, and I agreed that he did, although it was hard to tell. When Owen appeared, handing us our glasses and then sitting on the other side of Anna — there was no other place to sit in the small room — Anna smiled at him and patted his thigh. She left her hand there as she said, "I'm so glad you're here. I've been telling Owen for a long time he should track you down. He still feels guilty about what he did to you."

I flushed, and glancing at Owen I saw that he had flushed, too. That answered the question of whether he'd told her. "Anna," he said.

"What?" She made a guilty face. "I'm

sorry," she said. "I have an honesty defect."

"It's okay." I couldn't decide whether to be affronted or amused.

"Owen wishes he could put a filter in me." She smiled. "But," she added in a teasing tone, "it's what he loves about me, too." She turned to him. "Admit it!"

He gave her a mock frown, shaking his head, his cheeks still pink. "I admit nothing," he said.

"I'm really sorry." She held up her hands. "Let's blame the hormones. Or the sleep deprivation! Let's blame that."

"It's okay." I caught Owen's eye and looked away. "It's really okay. It was a long time ago. Let's talk about the baby."

"You might be sorry," Anna said. "I can talk about the baby a long time."

The baby's name was Emmet. He was five weeks old that day. He'd been colicky, but now he was sleeping more and more, to Anna's great relief. Anna coordinated educational programs for a museum, but was on maternity leave for another two months. Owen was a music publicist. He listed some of his clients, and I was impressed — I'd heard of several of them. They'd been married for three years. They'd met at a wedding — one of Owen's co-workers had married Anna's best friend. I asked question after question, hoping to distract them from asking any of me. In the back of my mind I heard Anna saying, "He still feels guilty about what he did to you." Watching Anna's mobile features as she talked, I wondered how any man who'd once loved me had ended up with this sweet, open person who seemed incapable of lying. I had always assumed some common thread connected all the people you chose to love, but if there was one between me and Anna I had no idea what it was.

Emmet woke and started screaming. It had been some time since I'd heard a newborn cry. I'd forgotten how desperate you became to give him what he wanted. It wasn't time for him to eat, but after bouncing him and trying all manner of toys, Anna sighed and said she'd better nurse him. "Take Cameron out for a beer," she said. "Then you guys can talk." Owen gave her a look, and she turned to me. "I'm sorry," she said over Emmet's cries. "I just can't help myself."

We went to a bar across the street, a dark pub-style place with a pool table and no one but the bartender inside. We made awkward chitchat, Anna's comments still in the air between us as we sat down with our beers. "I can't believe you're a father," I said.

"Me neither," he said. "It's weird, though. Anna seems like a mother now, and she didn't before."

"She wasn't before."

He laughed. "True."

"I guess we're grown-ups."

"More or less," he said. He clinked his beer against mine.

Halfway into the second beer, I said that Anna and I seemed very different.

"In appearance, maybe," he said, like he'd already given the matter some thought. "But you're both romantics. You think that everything is connected somehow. You think everything means something."

"I'm not a romantic." Irritated, I mopped at the wet circles my beer had left on the table.

"Well, you used to be," he said. "The way you were at the paper — convinced every story was so important." He shaped headlines in the air with his hands. "CORRUPTION IN FOOD SERVICES. THE STUDENT BODY PRESIDENT'S ILLEGAL PARKING PASS."

"Hey," I said. "That was crucial stuff."

"And you cried the first time we . . ." He stopped. "I'm sorry. Anna's rubbing off on me."

"No more beer for you," I said, pulling his empty bottle to my side of the table. "And I didn't cry."

"You did so." He looked indignant. "Remember? You were so embarrassed that you were crying; you just sat there with your hands over your face."

I thought of him trying to tug my hands away, his voice, half laughing, half worried, as he said, "This is happy crying, right?"

Now he leaned forward and said in a whisper, "I lost my virginity to you."

"I dimly recall that."

He shook his head at the memory. "I was pathetic. How many condoms did I throw away, thinking I hadn't unrolled them right?"

"About four hundred," I said. "I, of course, was only pretending inexperience to set you at ease. I'd been with a thousand sailors, a movie star or two."

He gave me a half-smile. "I better get us another round," he said. He refused to take my money. I watched him leaning on the bar, saying something to the bartender that made him laugh, leaving the bartender a three-dollar tip. I had forgotten how much

I liked him, in all the confusion over his breaking my heart.

I drank some of the fresh beer, for bravery, and then I said, "You were sweet. I'm glad it was you."

"Thanks," he said, his eyes serious. "I mean, really. Thanks. I was afraid I'd made you regret everything."

"Only some things," I said.

"I want to ask you . . ." He dropped his gaze to the table, running his finger along a crack in the wood. "If you're not a romantic anymore, is that because of me? Is that my fault?"

I laughed. "Are you asking me if you ruined my life?"

"Not ruined, exactly." He shot me a look. "Affected."

Part of me wanted to take this line of questioning as arrogance, but I knew that wasn't what he meant. "I don't know," I said. "You're the closest I've come to permanent, unless you want to count Oliver."

"Who's Oliver?"

I was sorry I'd mentioned his name. "He was my boss. It was complicated."

He nodded and muttered into the table, "Say no more."

I waited until he looked up. "I'm not saying I wanted to marry you."

He held up both hands, palms out. "Hey," he said. "I'd never presume."

The front door opened, and we both turned to see two young men come in, laughing and noisy. They got drinks and went to play a game of pool. Owen said, "For a long time I was worried I was a bad person. I was afraid any relationship I got in, I'd fuck it up, because it doesn't take that much to fuck it up. Then I fell for this girl — before Anna — and after we'd been dating about a year I found out she was cheating on me."

"What happened?"

He shrugged. "I tried to be understanding — you know, didn't want to be a hypocrite — but it was over pretty quick. That's not the point, though. The point is, that's when I stopped feeling bad about myself and started thinking about how you must have felt. Well, okay, I didn't stop feeling bad about myself. But when I told you that what happened with Sonia meant nothing, it was true. It did mean nothing. But when Lizzie said that to me, I couldn't believe it. Because of course it meant something to me."

At the pool table, one of the guys said, "Fuck!"

"Oh, ho," the other guy said.

"Why did you do it?" I asked.

Owen looked away. "Oh, I don't know. All the usual reasons." He lifted one shoulder and dropped it. "I'd feel stupid listing them for you. They're true, but so inadequate."

"No," I said. "I mean, why did you choose her? Why did you choose her over me?"

"I didn't choose her," he said. "I know why it felt like that. But I loved you. I chose you. I would have always chosen you." He grinned. "If I chose Sonia, it was for like fifteen minutes."

"Or fifteen seconds," I said, grinning back.

"Hey now," he said. "Not when I'm being confessional."

I sat back. "There's no such thing as permanent anyway."

"Well, I hope that's not true," he said.

"Sorry. I mean except for you and Anna."

"Except for us." He said, somewhere between joking and earnest, "I wish there were some way to make you a romantic again."

"I am who I am," I said. I hadn't meant to sound like I was sad about that.

We went back to the apartment. The

living room was empty. I started to speak, and Owen put his finger to his lips. He tiptoed to the closed bedroom door, then waved me over. I could hear Anna on the other side, singing "It's All Over Now, Baby Blue," making an effort to push her sweet, slightly off-key voice toward Dylan's rough cadences. "That's a lullaby?" I whispered.

Owen smiled. "In our world," he said.

I looked at the expression on his face — the tenderness in it, the pride — and felt at the same time a new affection for him and a physical sense of the distance between who we had once been to each other and who we were now. I couldn't imagine that only Sonia had prevented me from being the woman holding his baby on the other side of the door. Owen was a nice person. I liked him and his wife, and I thought from now on we'd probably exchange Christmas cards and have dinner on the rare occasions we were in the same town. But just as Oliver's things lost their meaning without Oliver, so without the love I used to feel for Owen, he'd lost his meaning for me. He used to be the hero of the story, but now he was just an average person again. I thought of Will, the one my feelings put the spotlight on now, and then I tried not to think of him.

Owen guided me back to the living room, so that Anna wouldn't catch us eavesdropping. "She's embarrassed about her singing," he whispered.

"Another thing we have in common," I said.

When Anna emerged with Emmet, saying he wouldn't sleep, I asked to hold him. He stared at me with that expression newborns have that suggests they're perplexed and angry to find themselves in a bright world of hard surfaces and hunger. "He really does look like Owen," I said, and Anna beamed. Owen put his arm around her and kissed her on the temple, and Anna said I had to stay for dinner.

As the evening wore on, I began to say that I should go, although Anna protested every time. We watched Emmet fall asleep in his swing. Anna offered to make me a bed on the futon, but I lied and said I was on my way to Connecticut to see some friends. I thought I'd drive until I got tired, and then I'd find another motel. I'd decide which way to go once I got on the highway. There was no place else for me to look for Sonia, and I couldn't bear the thought of going back to Cambridge to leave the package. I'd have to mail it. Oliver would have to understand that I'd done my best.

Determined to leave, I was saying my final good-byes when the buzzer rang. Owen and Anna looked at the sleeping baby, but he didn't stir. Together they sighed with relief. "I'll get it," Owen said.

Anna watched him go, radiating anticipation. "Who is it?" I asked, but she just shrugged.

After a moment Owen came back, wearing a puzzled frown. "Weird," he said. "It's Will Barrett."

"Finally," Anna said, and Owen and I looked at her. She smiled with guilt and excitement. I stood up, and she put a hand on my arm. "He called while you were out," she said. "He said you'd leave if you knew he was coming."

"He was right," I said.

"But it's so romantic," she said. "He drove all this way."

I looked down into her bright, hopeful eyes. "I can't," I said.

I went for the door. Owen was right behind me. "What's going on?" he asked. Eight years ago I'd packed my things while he followed me around his house with tears in his eyes, saying again and again that he loved me. I'd kept my resolution to leave him without a word.

"Déjà vu," I said. I opened the door and caught Will with his hand raised to knock. "I'm sorry," I said to Owen, and then brushed past Will and ran down the stairs. I heard Will pounding after me, but I made it to the street before he grabbed me by the arm.

He was breathing hard. "I'm not going to let you do this."

I yanked my arm from his grasp.

"You're not running away," he said. "I'm going to talk to you."

I turned and started walking down the street toward my car. He fell in step beside me. "I want to explain," he said. "I wasn't trying to deceive you. I just didn't want to ruin it."

I nearly laughed at that. I picked up my pace.

"I was afraid if I told you, this would happen," he said.

I reached the car and unlocked my door. He grabbed my arm again. "I'll stand in front of the car," he said. "I'll throw myself on the hood. Cameron. I'm not kidding."

"All right," I said. "Get in."

He kept one hand on the car as he walked around to the passenger door. I put the key in the ignition but didn't turn it.

"I want to explain," he said once he was inside.

"I think I got it." I put both hands on the wheel and stared out the windshield like we were going somewhere. "You're dating Sonia."

"But that's not what I want to explain."

"What do you want to explain? Why you made a fool of me? Why you listened to me babble about her life and never said a word? Why you lied to me? Yes, please explain."

He took a deep breath. "I didn't lie to you."

"Fine," I said. "Why you omitted the truth."

"I don't know why I didn't tell you."

"That's a good explanation. I can see why you drove three hours to give it to me."

He threw his hands in the air. "Will you just let me talk?"

"Okay. Talk."

"I'm not dating Sonia," he said. "I'm not in love with Sonia, and she's not in love with me, either. But when she broke up with Martin, on and off for a couple months . . . we're adults, we were lonely. Nothing's happened since she got engaged."

"I don't want to hear this."

"You said you did!" He let out a shaky breath. "You remember when Sonia and I broke up in college?"

"What has this got to do with —"

"Just let me tell it!" he snapped. Then he held out his hand, as though to calm us both. "Afterward I was sitting in the airport, feeling . . . I don't know what."

"Sad," I said.

He gave me a rueful smile. "Sad, yes. And then I looked up and there you were. When I saw you, when I saw that you had come to say good-bye, I thought, Of course." He looked at me like he expected me to understand.

"And?"

"I had this crazy feeling I should ask you to come back with me, that it would be perfectly natural if you got on the plane, too. And when I opened my door the other night and saw you there, I had the same feeling."

"That I should get on the plane?"

He sighed. "No," he said. "That you were the one I was meant to be with. That you were the one all along."

I thought of standing with him, watching those ducks circle, dancing with him at the prom, all the times I'd had that feeling myself. "I don't know," I said.

He took a deep breath. "I have to tell you one more thing."

"What?" I whispered.

"Sonia's in Clovis." He was wincing as he spoke. "Her mother had a breakdown. She went out there to take care of her. She didn't want anybody to know. She made me promise . . ."

"You knew this the whole time?"

"She made me promise," he said. He looked miserable. "I'm breaking my word to tell you now. She may never speak to me again."

"I can't believe this," I said. "It's just the same thing over and over."

"But it's not," he said. "I'm telling you I want to be with you."

I shook my head. "I can't do this again."

"What are you talking about? We dated before?"

I couldn't look at him. "I can't do it," I said. "I can't be with you."

"Cameron, please." His voice trembled.

I closed my eyes. "No," I said.

"Cameron . . ."

"No," I said.

He got out of the car and shut the door gently, with both hands.

I started the car, but then I just sat there

with the engine running and watched him walk away. When he was gone I leaned my head against the steering wheel. I had the heavy feeling that I was fated for departure. It seemed to me that I left everyone, even Oliver, packing my bag to abandon his house like a hotel guest fleeing the bill. Over and over my life blurred around me until I was nothing but the forward motion of my car. I left Sonia outside that gas station, and ever since I'd been driving away.

22

On the drive from the Amarillo airport to Clovis it was impossible to shake the feeling that I was going back in time. I hadn't been back to Clovis since Sonia and I had left for college twelve years before. The strangest part was not how much had changed but how much had stayed the same. Passing all the places we used to go was like being on the set of a movie about my life. I kept expecting to see a younger version of myself coming around the corner, wearing hoop earrings and a bright shirt with shoulder pads, my bangs curled and sprayed into place. There was a new mall, and signs announcing that a hardware chain was coming soon, but Main Street looked much as it had when we used to spend our Friday nights driving up and down it. Pickup trucks, dirt-brown buildings, the sun bouncing off metal and glass. The sky was so vast it seemed to absorb even the biggest and ugliest man-made things into nature, until it all became landscape, and I thought of climbing into the Bandolier cliff dwellings on that last trip with Sonia, turning to her to say, "Can you believe people used to live here?"

With my conscious mind I couldn't remember how to get to the pizza place, but my teenage self took over and made all the right turns. It was late in the afternoon, and the parking lot was empty. I sat in my bright blue rental car at the edge of the lot. This was the place where Sonia and I first met. I could see myself standing at the curb, hunching my shoulders to look smaller, and I could see her walking toward me, the sunlight shining in her hair.

The Grays' house looked smaller than I remembered, like it had shrunk in the rearview mirror and then stayed that way. Still, walking up the driveway with the package in my hand, every move I made seemed an echo of one I'd made before. Time had closed in a loop, two hands bringing the ends of a string together.

I was reaching for the doorbell when the door opened and Sonia stepped out. She didn't see me — she was moving fast, her eyes on her feet — and she ran right into me. "Oh!" she said. I felt the shock of her body against mine. She was physical, real, not just a character in my memory. I grabbed her arm to steady us both.

She was wearing ratty shorts, running shoes, a purple T-shirt left over from high school that said GO WILDCATS. She had her hair pulled back in a ponytail. Her cheekbones and the line of her jaw were more prominent than I remembered. She looked tired, I thought, or maybe she just looked older. She was staring at me with the same surprised recognition that was no doubt on my face.

"I can't believe you're here," she said. "I didn't really think you would come." She stepped forward, out of my grasp, to give me an unexpected hug. It was an intimacy I wasn't quite ready for. I hadn't expected to find her so happy to see me. Somehow, after all these days of looking, I hadn't expected to find her at all. I lifted my free hand to rest lightly on her back, my awkwardness making me feel inadequate to the moment. "Camazon," she said into my shoulder, like she was confirming that that was who I was.

She stepped back and looked at me again. She was smiling, but when I failed to speak, her expression grew uncertain. She bit her lip with her two front teeth and tugged at the end of her ponytail, smoothing it against her neck. It was a nervous gesture so familiar that for an instant she could have been fourteen. I blinked, but the shadow of her girlhood self remained, a double exposure.

"Hi," I said.

"I was just going out for the mail," she said.

"Oh."

We both nodded.

"I'll get it later," she said.

"Okay."

Behind Sonia a teakettle began to wail. Alarm flashed across her face, and she turned and ran inside and down the hall, leaving the front door open.

I stood there, reluctant to follow her. Being back here unnerved me more than I'd expected. In the year after my friendship with Sonia ended, I hadn't been able to stop myself from imagining the confrontation I might have with her, the biting things I might say. That year I had dreams where I defeated her, usually in some nonsensical way, like in a competition to buy a roller rink. But for a long time, I'd thought myself well past any such desire — I'd thought myself well past any desire to see her at all — and on the way here I'd thought only of giving her the package, seeing her open it, and leaving. Now I saw that of course it wasn't as simple as that. I didn't know quite what I wanted. I had the package in my hand, but it didn't seem sufficient reason for my being there. For one thing, I'd felt, when she hugged me, an unexpected desire to be a kid again, to once again be her friend.

I made myself step inside. In the living room, the furniture was older, shabbier, but otherwise the same. I ran my hand along the back of the couch. I could see myself sitting there with Will as he pressed the bloody towel to his head. I walked into the kitchen, and another me brushed past, running outside to stop whatever might be happening there.

Sonia was standing at the counter, wearing an expectant smile. "I thought you'd forgotten the way," she said.

"No," I said. I put the package on the table.

"Well," she said. "It has been a long time."

"Sonia . . . ," I started. I had a vague idea of asking after her mother.

"Do you want some tea?" she asked, her voice unnaturally bright, and I realized she was nervous, as nervous as I was. When I nodded, she listed the various teas on hand

and then went to make me a cup. I sat down at the table. She seemed to be deliberately making noise, clattering the mugs, banging the sugar bowl on the table even after I'd said I didn't want any. "Milk," she said. "Spoon." When all these things were arrayed in front of me, she sat down, gave me a quick smile, and then busied herself dunking her tea bag in and out of the water.

That day her mother had hit her in the backyard, I'd sat at this table with Sonia while her father consoled her weeping mother upstairs. Sonia had shown me her palms, shot through with splinters — fleeing her mother, she'd scrabbled up the wooden ladder on the swing set, and Madame Gray had pulled her back down. I'd found tweezers in the bathroom and, careful as a surgeon, removed every tiny sliver from her hands.

I didn't know now how Sonia could be here without thinking of that, how she could walk into the backyard without seeing her mother standing over her, ready to hit her with a chain, how she could look at her mother at all. I couldn't imagine what was happening with her mother now, to make Sonia come back here after all of that.

"How's your mother?" I asked.

Sonia seemed startled that I'd spoken. "What?" she said.

"How's your mother?"

"Oh," she said, "she's . . ." Her voice trailed off. Then she seemed to gather herself. She looked at me with determined cheerfulness. It was an expression I recognized. She was about to give a performance. "It's really pretty funny," she said. "It's like I'm the mother and she's the child. She keeps trying to sneak out. I caught her yesterday, and she said, 'Tell me what nine times five is and I won't go.' Luckily, I always remember that one. Forty-five. Why my brain can come up with that answer and no others I have no idea. Then she started in with some other ones — six times seven, and so on — but I said, 'Mother, we had a deal.' Except I said it in French, because for some reason she listens to me more when I speak French. Can you believe she's still playing the number game? It's funny. Just like old times, huh?" As she said "old times," her face, just for a second, was sad. "I'm sorry," she said. "I don't know why I'm being so flip. I just feel discombobulated, like I've gone back in time."

"Oliver says all times exist simultaneously."

371

"Feels like it," she said. "Here we are again."

"Do you remember . . . ," I started, and then I looked away. I'd been about to ask about the time with the splinters, which of course she remembered, and why did I want to bring it up now? What exactly did I want to remind her of? Her mother's cruelty? My own beneficence?

She waited for me to finish, but when I didn't she didn't press me. "It's so weird, being here with you at this table, feeling like I have to be polite to you," she said.

"You don't have to," I said. "Don't strain yourself."

She stood, abruptly, and dumped her tea in the sink. "I made it too strong," she said, but she hadn't even tasted it. She took out another tea bag, poured the water again. "I knew the second that was out of my mouth you'd take it the wrong way," she said.

"What way should I take it?" I said.

She turned and leaned against the counter. "I just mean, you're so familiar, but then you're not. I don't know the rules for how we should interact." She looked down at her mug. "When I saw you, my first feeling was relief, you know, like thank God, Camazon's here, she'll understand, I can tell her everything . . . but then I remembered that's not who we are to each other anymore." She looked up. "Is it?"

"There's a reason for that," I said.

"Yeah," she said. "I know." She sighed. "You know, I knew from what Oliver said that you were still angry at me. But I'd hoped you weren't just coming here to settle a score."

Though I'd been curious before, now I didn't want to hear about her secret correspondence with Oliver. I wanted to pretend he'd never written her at all, just as I wished I could pretend she'd never slept with Will. "How did you even know I was coming?" I asked.

"Will called me."

"Oh." My stomach tightened at this news. "I didn't tell him."

"No, but he thought it was a possibility. I thought you'd be torn between your desire to complete a task and your reluctance to ever see me again." She gave me a quick, sharp look.

"I was," I said.

"See how well I still know you?"

Was that sadness in her voice, regret, or just weariness? I wasn't sure. Her body gave nothing away. She was leaning against the counter, her hands cupped loosely around her mug, with every appearance of calm. She didn't even seem nervous anymore, as though in the last few minutes she'd decided I wasn't worth it. Now she wasn't even looking at me, her gaze traveling out the window toward the backyard. I couldn't gauge whether she really felt as indifferent, as confident, as she looked. I used to think I knew what was real, what was the mask. She used to teach me her cheerleading routines, so that I watched her at football games with a mix of pride and worry, because if she made a mistake, I'd know it, even if no one else did. But she didn't make mistakes. She was the only cheerleader who ever looked happy to be up in the air. The other girls wobbled and shook, their mouths set in fearful grimaces. Up she went, Sonia, with a broad grin. Her leg didn't even shake as the squad's only boy held her foot with both hands. He would pitch her into the air, and for a moment she would fly. No one but me knew how scared she was, every time, that she would fall. She said no one in her life had ever understood her the way I did, in that moment before we knew whether she had gotten it right.

Out of all the conflicting things I felt, looking at her now, the one that rose to the surface was a desire to provoke her, to make her angry. There's nothing lonelier than being angry at someone who's indifferent to your anger. It's like playing catch off a wall by yourself. Everything you feel just bounces back to you.

"Why did you write to me?" I asked. "Was it the challenge, to see if you could win me back?"

Her gaze snapped back to me. "That's one way of looking at it," she said, and to my satisfaction I heard an edge in her voice.

"What's another?"

"I told you why," she said. "Getting engaged made me think about my life so far, how I'd gotten here, what might've been different. And my mother was . . . having problems. After a long time when she wasn't. So here I am, about to do this adult thing, and these things are happening that are making me feel like a kid again. And I wanted to talk to someone who would understand."

"Sleeping with Will didn't do the trick?"

"No." She tried to look impassive but her left eye twitched. "I'm not going to talk to you about Will."

"Why not?"

"Why should I? What happened between

us is between us. What happened between you is between you."

"You don't see any connection? That's twice now we've shared a man."

"I wouldn't really say we shared them. They were both yours in the end."

"What do you mean?"

She took a long sip of her tea before she answered. "Will still hopes you're coming back," she said. "He's fallen for you."

"He told you that?" I was taken aback by this, and it struck me that I'd gone on assuming my feelings for Will were stronger than his for me.

"I could tell," she said. "When he falls he falls hard. Or didn't you notice?"

"Lying to me is a funny way to show it."

"Now he feels stupid. He's afraid he misread you, thinking you'd fallen for him."

"He misread me? I'm not the one who was sleeping with you."

"You're not going to make this one my fault," she said. "This is nothing like what happened with Owen."

"But it is."

"How?" she snapped.

"Because it is," I snapped back. "Because maybe I'm just the one they take when they can't have you."

There was a terrible silence in which my

words seemed to echo. If only I'd said something neutral, even cold or hurtful, instead of insecure and pathetic. I waited with dread for her to speak, sure I'd hear pity in her voice.

Instead, she seemed angry. "That's completely ridiculous," she said. "It's you he wants, believe me. And I'm telling you this even though it makes me a little jealous, how badly he wants you." She paused, and when she spoke again it was in a clipped, matter-of-fact way. "It's funny, I used to worry about you and Will, because sometimes it seemed to me you two were a better match than we were. But you never noticed that, because you're so busy protecting yourself it never occurs to you that everyone else is just as vulnerable. Thank God I didn't realize you were in love with him until we broke up."

"You knew?" I couldn't believe it, and all at once I felt like I was sitting there naked. "How?"

Sonia shrugged. "There was something about the way you were that day, the way you went to the airport after him. I just knew."

"And you were angry?"

"I didn't think you'd done anything," she said. "And you were with Owen by then.

But, yes, I was angry, at least for a while. Angry that you'd kept the secret from me."

I pushed to my feet. "That *I* kept a secret . . ." I stopped and took a deep breath. "Is that why you slept with Owen? Because you were angry at me?"

She slammed her mug down on the counter and took a step toward me. "I slept with Owen because my father had just died, and you weren't there."

"So it was my fault?"

"No, it was mine, and Owen's, too, by the way." Her voice trembled. "But it was one mistake." She jabbed a finger at the floor. "One mistake."

"It was a pretty big mistake."

"My father had died. Do you understand how that felt?" I was about to say I did, when she spoke again. "Don't you dare say you do, because you don't."

"I lost Oliver," I said.

"He wasn't your father!" she shouted. She looked alarmed at the sound of her own raised voice. She pressed her hand to her mouth, shushing herself, and cast a worried glance toward the front of the house. "My mother's asleep," she said.

"So what?" I said. "Why do we have to be careful of her? What are you even doing here with her? The woman's still shouting math problems at you."

She stared at me a moment. Then she said, "I'd tell you if I really thought you cared."

"What makes you think I don't?"

"You don't want to be my friend," she said. "You can't even forgive me."

"Do you have any idea how it felt to have you betray me, like our friendship meant nothing?"

"Do I have any idea? The last I saw of you was the back of your car. And now you come here saying I should leave my mother, who's the only parent I've got left. What if Oliver had gotten senile and started cursing at you and wetting himself? How long would you have stuck around then?"

"I would have."

"If he hadn't died I bet you would've left him, too."

"That's not true," I said, though suddenly it seemed like it was. I seemed to have a memory of driving away, Oliver waving at me from the window, each of us watching the other disappear.

"You would've said, Oh, just pop into the bathroom, Oliver, I'll be right out here waiting. And then you would've left him there, alone in a big cloud of dust."

"That's not true," I said, my voice rising.

"He would've tried to go after your car, but he wouldn't have been fast enough. And then he'd have been all alone. Because you'd have left him behind like garbage, like nothing between you ever mattered at all."

"That's not true!" I shouted.

"It is true!" she shouted back, shocking me into silence. "You left me alone!"

She looked furious, but her eyes were bright with tears, and the hurt and anger in her voice made me feel again what an awful thing I had done. I imagined Sonia waiting on that curb at the gas station, sure I would relent and come back. How long had she waited before she called her mother? How many hours more had she waited for her mother to arrive? I thought of the long drive home, Sonia staring out the window at the flat, brown land rolling by while her mother's voice, tight with fury, told her all the things that were wrong with her.

She stared at me now, breathing hard, her face flushed. She wasn't over anything, not the sight of her mother standing over her with a chain, not the sight of me driving away. Oliver was right — it was all still with her, her hurt and her anger and her guilt. We were together in that.

She sat down at the table, closed her eyes, and pressed her finger and thumb hard against the lids. "I'm not going to do this," she said. "I can't do this right now." She opened her eyes and grabbed the package. "I'll open this, and you can go," she said. She tore the paper off before I could protest. I didn't want her to open it. I no longer wanted to see what was inside.

From the box, Sonia lifted out several sheets of folded paper. Even from the back I recognized Oliver's spiky hand. She read the first few lines and then dropped the letter back inside. "This is really for you," she said. She seemed exhausted, drained of energy by opening the package, by screaming at me, maybe by the struggle it had taken not to cry. She pushed the box across the table toward me. "I'm going to check on my mother," she said. She rose from her chair as if she were as fragile as Oliver. As she left the kitchen she wavered and put her hand on the doorframe for support. I listened to her footsteps as she made her slow way up the stairs.

I sat down and lifted out the letter, my pulse thrumming in my throat. Beneath it was a picture in a frame. A young woman sat on a lawn, leaning back on her hands and smiling at the photographer like he'd just made her laugh. She wore a white dress, and her wavy dark hair tumbled over her shoulders. She was Billie, the girl I'd visited so often in the attic, the one now closed up in a box in the trunk of my car, which I'd left in the LaGuardia Airport parking lot. Only in this picture she didn't look sad. I heard again Oliver's voice as he said, "I did what you have done. I left her behind." I swallowed over the lump in my throat.

I sat for a few minutes with the letter still folded in my hand. It contained the end of the story, the last thing Oliver would ever say to me. Finally I unfolded it.

Dearest Cameron,

Here, at long last, are my memoirs, the first truthful accounting I've given of my life in nearly sixty years. You may do with this document what you will. If you'd like to pull back the curtain on my life, I wouldn't blame you for it. I myself would be unable to resist. Of course the truth might be embarrassing for Ruth, but perhaps you won't consider that a detriment.

My name is not Oliver Doucet, and I am not, by birth, a southerner. I was born Sid Murphy, in 1911, in a little town in upstate New York.

I imagine you understand now why I was such a recalcitrant subject. I wish I could see your face. There are certain drawbacks to a posthumous surprise.

I told the truth when I said my mother was a cold woman, my father a philanderer. There's not much more I wish to say about them, or about my early life in general. I did nothing to distinguish myself. I was, among other ignominious things, a shoe salesman. The only bright spot in those years was Billie, beautiful Billie with her movie-star name. We were friendly from childhood, but for one reason or another, mostly owing to my inability to believe she'd want me, we didn't become a couple until 1939. She was comforting me about a girl who'd recently left me for another man, and I blurted out that I didn't care because she, Billie, was the one I loved. Then I looked at her with such trepidation she laughed. Certain she was mocking me, I fled the room, but she pursued me. "You idiot," she said. "I've been in love you since I was fifteen."

I proposed not long afterward, but then I joined the service, and though she wanted to get married right away, I insisted we wait. I didn't want my first act on marrying her to be departure. How foolish that seems to me now.

I met the original Oliver Doucet in 1943 in Colorado. We had both been made official historians — he because he had actually been a history major in college, and I because among my jobs there had been a brief stint as a copywriter for an advertising agency. We had the same birthday. This was one of the first things we learned about each other, and then Oliver said, in his way of talking, which was almost always serious and mocking at once, that we were destined to be friends.

His parents were dead. His mother had belonged to a wealthy Oxford family — they'd been mayors, judges, famous hostesses — but there was only an aunt left now. His parents had left Oxford for a tiny town in Mississippi, where they'd joined a strange church — Oliver didn't much like to talk about that — so he'd seen this aunt only a handful of times, but he'd always had the feeling they understood each other, and he was to be her heir.

He died, not in combat, of course, but in a jeep wreck, in a compromising position with a young man from town. He'd left a letter for me, saying that if anything happened to him he'd like me to go see his aunt, and so after the war was over and I was discharged, I did. I had the same sense of duty, the desire to complete one stage of life before beginning another, that I trust has brought you to Sonia with this. I planned to see his aunt first, and then go home to Billie. The choice seemed small, but it changed my life. If I'd gone back to Billie right away I would have stayed.

All the way there on the train I prepared lies about him. I was going to make his death more heroic than it was — I was going to say he'd swerved to avoid a child playing in the road. I wasn't going to mention that he'd been drunk, leaving a bar with a questionable reputation, and certainly I wasn't going to say a word about his young man. But his aunt — my aunt, as I can't help but think of her — didn't believe my story. Perhaps I hadn't yet learned to lie with conviction. When she asked me for the truth, I told her. She said, "It's a shame." She shook her head. I waited for something more, and after a few moments I suppose my face displayed my surprise that nothing more was forthcoming. She shrugged. "I liked the boy," she said. "But I didn't know him very well." She sighed. "Still, I'll miss him. I refuse to leave this house to the Lamars" — the Lamars were distant cousins of hers. Then she looked me up and down and asked me to stay a few days.

I didn't realize it at first, but this was an interview. Every day, she quizzed me about my thoughts on society, art, government, and my upbringing and general lack of accomplishment. She told me stories about the town, the house, the family, watching me closely for signs of disinterest. I gave her none, because I liked her. I felt, as the original Oliver had, that we understood each other. When she asked me if I'd like to become Oliver Doucet, live with her and be her heir, I have to say I wasn't particularly surprised. I was ready for it. There was nothing in my old life, except Billie, that I had any wish to return to. As for my aunt, she was lonely. She wanted some family of her own. She took to me, my dear, exactly as I took to you.

I researched the family until I no doubt knew more about them than the original Oliver Doucet ever did. I think this, not my time in the military, is what sparked my interest in history. It didn't take long for me to believe I was Oliver Doucet. I belonged with my aunt, in that house. I was a historian, and when I started writing my books it became even clearer to me that I'd finally begun living the life I was meant for all along. Ruth's mother, my wife, was one of the Lamars — my aunt grumbled about this, but I think she was as pleased as I was that I was now related to my new family after all, if only by marriage, and later that Ruth was related to them by blood.

I never had any contact with anyone from my original life again — not my parents, not my friends, not Billie. I left them behind more thoroughly than even you've been able to. At first I meant to contact Billie, once I was settled in, but the more I became Oliver Doucet the harder it was to imagine reintroducing myself to her. What would she make of my new name, the accent I'd worked to acquire, my lies? If I brought her here, would she inadvertently expose me? It became more and more impossible to reach over the gulf between us. I hoped she wasn't still waiting. I hoped she thought I'd died. What a coward I was. Even on my wedding day I was haunted by the sight of Billie's face, the last time I saw her, when she looked at me with such sorrow at my leaving, such hope for my return. I tried to find her, after my wife died, but I had no success. She left town about a year after the war — a year, I imagine, that she spent waiting for my return — and after that I lost the trail. I don't know what became of her, if her life was happy or sad. Even now she appears to me, exactly as she was sixty years ago, and she asks, "Didn't you love me after all?" And the answer is, I did. I loved her like I've never loved anyone else in my life, and I spent much of my life lonely because I'd left that love behind. (In the end I wasn't lonely. I was never lonely with you.)

I suppose there are many lessons you could take from this story. I'm tempted to enumerate them, having always felt that in some way it was my duty to pass on wisdom to you. You could say this story tells you that there is no absolute truth about a life. You merely choose the story you want to tell, and keep telling it. To many a historian's despair, sheer repetition often serves to make a story true. I want you to see how many truths there are, that even the contradictory ones don't cancel each other out.

Or perhaps all I want you to know is this — I lied to you when I said the ring I gave you belonged to my aunt. I bought it for Billie, when I still intended to return to her. It was her you reminded me of.

Do you see why I sent you to Sonia, why I wanted you to learn these things in her company? Please don't choose loneliness, my dear Cameron, thinking it will protect you from grief. It will spare you nothing. I've left you now, and before that I lied to you every time I answered to my name. Do you not understand, even so, how much I loved you?

Oliver

Shock is not a strong enough word for what I felt when I finished reading. I felt like someone had put a bag over my head, rushed me off into the night, yanked the bag off in a foreign country, where even the light looked different, and told me this was my life. It was impossible to believe what I'd just read, that Oliver was somehow not himself. I turned the last page over to see if he'd written on the other side that he was joking, but all I saw was a blank.

Oliver had had no right to put my name on his family tree, which, after all, wasn't even his. He'd told me to make my own history — wasn't that a meaningless endeavor if that history was a lie? I'd thought that while I was with Oliver I was rooted somehow, but his claim to that house in Oxford, the rich past in the attic, had been as tenuous as mine. We'd just been two wanderers clinging to each other, pretending it was possible to stop running, pretending we belonged. I didn't know a Sid Murphy. I didn't want to. Even the idea of Oliver had abandoned me, and this was worse, in the end, than when his physical self had died.

I don't know how long I sat at that table, listening to myself breathe. What was I supposed to do now? I'd been taking direction from a man who didn't exist. Maybe I didn't exist, either, with no one to bear witness to my presence, no one to testify that I had combed Oliver's hair, felt the warmth of Will's skin, stripped off my clothes and plunged naked into water, twirled in circles with Sonia in her backyard. I sat there until I began to feel that if someone didn't touch me I would slowly disappear.

I crept up the stairs as quietly as I always had when Madame Gray was there. Sonia's room was still pink and white, a little girl's room with a woman's clothes hanging in the closet. She wasn't in there, and I heard a soft murmuring of voices coming from the end of the hall. I'd only ever seen Madame Gray's room in quick glimpses. It was on a dark side of the house, and was made darker still by the lowered blinds. I'd thought of it as a cave, as the lair of a dragon from one of Sonia's father's stories. Now, as I walked toward the half-open door at the end of the hall, I felt a childish nervousness about what I'd see on the other side, like when you wake in the night, frightened by something you can't name, and force yourself to look inside the closet.

Sonia was perched on the edge of her mother's bed, her back to me. I could see the shape of her mother's body beneath the tangled sheets, but Sonia's position obscured my view of her face. For a long moment they sat there in silence. Then Madame Gray lifted her hand and touched Sonia's head, and I knew what Sonia was doing here. Her mother had tried to kill herself. A large white bandage was wrapped around her wrist.

I wondered how she had done it. Had she threatened suicide on the phone to Sonia and then nicked herself with a razor, or had she cut her veins open, lengthwise, in the tub, and watched the water turn red? Had she only wanted Sonia's attention, or had she really expected to die? I wanted to ask Sonia these questions, but I knew she would only look at me, incredulous, and ask me what difference it made. Her mother needed her, and here she was, no matter what the woman had done. Was that weakness on Sonia's part, or strength? Her whole life, she'd loved a person who gave and withdrew her affection at every turn. No wonder she thought of me as a coward for fleeing the moment something went wrong.

As I watched, Madame Gray began to stroke Sonia's hair, and Sonia bowed her head and submitted to her mother's touch. She let out a long, shuddering breath. *"Je t'aime,"* she said.

Here was the secret of this house, the thing it took bravery to face — that to go on loving someone means to over and over allow the necessary pain. Standing there in the doorway, I had a moment of empathy so total that I felt I was Sonia — we were, finally, singular, as we'd once imagined ourselves to be. For the first time since we met I didn't just witness Sonia's life, I lived it. I struggled, between my mother's blind hatred and my father's blind love, to figure out which one I deserved. I heard my own mother say she wished I had never been born. I watched as my best friend abandoned me. I felt what it was to be negated in that way, and I understood that if hatred can negate us, love can create us, and when we lose it we don't know who we are.

The moment passed. I was only myself again, and that seemed a lonely thing to be. I crept back down the stairs, intending to leave, but I couldn't bear the thought of being any more alone than I was here in this house with the two of them upstairs. I went out the back door into the yard. It seemed to have shrunk, too, barely big enough now to contain me and the swing set that still stood in the corner. Someone had fixed the swing. Over the fence, I saw the roof of another house, and above it dark electrical lines cutting through the enormous sky, the scene made watery and unreal by the tears in my eyes. I crossed to the swing set and sat on one of the swings.

Oliver's letter was still in my hand. I unfolded it and read it again. This time I didn't think about the lies revealed. None of that seemed to matter. I read out loud, "Didn't you love me after all?" and nobody answered, because even though Oliver said he loved me, and I believed him, now he was just a piece of paper in my hands. I felt what Sonia felt after her father died, that I was nothing at all, and I knew that when you felt like that you would hang on to anything that presented itself, like a flimsy raft in a vast ocean, anything that made you feel you were here, you were real, and someone wanted you.

"Oliver's dead," I said, my voice trembling. "He's dead." At the sound of those words in my own voice I felt shocked. It was like I was learning of his death for the first time. As I leaned back, pumping the swing, tears ran down my temples and into my hair. Sonia and I used to come out here and swing like children even as we planned our adult lives, all the things we were going to do and be. I pictured Sonia leaning way back, her hair brushing the ground, her eyes closed against the sunlight, her mouth open in laughter, her feet shooting into the air. And then I heard my father say he was proud of me, twirled with Owen through the newspaper office, and watched *The Philadelphia Story* with Oliver, laughing at his Katharine Hepburn imitation. I lay in bed with Will as he put a line of kisses down my arm and asked me to stay, but try as I might I couldn't live in that moment, because I was also in that other one, when I sat there and did nothing while he walked away. How much had I lost, racing down the highway with everything I owned in my car, trying to arrange my life so that I had nothing to lose?

I stopped the swing and sat there with the letter in my lap, my face in my hands, sobbing like a small child who cannot find comfort. I was alone. For the first time I felt nothing but my grief, and it was like a cave, like being in the attic with all the lights off, and I didn't want to leave. I stopped crying only because my body couldn't do it anymore, and then I became aware again that I had a body, that I was in Clovis, in Sonia's backyard, on a cool, bright afternoon. I wiped my eyes on my shirt and sat there blinking like I was new to the light. I took a deep, shaky breath, and then I sensed movement beside me and jumped.

Sonia was sitting in the swing next to mine.

For a moment she went on swaying, watching her feet trail in the dirt, and I thought she wasn't going to say anything. Then she looked at me. My face was sticky and stiff with salt, my hair damp around my temples. My eyes felt swollen. "Oh, Camazon," she said, her voice tender. She reached over and tucked my hair behind my ear. "You're a mess," she said, and then she took my hand.

My father once told me that a happy ending is just the place where you choose to stop telling the story. So this is where I choose to stop. More things are still going to happen, of course, some good, some bad. Some things never get any better. When people die they stay dead. None of us knows why we love, or why we stop loving, or why everyone we love we lose.

When Sonia and Martin get married, I'll be there, among the guests, while Suzette stands at her side. On my thirtieth birthday Will and I will walk along the beach in Gloucester, and I'll hear him shout over the wind, "Cameron, let's go home," and I'll know that this is what you live for — to hear someone say, "Let's go home," to hear someone you love call your name.

But this is where I choose to stop. I'm sitting beside Sonia in her backyard, and as I hold her hand I'm holding hands with the person she is and the person she was when I first met her, and she's holding hands with the person I am and the person I used to be. They're all there — all the people we were and will be, linked like a chain of paper dolls, girls and women, unfolding and unfolding from the moment when one fourteen-year-old said to another that it was a beautiful day.

Acknowledgments

I couldn't ask for a better editor than Sally Kim, whose insights into and support of this novel have been immensely helpful. I continue to owe a huge debt of gratitude to my agent, the incomparable, indefatigable Gail Hochman. Thanks, too, to her assistant, Joanne Brownstein, and to Shaye Areheart and everyone else at Shaye Areheart Books.

I'm grateful to Vanderbilt University and Sewanee, the University of the South, for support during the writing of this book. Thanks especially to Mark Jarman, Wyatt Prunty, Cheri Peters, Phil Stephens, and John and Elizabeth Grammar.

Many thanks to my sources: Samantha Wood, Terry BenAryeh, Shivika Asthana, Caroline Kim-Brown, and Carolyn Ebbitt. And thank you to everyone who offered comments on the various versions of this novel: Leigh Anne Couch, Juliana Gray, Dana O'Keefe, Manette Ansay, Margot

Livesey, Alice McDermott, Elwood and Nina Reid, and especially Matt O'Keefe.

And last, thanks to my daughter, Eliza, whose impending birth compelled me to finish this novel on time.

About the Author

Leah Stewart is the author of *Body of a Girl.* She has taught at Vanderbilt University and Sewanee, the University of the South. She lives outside of Chapel Hill, North Carolina, with her husband, writer Matt O'Keefe, and their daughter.

Visit her at www.leahstewart.com